Em
and Other Writings

Legacies of Nineteenth-Century
American Women Writers

Emily Hamilton
and Other Writings

SUKEY VICKERY

Edited and with an introduction by

SCOTT SLAWINSKI

University of Nebraska Press
Lincoln & London

Library of Congress Cataloging-
in-Publication Data
Vickery, Sukey, 1779–1821.
Emily Hamilton and other writings / Sukey Vickery ; edited and
with an introduction by Scott
Slawinski.
p. cm. — (Legacies of nineteenth-
century American women writers)
Includes bibliographical references.
ISBN 978-0-8032-1785-0 (pbk. : alk.
paper)
I. Slawinski, Scott. II. Title.
PS3129.V54E65 2009
818'.309—dc22

2009005432

For Susan and Sharon
and, as always, for Sally,
lovers of reading all.

Contents

Acknowledgments

A number of people have been important to the preparation of this edition. To begin, I thank the series editors, Sharon M. Harris and Karen Dandurand, for their interest in the project, and additionally to Sharon for mentioning the series to me, providing helpful guidance regarding the editing process, and supplying valuable feedback to an early version of the introduction. Karen Dandurand's evaluation of the final draft of the introduction was also much appreciated. Both Sharon and Carla Mulford provided key suggestions for identifying the many quotations Vickery employs in *Emily Hamilton* and for the list of contextual readings. I am grateful to the anonymous reviewers tapped by the University of Nebraska Press for their enthusiasm concerning the project and their ideas for the preparation of this edition. Ladette Randolph, Kristen Rowley, and Ann Baker at the University of Nebraska Press ably guided this edition through the submission and publication process. Colleen Clark proved a thorough reader and careful copyeditor of the entire manuscript. I am especially grateful to the press for its flexibility in allowing me extra time to complete the project; the edition is much better for it. I thank the librarians and staff at the American Antiquarian Society, and Thomas G. Knoles in particular, for their help regarding Sukey Vickery's manuscripts; I further thank the AAS for its kind permission to publish the manuscripts. Don Lennerton of the Leicester Historical Commission supplied me with useful information about Vickery and without his precise directions I would never have found as quickly and efficiently as I did the cemetery containing her gravesite. The English Department of Western Michigan University has been very supportive of this project, particularly the former chair, Arnie Johnston, and the current chair, Richard Utz, and I thank the department as a whole for recognizing the importance of editorial work in the field of English studies. As always, my cats, Emmy, Gracie, and Sticker, continually reminded me to take notice of the essentials of life: to sleep, to eat, and most especially to *play*. Finally, I thank my wife, Sally, for her willingness to be my collating partner, for her incisive comments regarding the volume's introduction—there is no one better at editing my writing—and for her moral and emotional support during the editorial and publication process. I am grateful she is my partner, period.

Introduction

In the early 1940s, when John Barnard Bennett was researching his master's thesis—a biography of author Sukey Vickery—one of Vickery's descendants made a fortuitous donation to the American Antiquarian Society: a handful of surviving manuscripts penned but never published by Vickery. Among the personal letters and manuscript poems one might expect to find in such a donation is a diary fragment that is hardly a page long. Dating from December 1815—a dozen years after Vickery ended her public career as an author—the fragment documents five days of Vickery's later life as wife and mother. Reporting such commonplace events as her daughter's progress with spinning and the disappearance of one Mr. Green, this fragment likely was part of a larger daily record of her life that is now lost. Its mere existence nonetheless testifies to Vickery's continued interest in and commitment to writing. In addition to revealing that she continued to compose in private, however, the diary also demonstrates Vickery's dedication to her own children's literacy and education. The first entry records that her daughter Eliza had already learned the basics of writing and that Vickery was just beginning to show her daughter Amanda how to use a pen. In fact, four of the five entries deal with her children's education, which also included science and mathematics, so concerned was she with "their improvement and future usefulness." Why this fragment—and not the rest of the manuscript—survived the intervening 130 or so years we do not know, but that it shows writing was integral to Vickery's life is undeniable. It and her other surviving works clearly suggest Vickery's self-conception as an author, one who gained considerable fame from her published verse and wrote a heretofore unacknowledged significant early American novel.

On June 11, 1779, Benjamin and Susannah Vickery might have sat in their small one-story home in Leicester, Massachusetts, wondering when their newest child would be born, what that child would be like, and how it would contribute to their family life. Perhaps they even began planning out the new arrival's future. They certainly could not have anticipated that they would bring into the world a poet and novelist whose works not only would be published in her own lifetime but would return to print over 225 years after her birth. But so it was to be, and the next day, June 12, Susannah gave birth to a daughter and named her Sukey, a shortened version of the new mother's name.

The Vickerys had come to Leicester during the siege of Boston in 1775. Having most likely had his tailor's business severely disrupted by the coming of the American Revolution, Benjamin Vickery packed up his wife and child and, leaving behind their home in Charlestown, headed west toward Worcester. Benjamin Vickery's family had lived in Hingham, Massachusetts, for three generations, ever since their emigration from England. His grandfather had performed military service in 1675, which eventually netted his father a grant of land in 1725. Opting not to remain in Hingham, Benjamin made his way to Boston and became a tailor. He married his first wife, Elizabeth Foster, on June 26, 1755, a union that produced the child he took out of the Boston area during the siege. Their union, however, ended with the death of Elizabeth, and the wife he brought with him to Leicester was Susannah (Barter) Vickery, whom he had married on November 22, 1764. At the time of their move, Leicester had a population of 1,078, but not one of the residents was a tailor.

Benjamin Vickery rented out what was known as "the little Bowdoin farm," which consisted of a house and barn, and set up his tailoring shop. Though the structure was demolished when the Vickerys stopped living there, the site of the house became known as

Vickery Knoll. With little to distinguish the family from their neighbors, not much is known of Sukey Vickery's early life. John Barnard Bennett speculates she was christened in the meetinghouse of the Congregational Society of Leicester and spent her childhood doing chores and playing. The year 1788 brought a change to Sukey's life, however, as the historical record reveals that the future poet was enrolled in the Leicester Academy, a private school founded in 1784. While it frequently struggled financially, the school survived, and it was there that Sukey received her education and was most probably exposed to classic and contemporary English poetry, giving her the literary foundation she demonstrates in her quotations from other works as well as through her own poetry. While little is known of Sukey's life at school, fellow student Ruth Henshaw did record in her diary entry for June 23, 1792, that Sukey Vickery took part in a play called *The Hypocrite*.

In addition to her education, once she came of age, Sukey Vickery probably participated in dances, visited distant friends, and courted. Before courtship crystallized into marriage, though, Vickery had produced nearly all of her extant writings. Her heretofore unpublished manuscripts reveal that she had been composing poems at least as early as 1800, but her first published piece appeared in 1801 in the *Massachusetts Spy*. In all likelihood Vickery's choice of the *Spy* was greatly influenced by the fact that it was published locally in Worcester, but she also undoubtedly knew that it was one of the most successful newspapers in New England. Moreover, the publisher of the *Spy* was a known Federalist, so she must have figured that a poem focusing positively on John Adams would surely receive a favorable reception. Begun in 1770 by Isaiah Thomas Sr., the *Massachusetts Spy* quickly evolved into a deeply partisan newspaper on the side of the Patriot cause. By early 1775 the newspaper's circulation had reached 3,500, and while subscriptions dropped significantly over the course of the war, reaching a low of 231 in 1780, the newspaper survived and became very successful once peace was restored. It was a highly respected and established newspaper, famous throughout the region. Vickery could not have selected a better publication in New England to gain exposure for her work.

Vickery's first published poem, "LINES, Addressed to JOHN ADAMS, ESQ. late PRESIDENT of the UNITED STATES," contains her own meek, tentative self-introduction. Truly unsure of her talent or perhaps posing as a humble young lady who fears being labeled a bluestocking, Vickery tells Thomas, "Should you think them worthy to be inserted in your Paper, though I dare not think you will, a constant Reader will be gratified. But should this simple production be thrown aside, my youth and inexperience must be my excuse for venturing to offer it to the Public." The publication of this first poem praising the retiring President Adams and the new nation must have encouraged her to continue submitting her poetic creations; her work would appear a total of sixteen times in the *Spy* between the printing of this first piece on April 15, 1801, and that of her last on October 20, 1802. Her last published poem is also her last extant poem, and whether she continued to produce poetry for herself remains in the realm of conjecture.

Ranging considerably from elegies for departed friends to philosophical ruminations on the passing of time to encomiums for the beauty of the natural world, her published poetry did not directly fade into obscurity once the next issue of the *Spy* appeared, for Fidelia, as Vickery was known in print, attracted admirers who wrote poetic epistles to her and praised her verses. Two of these—Theodorus and Frederic—addressed poems specifically to her and garnered responses from her, imitating the Della Cruscan trend popular in England at the end of the eighteenth century, where couples exchanged verse epistles filled with flirtatious expressions of admiration. Her third admirer, Eugene, did not directly address his poem to Vickery, but he did praise her as he tried to clear a poetic space for himself. Praise for the young poet from Leicester appeared even as far away as Vermont, in the *Federal Galaxy*, under the title "Tribute to Merit."

To the anonymous author of the piece, verses by Theodorus and Fidelia "are as a cool spring in the arid deserts of Arabia, or the solitary blue and yellow flower in the gloomy region of Nova Zambia." Despite the praise from her admirers and the *Federal Galaxy*, Vickery fell publicly silent after publishing a verse epistle to Frederic in response to the sonnet he had addressed to her.

Fidelia's silence possibly had to do with a turn in her literary career, for by 1802 she had written and submitted a novel to Isaiah Thomas Jr., who had just assumed control of his father's business. The story of the courtship trials and triumphs of three female friends, Vickery's epistolary novel *Emily Hamilton* appeared in print in 1803. Word of this new production from Fidelia had reached Thomas Jr. as early as February 13, 1802, as a letter from Vickery to him documents. Like many of her contemporaries, she was chiefly concerned with maintaining her anonymity: "On supposition the little work above alluded to ever should appear in print, I shall never consent to have my name or that of Fidelia appear to it." Vickery's motives for remaining anonymous are likely various. She was almost certainly influenced by the trends of the day, which favored pseudonymous publication, and by her own sense of Christian humility, but like her self-introduction to her first published poem, her desire for anonymity also likely represents a degree of anxiety about publicity, especially for a young lady of marriageable age. While her concern for being labeled a bluestocking might have diminished with the publication of each poem, Vickery also quite probably felt uncomfortable with her new genre. Eighteenth-century Americans thought of poetry as noble and a sign of literacy and education, but the novel, as Cathy N. Davidson has made clear, was a disreputable genre. According to its critics, novels contributed to idleness, unfitted readers for their social stations in life, and implanted a dangerously high degree of depravity in readers. Novels, in short, were immoral productions, as Vickery's contemporary, the Reverend Samuel Miller, testifies: "Every opportunity is taken to attack some principle of morality under the title of a 'prejudice,' to ridicule the duties of domestic life, as flowing from 'contracted' and 'slavish' views; to deny the sober pursuits of upright industry as 'dull' and 'spiritless;' and, in a word, to frame an apology for suicide, adultery and prostitution, and the indulgence of every propensity for which a corrupt heart can plead an inclination" (qtd. in Davidson, *Revolution and the Word* 47).

Vickery appears to have seen herself as walking a tightrope of propriety now that she had turned her attention to writing fiction. In addition to expressing an anxious desire to maintain authorial anonymity, Vickery's letter also explicitly states that she has drawn on real incidents from life, arrived at through either hearsay or (presumably) direct observation, as source material for her novel's content. Her assertion of the truth of her novel coincides with her care "not to write any thing that could have a tendency to injure the minds of the young and inexperienced." Vickery obviously felt some need to justify her choice of genre, as did many of her contemporaries who made similar claims about their own work.[1]

While Vickery's concern for the truthfulness of her novel serves as a connection to her predecessors, her claims about the composition of *Emily Hamilton* anticipate statements by women authors of the nineteenth century. Vickery tells Thomas that she composed her novel during her leisure hours, especially late at night when her writing would not impose upon the family and her responsibilities to it. Such a claim is quite in line with those made by later women writers who felt a need to assure their publishers and sometimes their readers that they had not neglected their families while they wrote. Vickery also claims ignorance of copyright law but hints that she hopes some small financial gain might be realized through her book. She closes her letter with a willingness to defer to Thomas's "superior" judgment regarding her manuscript's worth. Her dance with Thomas over the submission of her work bears some resemblance to what Susan Coultrap-McQuinn defines as a woman writer's relationship to the Gentleman Publisher of the mid- to late nineteenth century.

According to her, "publishers were responsible for instrumental activities and authors for inspirational, expressive ones, [just] as men were supposed to be responsible for business and women for spiritual and emotional affairs; under this model, Gentleman Publishers usually gave their writers responsibility for their own sphere, providing some guidance when necessary." Thus, "insofar as these associations called for submitting to the wisdom or care of their publishers, while taking responsibility for their own sphere of activity, women writers were also in a familiar male-female relationship" (38). Vickery's deference, then, to Thomas's judgment regarding her manuscript, copyright, and payment anticipates an author-publisher relationship that would become much more intricate as the century wore on.[2]

The historical record is silent regarding whether Thomas Jr. responded to Vickery's inquiry concerning copyright, but he did publish the novel by subscription. In selecting Thomas's shop to publish her novel, Vickery could not have chosen a better operation, at least in New England. Isaiah Thomas Sr. had built up a notable publishing business by the time he turned control over to his son in 1801 or 1802. Thomas Sr. had taken over a print shop from Zechariah Fowle in 1770. In addition to beginning the *Massachusetts Spy* in 1770, Thomas began producing an annual almanac in 1771 and, briefly, a magazine called the *Royal American*. The Revolutionary War induced him to move his operation to Worcester in 1775, where he would remain for the rest of his life. Thomas's business ventures thrived in the prewar years, suffered rough times during the war, and expanded tremendously once the war was over. In 1778 he began publishing his almanac out of Worcester, and by the mid-1780s he was producing lucrative editions of George Richards Minot's *History of the Insurrections in Massachusetts* (which chronicles Shay's Rebellion), the Massachusetts Constitution, and a collection of the state's laws. From 1789 to 1793 he brought out the *Massachusetts Magazine; or Monthly Museum of Knowledge*; despite frequently operating in the red, it was one of the longest-running periodicals in the early United States and in recent years has achieved respect among scholars for its content. The number of Thomas's publications exceeds those printed by every publisher preceding or contemporary with him, including Benjamin Franklin, who published approximately eight hundred books to Thomas's nine hundred. Thomas brought out works by some of the major authors of the eighteenth century, including Richardson, Goldsmith, and Rousseau. Also to his credit are the presumed first American novel, *The Power of Sympathy*, collections of poems by Sarah Wentworth Morton and Mercy Otis Warren, and two of the most successful books of all time, Noah Webster's spelling and grammar texts.

The firm was still running on the momentum and prestige established by his father when Thomas Jr. began printing Vickery's poems in the *Spy* and when he published her novel in 1803. Much has been made of the quotation against novels by someone named Kelly— Bennett speculates it is Irish author Hugh Kelly—which Thomas Sr. inserted on the flyleaf of his personal copy of *Emily Hamilton*: "The perusal of Novels generally tend[s] to *enlighten* than to *distract* the Mind," but if even a single line serves to "excuse a vice," then parents and guardians should "expel Such Books from their Homes." This ambivalence toward the utility of fiction did not stop either Thomas from publishing other novels, nor did it stop Thomas Jr. from advertising *Emily Hamilton* and trying to drum up sales for it. He advertised the novel's publication in the October 20, 1802, copy of the *Spy*. Although Vickery insisted on publishing the novel anonymously, the authorship of novels in the early republic was often an open secret locally, and therefore using the *Spy* to advertise the book might have been Thomas's attempt to capitalize on the fame Fidelia had achieved as a poet in his column "Blossoms of Parnassus." A book of 250 pages, *Emily Hamilton* sold for seventy-five cents, according to the ads in the *Spy*, making it an expensive purchase to most consumers of the era. Thomas published the novel by subscription, advertising it as such in October 1802, and later encouraged subscribers to send for their copies at the earliest date after the novel came out in June 1803. As no second edition of *Emily Hamilton* ever appeared, the book must have sold slowly.

Eventually, Thomas sent a copy to the editor of the *Monthly Anthology and Boston Review*, and in May 1805 the novel received a paragraph-length mention. Speculation has asserted that the reviewer was the Reverend John Pierce, a onetime English preceptor at Leicester Academy and a minister, but the suggestion remains unproven. The anonymous reviewer expends about half the review in discouraging women from writing novels, noting that no American woman, with the exception of Susanna Rowson, "has written a novel which can be read with any pleasure." Only if "the amusement and instruction which they can furnish will extend beyond the circle of their own partial friends" should women attempt to write novels. Despite this attitude, the critic notes that *Emily Hamilton* deserves (qualified) commendation: "The style evidently displays the youth of the author, though more simple and correct, than that in which young ladies generally write. The sentiments are common, but just; and though the incidents are neither very numerous nor interesting, they evince considerable ingenuity." Perhaps he was influenced by the sentimental image of the novel's author spending her youthful days supporting her elderly parents through the use of her sewing needle, as Thomas's letter apparently intimated. Given the lack of specificity in this review, the absence of excerpts (a common practice of the time), and the lengthy attack on women writers, one cannot but wonder whether it is a "puff" piece, designed to draw attention to the book without the reviewer actually having to read it, written mostly as a favor to Thomas. Considering that the titular character falls in love with a married man and that the novel's events include a near drowning and possibly an adulterous affair, the characterization of the sentiments as "common" and the incidents as uninteresting seems entirely misguided. After the publication of this review, *Emily Hamilton* appears only in the stock books of its printers. Though fewer than three hundred copies were likely printed, according to Bennett, the book remained in stock for many years. Thomas's inventory reveals that in 1805, twenty-six copies of the novel remained in sheets; a year later, one bound copy and the same number in sheets remained with Thomas, and the number in sheets remained constant for 1808. In 1809 and 1811, ten and then nine bound copies remained in the shop, and in 1813, three bound copies remained. With its irregular sales, the book never achieved bestseller status.

The publication of *Emily Hamilton* marks the last time Vickery appeared in print. It is possible that Samuel Watson (1782–1872), a local clothier, was already courting Vickery when her novel appeared; if he was not, he soon would be. On October 14, 1804, Miss Vickery became Mrs. Watson. During the sixteen years of her marriage, before her untimely death at the age of forty-one, Sukey Vickery Watson gave birth to nine children—seven girls and two boys—who appeared roughly every two years between 1805 and 1820. With a large family to support, her husband struggled financially before achieving success in his later years. Aside from noting that Vickery joined the First Congregational Church of Leicester in 1810, the historical record is rather silent regarding her later life. As we have seen, though, her married life did not prevent her from writing. While Bennett foregrounds "the total absence of evidence of any other pages of the diary" (52), one suspects—and expects—that she probably maintained a diary for many years. The 1815 fragment provides only a tantalizing glimpse into the life of the married Sukey Vickery, but the concern she expresses for her daughters' learning is not very different from the characters' concerns in *Emily Hamilton*. Since the diary reveals that Vickery instructed her daughters in domestic tasks, writing, and arithmetic, it is not difficult to imagine her carrying out the precepts of Judith Sargent Murray, educating her daughters beyond mere lessons in domestic chores. Five years beyond the diary's date, on June 17, 1820, Vickery died and was buried in Rawson Brook Cemetery in Leicester. After a considerably longer life, Samuel Watson was laid to rest beside her. Her gravestone, with an image of an urn beneath a weeping willow, also appropriately includes some verses:

> In lively hope of heavenly bliss,
> She closed her eyes in peace and love;
> She bid farewell to earthly cares,
> To join the heavenly throng above.

Her Poetry

Not much has been written about Sukey Vickery's poetry. Cathy N. Davidson has called it "clearly derivative in form and tone" and suggested that "to a modern reader [it] seems both overinflated and underdeveloped" ("Female Authorship" 7). She dismisses it quickly in order to focus extensively on *Emily Hamilton*, as does Amy E. Winans, who, in a brief paragraph about Vickery's verse, charges that it is "rather conventional in form" (380). For some appreciation of Vickery's poetic efforts one must look back to John Bernard Bennett's 1942 thesis, where he even goes so far as to suggest that marriage might have committed "larceny" upon American letters in stealing away a developing poet. Standing distinctly opposite to the most recent assessments, Bennett considers the poetry of greater interest than Vickery's novel; moreover, he believes her religious poetry to be her best. Even so, he cannot get beyond the charge of conventionality and considers her technical skill to be limited, something that became readily apparent to him in Vickery's longer efforts. That Vickery stayed close to eighteenth-century aesthetics cannot be denied; she wrote mostly in rhymed couplets, eschewed experimentation in meter by sticking with trimeter, tetrameter, and pentameter, and used the iamb almost exclusively. Yet Bennett gets it right when he claims that her poetry reveals "a strength of thought" (64). While her verse is noteworthy for its remarkable technical proficiency, its greater significance lies in what it reveals about Vickery and what was important to her.

In her two political poems, one of which was published while the other remained in manuscript, she reveals her informed engagement with contemporary politics and her own Federalist leanings. In the published poem, which appeared in the *Spy* just as John Adams was leaving office in 1801, she offers considerable praise for the former president, who she feels has been treated unfairly by his detractors. For Vickery, time will vindicate the controversial president:

> Thy name by all the great and good rever'd,
> Shall by Columbia's Daughters be ador'd,
> With that of thy copatriot WASHINGTON.

For the subject of her manuscript poem, Vickery took the dawning of the year 1784, the first year marking the acknowledgment of the United States as a nation independent of Britain. In it she has high praise for typical figures such as Washington and Franklin, and she touches on the "rising glory of America" theme that was so popular for the era.

For the most part, though, Vickery's poetry deals with religious topics or her natural surroundings. This is, perhaps, best demonstrated by her "Address to PIETY," which interweaves the two. Without piety, she proclaims, "every charm in nature flies, / No smiling prospect cheers our wand'ring eyes." Indeed, nature does not just lose its appeal but becomes menacing unless viewed through the lens of piety. So, too, with the night, when "Imagination calls some spectre forth, / And tort'ring fancy wakens all her pow'rs." According to Vickery, it is piety that disciplines these faculties, calms the mind, and soothes the spirit so that "new charms adorn each scene" and "No horrid visions agitate the breast, / But gentle slumber lulls our cares to rest." It is this poem that spurred Theodorus to begin his public poetic addresses to Vickery and brought her the first fruits of poetic fame. Comparable to "Address to PIETY," the elegies to "Miss H" and "Miss E****" depict a deep belief in the Christian faith, particularly in the resurrection, which she uses to comfort the mourners. Moreover, by again resorting to natural imagery, Vickery deepens her poetic message by turning the elegies into not just reflections upon absent friends but meditations upon the transience of earthly existence. Perhaps her dedication to her spirituality is best exemplified in "Resignation," where the poem's speaker states unequivocally that she will place her faith in God—even in the face of violent thunderstorms and earthquakes—to find peace. In fact, her desire for contentment reappears in several poems, not all of them religious.

The two elegies suggest another of Vickery's favorite themes, for she returned several times to the vanity of an earthly existence, and readers will likely wonder whether Ecclesiastes was a favorite with her among the biblical books. She first touches on this topic in her second published poem, "BEAUTY," where she notes that physical characteristics will dissolve over time. Vickery addresses Beauty as "thou tyrant, whose despotic sway, / Enslaves thy thousands in one fatal day" while pointing out that "Thy radiant charms must all decay with youth." Vickery spotlights various features that decay with age, but she also admonishes "Ye fair" to "be wise, while yet tis in your power":

> Improve each fleeting day, each passing hour;
> Enrich your youthful minds with virtuous lore,
> That will remain till time shall be no more.

Even in this early poem, Vickery expresses the same commitment to (female) education that is found in the journal fragment. Moreover, while her poem is primarily a religious argument, its language is suggestive of a political message as well, coupling tyranny with vanity and education with virtue. Vickery returns to the theme of earthly vanity in "Evening Reflections" and an untitled poem she published. Whereas the implied audience of "BEAUTY" is female, the stated audience of "Evening Reflections" is male. Vickery admonishes men to leave off their pleasure-seeking and return to their wives and families. Her argument is religious, political, and feminist. Not only are the men sinning with their "gambling, drinking, strife and noise" but they are also destabilizing their homes, the foundation of the republic. "Evening Reflections" also connects drunkenness with domestic abuse, making it an early precursor to the arguments of mid-nineteenth-century feminists who perceived temperance as a feminist issue. Similarly, in her untitled poem, Vickery's speaker claims:

> I never will sigh for the bubbles [baubles?] of earth,
> From them I can never true happiness find,
> I regard not the honors of fortune and birth,
> They're nothing, compar'd with a calm easy mind.

Repose, for Vickery, is found in an untroubled mind, brought about, as we have seen in "Resignation," by God and the natural environment with which she has surrounded herself in the poem.

While these poems primarily express a deep commitment to spiritual fulfillment, a deep appreciation of the natural world should, by now, also be obvious. Many of her poems employ natural imagery to convey her message, and her most pious verse frequently draws on things from the natural world to illustrate her larger point. Nature as a poetic subject can be found in early poems such as "Address to PIETY," in the middling poems of her all-too-short career, such as "Evening Reflections," and in some of the last poems she published, such as "Summer." The Vickery that emerges from this poetry is deeply appreciative of the world around her. Her contemporaries discerned her interest in nature as well, for Theodorus frequently imagines her gracing pastoral settings and roaming among pleasant woods and brooks. It is tempting to think of Vickery as a proto-Romantic, the way Philip Freneau frequently is, but her use of natural imagery is either for mere pleasure or for religious ends rather than sublime inspiration. Furthermore, while she is obviously familiar with eighteenth-century aesthetics concerning poetry—she must have known Pope's poems or Thompson's *The Seasons*—she is not strictly working within the pastoral either. What her verse does is vividly portray the natural world as residents in the early United States must have experienced it, must have been inundated with it.

Vickery's writings also reveal a deep commitment to a realistic view of the world and a realist aesthetic in her work. While this reaches its highest achievement in *Emily Hamilton*, one can see in her poetry an unflinching look at the world. Her poems dealing with the fading of all that is earthly are certainly informed by her religious convictions, but readers will also find a hard look at earthly existence. In her elegies, there are no excessive calls for tears such as might be found in more sentimental poems. Vickery instead tries to represent the character of each person as accurately as she perceived it. While she does not strive for a precisely balanced view of the dead by criticizing them, she does realistically view death as a part of life. Similarly, her polemic in "Evening Reflections" against taverngoing provides a similarly hardheaded look at the damage done to families by drunken husbands. Perhaps her aesthetic is best set forward in her unpublished poem "A tale for those who deal in the marvelous," in which she relates the conversation passing between two sisters who hear a sound in the dark night. While their imaginations run wild with all sorts of possibilities as to the nature and cause of the sound—including witches, spirits, and children groaning in their death pangs—the eventual culprit is not one of these fantastic images but a snoring cat. From this experience, one of the sisters adopts the practical resolution to investigate immediately any sound that goes bump in the night.

Only a fraction of Vickery's poetry is dedicated to answering the addresses of her admirers, and yet these are the poems for which Vickery has garnered the most attention as a poet. Totaling five out of twenty-one published and unpublished poems, her verse epistles to Theodorus, Eugene, and Fredric were, according to the anonymous reviewer of Vermont's *Federal Galaxy*, "as superior to the turgid song of Della Crusca, as they are to that *low* poetry which now abounds in European publications, under the name of *ballads*, in which simplicity is made much too simple." Whether his references to ballads and simplicity indicate that the reviewer was thinking of the emerging Romantic aesthetic pioneered by William Wordsworth and Samuel Taylor Coleridge remains open to conjecture. The applause garnered by Fidelia and Theodorus and the general appreciation for poetry written in the Della Cruscan style would not last, however, and by the time Bennett was writing his thesis in 1942, he could call that popular vein of eighteenth-century poetry "one of those misguided movements which have marked and will continue to mark the course of poetry" (57). In the specific case of Vickery and her admirers, Bennett remarks, "While such a thing as a good conceit was beyond their feeble grasp, they have abated not a whit the 'bombastic classicism' which marked their predecessors" (60). More recent scholarship dealing with the British Della Cruscans has in a limited fashion revived their reputation, but the American branch of the school remains in obscurity.

Who were the Della Cruscans and what did this "movement" encompass? The name "Della Crusca" comes from the Italian *Accademia della Crusca*, located in Florence. Founded in 1582–83, the academy was abolished, along with two other Florentine academies, by the Grand Duke Leopold in 1783 and replaced with *Real Accademia Fiorentina*. Among those residing in Florence at the time was Captain Robert Merry, an Englishman, who began writing poetry under the name Della Crusca. Forming a literary circle that included Florentine locals and British expatriates, these poets first published *The Arno Miscellany* (1784) and then *The Florence Miscellany* (1785). Several poems from the latter anthology began to circulate in European periodicals, and by the time Merry returned to England, his poetry had already achieved a degree of fame. It was not, however, until the British periodical *The World* appeared in January of 1787 that the Della Cruscan movement garnered widespread acclaim and achieved its highest notoriety. On June 29, 1787, Merry placed his first poem in *The World* under the pseudonym Della Crusca; on July 10,

Hannah Cowley, writing under the pseudonym Anna Matilda, responded, beginning the poetic correspondence that held countless readers in breathless suspense. Through numerous editions of *The World*, Della Crusca and Anna Matilda flirted, courted, fell in love, met, and then fell out of love and ceased writing to each other entirely, not unlike many a modern-day virtual romance begun in an Internet chatroom. The cessation of their poetic correspondence was due to the actual meeting of Merry and Cowley on March 31, 1789. Despite hints in her poetry, Merry was surprised to find Cowley was married, a mother, and many years his senior. In his disappointment, and aiming to close the relationship of Della Crusca and Anna Matilda, he wrote "The Interview," which appeared in *The World* on June 16, 1789. Cowley's response appeared three days later, ending the two-year romance that had captivated its readers. The verse correspondence between these two "lovers," in fact, gave birth to several other poetic correspondences, including Laura Maria's with Leonardo (another of Merry's pseudonyms) and Cesario, and Julia's with Arno. Despite the proliferation of verse exchanges, two years after the cessation of correspondence between Merry and Cowley, the Della Cruscan movement met its own end in the form of William Gifford's *The Baviad* (1791), a highly satirical poem designed to crush the Della Cruscan movement on aesthetic grounds. Gifford was successful beyond his wildest expectations, for he not only stamped out the movement in his own day but also consigned it to the dustbins of literary history for nearly two hundred years.

All this was occurring, of course, while Vickery was still a young child, but the Della Cruscan mode managed to cross the Atlantic and gain a foothold in the new nation, especially once the *Columbian Centinel* invited contributions from Philenia and Alfred, a correspondence that carried on for several years. Thomas's *Massachusetts Spy* was printing Della Cruscan poetry before Vickery came on the scene, and the movement continued to flourish for some time after she ceased publishing poetry in the newspaper. In his thesis

Bennett points out that Vickery and her admirers departed significantly from the conventions established by their Della Cruscan predecessors in Boston and London. While the women in the other exchanges pursued and were pursued by their admirers, Vickery was strictly the addressee, and whereas actual courtship took place in the other correspondences, Vickery's exchanges had more to do with admiration than affection. Furthermore, Bennett notes, in England females outnumbered males writing Della Cruscan poetry, while Vickery attracted three male admirers. Bennett calls these "minor changes" (60), but it certainly seems that Vickery and her admirers were adapting the Della Cruscan mode for their own purposes.

The correspondence between Vickery and Theodorus began only after she had published several pieces in the *Spy*, including "Address to PIETY," the poem that inspired him to write to her. His verse epistle, simply titled "To FIDELIA," appeared on June 10, 1801. In it he proclaims:

> Mid forests dim and meadows green,
> I know thy angel form is seen,
> With pensive steps and musing eye,
> Tracing the works of DEITY!

Having set Vickery in the natural imagery her poems evoke and having praised her efforts, he closes his epistle with a charge to "never cease thy charming strain— / But strike thy well strung harp again." Vickery composed a response eight days after the appearance of Theodorus's poetic accolades, which Thomas published on July 1. In her response, she reciprocates Theodorus's praise for her with admiration for his lines, claiming that if she possessed his talent, "Then should my numbers graceful flow, / And bid the heart with rapture glow." Vickery's verses, however, also "correct" the vision of her that Theodorus has presented to the public, as if she were seeking to maintain control over her own public imagine. In place of his vision of an angel of piety, she offers a realistic vision of herself as content but aware that anxieties are always on the horizon; with this thought in mind, she closes the poem with a wish for his happiness. This sort of exchange, where Theodorus offers an imaginative vision that Vickery wrests away from him in an attempt to define for herself her own public image, repeats itself in their second epistolary intercourse, initiated by Theodorus on September 2, with Vickery's response appearing on October 14. Before Theodorus could launch a third exchange, though, Eugene interjected himself into the *Spy*. While his poem merely invokes Vickery's name rather than directly addressing her, their epistolary interaction mirrors her exchange with Theodorus. Eugene praises her poetry and overtly sets it in the tradition of Della Crusca and Anna Matilda, but his chief aim is to bewail the "cruelty" of "Laura." Vickery answered Eugene, even though his poem was not directly addressed to her, but her response was probably not what he had hoped it would be. Although she is sympathetic to his plight, ultimately she commands him to shake off his mourning rather than offering to soothe his pain, to act like an adult instead of "affliction's child." Eugene chose not to respond to Vickery, leaving his silence open to interpretation, but one cannot wonder whether the hardheaded realism in her response silenced him. Theodorus, too, goes silent after their third exchange, perhaps because he finally seems to have learned that she demands the right to define her own public persona rather than have him do it for her. While his third poem presents the usual praises, he also cedes to Vickery her right to self-definition in his poem and merely asks her to provide another instance of her poetic talent, a request she grants in her response. Having reached what seems to be a mutual understanding, it appears that their poetic relationship had nowhere else to go, and so Theodorus, too, ceases to write to Vickery. A final exchange occurs between Vickery and Frederic. In his poem, Frederic's praise of Vickery extends to comparing her with "Philenia"—Sarah Wentworth Morton, one of the most respected women poets of the age. Frederic raises Vickery above Morton, and this is too much for her to tolerate. Her response steadfastly corrects him and restores Morton to her high place in the poetic canon of the time. Having done this, Vickery closes out her poetic career, never printing another piece in the *Spy* and leaving no extant poems later than 1802. Did Frederic's praise decide Vickery in favor of silencing herself, of refusing the laurels she was beginning to accrue through her publications? Or had she perhaps turned her literary talents in another direction?

Her Novel

Whether Vickery chose to forsake poetry for a new literary direction or was driven from the field by anxiety over her growing fame and Frederic's high-flown praise, it is a fact that her novel *Emily Hamilton* was published anonymously by Thomas less than a year after her last poem appeared in the *Spy*. Indeed, Vickery might well have chosen to concentrate on novel writing in place of verse, with the hope, as her letter to Thomas explains, of making a small living from it: "I am quite ignorant of the manner of disposing of copy rights, and a faint hope that I might possibly gain something by it induced me to mention it in confidence to Mr Greenwood." Given this statement, it is quite possible that Vickery envisioned a novel-writing "career" if *Emily Hamilton* did well. Since she obviously understood the importance of sales, she must have been disappointed when her novel did not become the next *Charlotte Temple*. That it did not is hardly surprising. As William Charvat, Cathy N. Davidson, and others have shown, a bestseller like *Charlotte Temple* was the exception rather than the rule when it came to novel writing in the early republic. Most printing houses were small and their business limited to the immediate area. While Isaiah Thomas did have a network of booksellers with whom he dealt—which he put to use in distributing and advertising *Emily Hamilton*—the few, poorly established roads and seasonal changes that limited shipping opportunities remained a reality of life. Moreover, any author situated in America who wished to write novels faced the additional challenge of foreign imports, especially novels from Britain. Without an international copyright agreement, printers in the young United States easily and with impunity pirated novels produced across the Atlantic. Samuel Richardson's *Pamela*, Daniel Defoe's *Robinson Crusoe*, and Oliver Goldsmith's *The Vicar of Wakefield*, to name only a few, remained steady sellers in the early republic, and these books could be produced at a fraction of the cost of an American-authored novel since the prices of pirated editions were untouched by royalty payments. Editions of early American novels ranged from first printings of only a few hundred to about 1,500 copies with the goal of selling several hundred to cover costs. Many books were printed by subscription, but even such "guaranteed" sales—assuming buyers did not renege on their pledges—did not always bring financial success; a publisher, in fact, might print only one novel in his entire career. Ultimately, authors in the early republic rarely profited from the publication of their novels, and many produced only one work of fiction in a lifetime.

While publishers and authors had their troubles, so too did readers. Cathy Davidson remarks in her groundbreaking study of the early novel that the cost of novels was in and of itself prohibitive. She speculates that the cost of a hardbound novel in the early republic might have been three to four times that of today's hardbound novel (that is, compared to mid-1980s cover prices). A "more meaningful measure," she suggests, "would be in terms of a late eighteenth-century economy":

> In 1800, a carpenter in Massachusetts earned $1 per day, an unskilled laborer half that much. A pound of sugar cost $.13, a pair of leather shoes $.80, and cotton cloth $1 a yard. A novel typically cost between $.75 and $1.50 (although one pirated edition of the popular *The History of Constantius and Pulchera*, paperbound and only 11-cm. high, sold for $.25). A common day laborer in Massachusetts had to

work two days to buy a copy of *Wieland* (1798). For the same amount, he could purchase a bushel of potatoes and a half bushel of corn. (25)

Moreover, members of the middle classes, who possessed significant-enough leisure time to read, were just getting strongly established at the time of *Emily Hamilton*'s publication. Clearly, authorship in the early republic was limited at the production and consumer ends of the market, and with Vickery's novel priced at $.75, these factors essentially extinguished any hope of substantial remuneration that either Vickery or Thomas might have held, even with the advantage of Thomas's advertising, reputation, and network contacts. The slow sales of the book might very well have forced her to give up any dreams of novel writing as a career, and her courtship with and marriage to Watson probably sealed her fate as a former author.[3] Whatever Vickery's motives for abandoning her career as a writer, her one novel stands as an unacknowledged gem of the early republic.

For more than a century it was not publicly known that *Emily Hamilton* had come from Sukey Vickery's pen. She unequivocally states in her letter to Thomas that she does not wish her name made public: "Had I known Mr Greenwood would have mentioned my name as the authoress of the Novel, I believe I never should have ventured to have had it thus exposed. It is, and ever has been, my wish to remain unknown." Her desire for anonymity was not unusual; contemporaries such as Sally Wood steadfastly maintained their anonymity, and even a bestselling author such as Hannah Webster Foster printed *The Coquette* under the cover of "*By a Lady from Massachusetts.*" The first attribution of *Emily Hamilton* was made not to Vickery but to one "Eliza Vicery" in an 1899 bibliography by Charles Lemuel Nichols, who was often subsequently cited as an authority. Had Nichols consulted notes by a clergyman named Samuel Jennison (notes now housed at the American Antiquarian Society), he would have realized his mistake and corrected it. Jennison, an amateur historian living in

Worcester at the dawn of the nineteenth century, rightly attributed *Emily Hamilton* to "a young lady of Leicester" whose last name was Vickery. His notes, however, never reached publication, and they only establish the last name of *Emily Hamilton*'s author. It is Joseph Denny's published recollections that confirm her first name. One of the earliest settlers of Leicester, Denny composed a series of reminiscences in 1873, and one of these correctly establishes Sukey Vickery as the novel's author. A final piece of evidence is the copy of *Emily Hamilton* housed in the Leicester Public Library, which is apparently Vickery's own edition of the novel, donated by her daughter Harriet. On the reverse of the title page is written "The authoress of this 'Novel' was Miss Susan Vickery, of Leicester, Massachusetts" (qtd. in Bennett 4–5), and the book's card catalog entry reads "Vickery, Susan." Although the library's copy supplies an incorrect first name, examined in conjunction with the other evidence, the entry confirms Vickery as having composed *Emily Hamilton*. Thus, the mystery of the novel's authorship remained unsolved until Bennett's detective work in his 1942 thesis firmly established Sukey Vickery as the author.

Although holding rigidly to convention by insisting upon her anonymity, Vickery chose a strikingly original path for the plot of her novel. While Charles Brockden Brown was admired by later generations as the "father of the American novel," it was not his books but those by Susanna Rowson and Hannah Webster Foster that sold well. Both Rowson's *Charlotte Temple* and Foster's *The Coquette* became bestsellers when they appeared in the 1790s and remained so through the nineteenth century. The former told through the voice of a narrator, the latter through a series of letters, each famously describes the seduction, impregnation, abandonment, and ultimate death of their heroines. While the novels' plot structure might subtly criticize the injustice of a patriarchal system, the overt theme of each is plain. Though Charlotte Temple and Eliza Wharton are the heroines, readers should seek to avoid their mistakes and fate; unlike Benjamin Franklin's life as he presents it in his *Autobiography*, their lives are not "fit to be imitated." It would take the novels of Catherine Maria Sedgwick and other authors of the 1820s and 1830s to develop the model heroine, the woman whom women should strive to be. This type of heroine achieves its greatest success in the form of Ellen Montgomery in Susan Warner's *The Wide, Wide World* and Gertrude Flint in Susanna Maria Cummins's *The Lamplighter*, two of the most popular books of the 1850s. Books by Sedgwick, Warner, Cummins, and their contemporaries form the center of Nina Baym's classic study, *Woman's Fiction*. Baym and the critics who followed her have noted the change from anti-models such as Charlotte and Eliza in the late eighteenth and early nineteenth centuries to the models found from the 1820s onward. *Emily Hamilton*, however, challenges this neat progression. Published in 1803, the book offers us not one but three heroines worthy of imitation by its readers: Emily Hamilton, Mary Carter, and Eliza Anderson. Readers are also treated to a host of other admirable women as well. Vickery was attuned to the reading public enough to include a seduction story in the novel, but she never foregrounds it; the seduction happens "offstage" and is only tangentially important to the rest of the novel. It serves more to testify to the injustice offered to women by men, akin to the story of Mrs. Henderson, who also remains offstage in the novel, discussed only by the main characters and offered sympathy for her marriage to a drunkard. What *Emily Hamilton* offers is an opportunity to reexamine the course of literary history: Is the novel the exception that proves the rule, or is it one among several that suggest the turn to model heroines occurs not in the 1820s but at least as early as 1803?

Emily Hamilton offers another opportunity to reexamine and perhaps revise how we narrate the course of American literature. Rebecca Harding Davis is the woman most frequently associated with early realist fiction in America, but she began her writing career in 1861, with "Life in the Iron Mills." Yet both Cathy Davidson and Amy Winans mark Vickery's own realist aesthetic, and Judith Fetterley has pointed out that "American women writers were realists well before the Civil War" (10). That Vickery's own form of realism has been overlooked is, in a way, unsurprising. In addition to employing such unrealistic devices as the intrusive and moralizing narrator, Vickery's contemporaries populated their novels with sensationalistic events such as spontaneous combustion, extremely odd coincidences, secret midnight flights, frightening abductions, and—at least once—a gothic castle in the middle of Connecticut. Vickery eschewed the sensationalism of her contemporaries and offered her readers in its place a carefully planned realism, evidence of which can be found immediately on the title page of *Emily Hamilton*, where she claims the novel is "*FOUNDED ON INCIDENTS IN REAL LIFE*." Of course, contemporaries such as Rowson and Foster also made such claims; *Charlotte Temple* was a "Tale of Truth," and *The Coquette* was "Founded on Fact." The wording of both of these claims, however, allows for a degree of imaginative embellishment. Rowson deals in "truth," suggesting that the gist of her story is truthful, though not literally so. Foster's claim does have a basis in fact—her heroine Eliza Wharton is based on a real Elizabeth Whitman—but once this fact is recognized, she seems to imply, the rest of her tale of woe can be imaginative. But Vickery founds her tale on real-life incidents, as if to emphasize her thrust toward a realist portrait of life itself. She immediately reinforces this impression in her introduction to the novel. Acknowledging that her audience will in all likelihood consist chiefly of women readers, she quickly moves to the heart of the matter: fiction's supposed ability to ruin young women's minds. In answer to this charge, she draws a distinction between dangerous novels and those that provide "instructive amusement":

> Those which carry us too far from real life, and fill the imagination with a thousand enchanting images which it is impossible ever to realize, conveying at the same time an idea of perfect earthly happiness, ought never to be read till

the judgment is sufficiently mature to separate the truth from the fiction of the story. But those which are founded on interesting scenes in real life, may be calculated to afford moral instruction to the youthful mind, in the most pleasing manner.

The difference between two types of novels is here made clear; while she acknowledges that truth and fiction mingle in novels, some— like *Emily Hamilton*—are clearly more realistic than others. She has not, she claims in the final paragraph of her introductory remarks, consciously written anything to injure young minds—she has not, in short, written one of those novels that "carry us too far from real life." It might be tempting to dismiss Vickery's word choice as just another way of claiming hers is a truthful tale were it not for one of her surviving letters. Vickery transcribed *word-for-word* into *Emily Hamilton* a letter she wrote to her friend Adeline Hartwell in which she recounts the fate of one Mrs. Anderson, who married a drunkard. In the novel Mrs. Anderson becomes Mrs. Henderson, but the story remains precisely the same. This surviving letter brings into sharp focus the seriousness with which Vickery treated her commitment to a realist aesthetic. Whether the life experiences of Emily, Mary, and Eliza similarly mirror those of real-life equivalents remains to be seen (and might never be known).

True to the preface, the female correspondents in *Emily Hamilton* face realistic challenges regarding their potential spouses, ethical choices, and inner lives. There are no dashingly seductive army officers, corrupt members of the Illuminati, plague-ridden cities, or suggestive threats of sexual impropriety. In place of these, Vickery sets before her heroines a series of emotional and intellectual challenges in order to represent more fully the real nature of friendship, courtship, and (eventually) marriage. As both Davidson and Winans observe, part of the challenge of courtship and marriage is the retention of old friendships. Rather than present married life as the tomb of friendship, as Eliza Wharton calls it in *The Coquette*, Vickery chooses to depict women who are participating and achieving success in the marriage market but who do so without sacrificing their longtime friendships. They instead work to retain those relationships through friendships with each other's spouses and frequent visits to their respective homes. Moreover, the emotional engagement remains intact for the length of the novel. Where Eliza Wharton's friend Lucy Freeman Sumner becomes emotionally distant, taking more pleasure in her home life than in anything else—including answering her friend's numerous letters—Mary Carter, once married, remains deeply attached to her friends and interested in their lives, even after the birth of her first child. In fact, a by-product of the exchange of letters of these distantly located friends is another aspect of Vickery's realist aesthetic. In his study of "epistolary practices," William Merrill Decker remarks that fictionalized letters do not include a sense of time and distance: "Examining works like Richardson's *Clarissa* and Hannah Foster's *The Coquette* after reading authentic correspondence, one immediately notices an absence among fictional letters of the insistent spatiotemporal referencing that characterizes a genuine epistolary exchange" (246n8). *Emily Hamilton*, however, does include such comments on distance and the passage of time between visits.

Courtship and marriage, of course, are central to *Emily Hamilton*'s plot, and here, too, Vickery remains true to her times, incorporating various aspects of eighteenth-century expectations. No doubt, as a young woman in her early twenties, Vickery was intimately familiar with the conventions leading up to marriage, perhaps even deeply involved in them with Samuel Watson by the time she was writing her novel. In *Hands and Hearts: A History of Courtship in America*, Ellen K. Rothman details the rituals involved in courtship, and many of these same details can be found in *Emily Hamilton*. For example, she remarks that by "the last quarter of the eighteenth century, middle class Americans enjoyed considerable autonomy when it came to choosing their future mates" (26). Indeed, the state of one's heart and not the inclinations of one's parents became central to deciding whom to marry. Parental consent became more of a formality as time passed, and the legal requirements involving it steadily eroded. Vickery herself, while she places marginally more emphasis on the parental role in her novel than Rothman's findings suggest, stays mostly within these boundaries. Mary Carter, when she marries, has the blessing of her guardian grandparents, but her marriage is not contingent upon their consent; this generally holds true for Emily's wedding as well. Rothman notes that "most couples were prepared to marry without their parents' blessing, [but] they much preferred to marry with it." Moreover, overbearing parents who sought to impose their will on their children often found their aims subverted or resisted: "Secret engagements, conditional engagements, clandestine marriages were the result [of parental interference]; and public opinion was inclined to hold parents responsible for such undesirable situations" (29). The condemnation of tyrannical parents is not surprising, as Jay Fliegelman notes in his *Prodigals and Pilgrims*; the American Revolution was framed, after all, as a revolt against a tyrannical parent and an affirmation of "affectional and voluntaristic marriage" (129).

Vickery ably and realistically represents all of this in her novel. When Mr. Hamilton attempts to assert his will over his daughter by promoting Lambert, even in the face of her reservations about the man, Emily resists, albeit clandestinely, by attempting to avoid Lambert's company and coming out of her room to visit with him only when called upon. She extends herself only as far as politeness requires and not one step further. And when the truth of Lambert's character is revealed, her father apologizes for his interference and gives her free rein in her choice of a mate, recognizing, perhaps, that Emily is a better judge of future husbands than he is. Emily writes, "When I told them [her parents] that I had consented to receive Lambert's visits only to please them, and that he had no share in my affection, my father took my hand, and assured me that in any future instance of the kind, he never wished me to sacrifice inclination to duty." In fact, as Rothman documents, "friend" was a common appellation for kin during the colonial period, and as Fliegelman notes, friendship—or mentorship—was a way of avoiding the difference in power that the word "parent" implied. It supplied a sense of equality—or future equality—that was inevitable with the growth of children into adults. Emily frequently calls her parents her "friends," and Mary's grandparents, despite their considerable advancement in years, are still referred to in the novel as Mary's "friends."

If parents were friends whose relationship with their children should primarily be one of advising and guiding, tyrannical parents were bad parents. Mr. Hamilton's promotion of Lambert as a suitor is, from the point of view of the novel, wrong. Sympathy quite clearly lies with Emily and her judgment, which the novel's construction bears out when her estimation of Lambert is validated by facts from his past.[4] Condemnation of tyrannical parents reaches its fullest form, though, in the case of the fathers of Edward Belmont and Clara Belknap Belmont. The novel makes clear that the Belmont marriage is not one of love but is realized through a bargain between the fathers. Clara is even in love with another man at the time, a match her father opposes based not on rational reasoning but on prejudice (Le Fabre, the man she loves, is a Frenchman). This marriage is an unhappy one, a fact represented—though not revealed clearly—from the first appearance of Edward Belmont in the novel. To complicate the Belmonts' marriage further, Vickery appears to hint ever so subtly that Clara is an adulteress. To be sure, *Emily Hamilton*'s author is genteel enough not to establish this openly, but the suggestion that Clara frequents Le Fabre's company, in fact prefers it to her husband's, suggests that they might be involved in an adulterous affair. While one might debate whether Vickery meant to imply infidelity, she is quite clear in her representation of both Belmonts as miserable. Edward, after he learns of his wife's past and her present feelings, becomes melancholy, is even regretful of his marrying once he meets Emily, while Clara longs to be in the company of her former lover, and her unfulfilled desire leads to her decline and eventual death. Such are the fruits, the novel argues, for parents who act like tyrants rather than friends and advisors to their children.

Just as Vickery is true to the prevailing attitudes regarding parental involvement in children's lives, she is also faithful to the haggling that takes place over setting the wedding date. According to Rothman, women often chose the wedding date, but "very few selected the earliest possible one" (72). While finances, age, personal or family health, and the weather are all found as excuses in diaries and letters of the time, often women claimed they wanted "to prolong the period of their power" (qtd. in Rothman 72). Mary Carter cites just such a reason when she confides to Emily, "When I am married I expect to submit to his authority, but surely I ought to exercise my power as long as possible now." Rothman further notes that "women consistently sought longer, and men shorter, engagements" (72), women being less eager to enter into marriage than men. So it is in *Emily Hamilton* as well, as Mary relates to Emily how "Mr. Gray is importunate, and earnestly solicits that he may call me his, on the first week in March; I endeavor to have the ceremony deferred a month longer, at least; but his uncle and my friends are all on his side, and I have not much hope of prevailing." Although Vickery was single while she was composing *Emily Hamilton*, she was obviously quite familiar with the rituals and conflicts associated with the approach of marriage, perhaps through the experience of friends who had already married, and she accurately represented what she observed.

While she demonstrates her realist aesthetic in her representation of American society, Vickery also prefigures Henry James in her dedication to psychological realism. While James probably would not ultimately have approved of *Emily Hamilton*, were he to have read it, he might have at least appreciated how Vickery details the inner life of her characters, especially that of her titular character, whose letters occupy most of the book. In his preface to the New York Edition of *The Portrait of a Lady*, James remarks that he thought first of the character of Isabel Archer, around which the events and all the other characters of the novel essentially revolve. The centrality of Isabel Archer can be likened to that of Vickery's Emily Hamilton. Once Emily unwittingly falls in love with a married man, a significant portion of the novel is dedicated to the illustration of her struggle to overcome her emotions rather than to the exploration of following the dictates of passion blindly—a significant break with other, more popular novels of the period. Structuring her book around this conflict allows Vickery to display her main character's inner mental and emotional strength, ultimately developing an early strain of psychological realism that matured in novels by antebellum women and Nathaniel Hawthorne as well as in those by Henry James.[5]

We see Emily's struggles made plain in several letters, where the chief contest comes between passion and reason. This is not far from Foster's Eliza Wharton, who is advised to let her reason conquer her fancy (or imagination). The depth of Emily's struggle is revealed several times throughout the novel, but one of the most explicit passages occurs in letter 52:

> I retired early, but in vain did I endeavor to obtain repose; reflection kept me waking, but no consideration shall tempt me to act ungenerously with regard to Devas. I will be just, though I suffer more than I have ever yet done, to extirpate the idea of Belmont from my heart. Ah! my dear parents, could you see the heart of your darling Emily, torn as it is by conflicting passions, how would your aged bosoms bleed to behold such a strange medley of love, hope, anxiety, distress and remorse. My constitution is naturally good, but I perceive the agitation of my mind and the long anxiety I have suffered, has sensibly impaired my health. I have reasoned with myself till I have been perplexed almost to

distraction. I feel mortified at my weakness, but neither my pride nor my reason can teach me to banish entirely from my heart, a man, who, though he is the worthiest and most amiable of his sex, I wish I had never seen.

Vickery, however, is not content to rest in simply representing how Emily struggles with the knowledge of her own feelings, how she attempts to exert reason over emotion and fancy. She further complicates the situation by having her heroine learn that she is in turn loved by the object of her passion. Belmont's unwitting declaration along the garden wall brings Emily to a new depth of misery: "I went to my chamber and wept till my tears refused to flow any longer. The idea that I was beloved by him never entered my heart; and now the certainty of it renders me miserable." Always, in these letters, the focus remains on Emily's inner life, her struggle to deal with her emotional state, to let her reason dominate.

Moreover, while Emily Hamilton's inner conflict is central to the plot, the other characters also receive their due. Eliza Anderson deals with a faithless suitor, Mr. Gray mourns for his dead fiancée, and Mary Carter not only helps Mr. Gray overcome his grief but also articulates the pleasures and challenges of married life as Mrs. Gray, including how to balance her female friendships against her responsibilities as a wife. In fact, the entire novel is told from the point of view of the women. While Vickery was no doubt writing what she knew best, she also stays close to the "real life" experiences of women in 1803 America.

Another aspect of Vickery's realism is the rather remarkably unsentimental nature of *Emily Hamilton*. This is not to say that the novel is devoid of sentiment, but rather that Vickery "tones down" the emotional content in the interest of aligning the actions and experiences of her characters with those of her readers. One would expect to find, for example, heightened expressions of emotion when the women learn of the death of their friend Ashley, when Eliza's suitor proves faithless, or when Emily learns that one of her suitors has seduced a neighbor. But readers are simultaneously presented with young women who meet these challenges rationally and effectively rather than with overflowing and sustained grief. Similarly, there is considerably less overt moralizing in this novel than in those of several of her contemporaries. This is not to say that Vickery's characters are not susceptible to lecturing their correspondents and, by corollary, the readers of the novel, but the novel emphasizes plot and the psychology of her characters far more. Here, too, the epistolary format aids Vickery in her aesthetic goal, for when she does incorporate an overt moral lesson into the novel, she does so realistically through the voice of her characters; moreover, such lectures occur within the context of the larger action and are, therefore, not the main focus of any one letter, blunting the attention they might otherwise call to themselves. Mary Carter might reflect at length on the evils of card playing or the social strictures imposed on fallen women, but the moral center of the novel resides much more in how the characters think about and react to their personal experiences than in abstract lessons that purposely draw attention to themselves. Even William Dean Howells, the Dean of American Realism, might have appreciated Vickery's efforts, though perhaps not the final product.

If Vickery practices her realism through her characters and their situations, the epistolary format allows her to spotlight another key element of the novel: the statement it makes with regard to women's role in society. Vickery clearly stakes out a claim to women's independence of thought and action. Recall, for instance, that Mr. Hamilton does eventually tell his daughter that he and her mother will be guided by Emily's choice of a spouse. The novel foregrounds the importance of this lesson in the shape of Mrs. Belmont, whose separation from Le Fabre eventually destroys her happiness and herself. Happiness in marriage, in fact, is a key element in the novel, and the epistolary format allows the correspondents to explain their expectations regarding their spouses. In this novel, happiness consists not in a large fortune, but in *both* partners' satisfaction with their spouses. In short, women's happiness counts, and mutual compatibility is the message conveyed to readers. Such emphases place Vickery in line with what historian Jan Lewis has identified as the "republican wife," for whom mutual happiness, friendship, and a sort of equality in marriage were ideals to seek; financial gain was to be eschewed. It should also be observed that the novel consists only of letters by women, spotlighting, as Amy Winans has noted, the importance of women's friendships. This is a female-centered novel, with the male characters discussed and described solely by the women. Thus, through Vickery's technique, we must judge the male characters through the eyes of the female characters. This, too, lays claim to the importance of women's lives and perspective, making women's role in life central to the novel.

While the novel is overt in its statements about women and social conventions, it also makes some interesting, albeit subdued, statements about wealth and commercialism. Though not in the foreground, the marketplace plays a significant role in *Emily Hamilton*. For one thing, the two characters who are most associated with attempts to accumulate wealth in the novel die in the end. The first, Lambert, is out to make a financially rewarding marriage for himself. He expends a great deal of energy trying to win Emily Hamilton's hand, even after her rejection of him once he is found out to have seduced, impregnated, and abandoned another woman. The rake of the novel, Lambert follows the usual path of descent until he winds up under a death sentence, all of which happens "offstage," as his story is told via hearsay and gossip, never by his own first-person accounts. Charles Devas, the second character who sets out to make his fortune, is not a rake; he honorably sets forth to make money through honest work, intending to return and win Emily's hand. His uncle commissions Devas to attend to some business ventures in Baltimore; he further establishes generous terms for his nephew, thus enabling Devas to make his fortune and win Emily's regard and hand. But before he can return to marry Emily, his ship sinks and he is lost. Clearly, fortune hunting, legitimate or otherwise, is not reinforced in this novel, and it is the characters who already possess wealth who come out all right in the end. Nothing untoward happens within the timeline of the book to Emily's happily established parents, to her friends' parents, or to her near neighbor and chief love interest, Belmont. All of these characters possess wealth, property, and stability at the novel's outset. While Vickery presents a progressive view of women's lives and needs, she suggests a conservative attitude toward hunting for wealth and social mobility (at least by males, since Mary and Emily both rise in status through marriage).

Unquestionably, there is a richness to Vickery's writings that warrants considerably more scrutiny than they have heretofore received. Like many of her contemporaries, she wrestles with the issues of her day, particularly those pertinent to her own social position, be they marriage, women's rights, financial anxiety, or the life of the mind and spirit. These same issues remain with us today, making Vickery's work resonate for twenty-first-century readers, and perhaps it is in this century that the young poet and novelist of Leicester will finally find the national readership that eluded her in her own lifetime.

Notes

1. Foregrounding the truth of her tale was also a good marketing strategy, since most of the published novels of the day stressed their own fidelity to fact; even the gothic author Charles Brockden Brown asserted that *Wieland* had its origins in historic incidents.

2. Hawthorne, for example, sometimes requested that William Ticknor accompany him on trips, pick out his suits, order his cigars, pay his bills, buy postage stamps for him, and select a pet dog; Susan Warner asked G. P. Putnam to sell her picture of George Washington for her (Coultrap-McQuinn 37).

3. Vickery's contemporary, Maine novelist Sally Sayward Barrell Keating Wood, provides a pertinent example, since she produced her (known) fiction only during periods of widowhood, not during her two marriages.

4. The vindication of Emily's power to choose a husband without interference contrasts sharply with Foster's *Coquette*, where family and friends constantly push Eliza Wharton to marry Boyer, whom she does not love.

5. Cathy Davidson draws a connection specifically to *The Scarlet Letter*, though not in terms of psychological realism: "The novel [*Emily Hamilton*] anticipates *The Scarlet Letter* in its sympathetic portrayal of a woman who transgresses against her marriage vows but whose transgression is shown to have, much as Hester Prynne's, a justification of its own" ("Female Authorship" 11).

Works Cited

Bennett, John Barnard. "A Young Lady of Worcester County." Master's thesis. Wesleyan U, 1942.

Coultrap-McQuin, Susan. *Doing Literary Business: American Women Writers in the Nineteenth Century*. Chapel Hill: U of North Carolina P, 1990.

Davidson, Cathy N. "Female Authorship and Authority: The Case of Sukey Vickery." *Early American Literature* 21 (Spring 1986): 4–28.

———. *The Revolution and the Word: The Rise of the Novel in America*. New York: Oxford UP, 1986.

Fetterley, Judith. Introduction. *Provisions: A Reader from 19th-Century American Women*. Bloomington: Indiana UP, 1985.

Fliegelman, Jay. *Prodigals and Pilgrims: The American Revolution against Patriarchal Authority, 1750–1800*. New York: Cambridge UP, 1982.

Lewis, Jan. "The Republican Wife: Virtue and Seduction in the Early Republic." *William and Mary Quarterly* 44.4 (October 1987): 689–721.

Rothman, Ellen K. *Hands and Hearts: A History of Courtship in America*. New York: Basic Books, 1984.

Winans, Amy E. "Sukey Vickery." *American Women Prose Writers to 1820*. Ed. Carla Mulford, Angela Vietto, and Amy E. Winans. Vol. 200 of *Dictionary of Literary Biography*. Detroit: Gale, 1998. 380–84.

A Note on the Text

Emily Hamilton was published in 1803 by Isaiah Thomas Jr. and was never republished. The text is taken from this first edition, a copy of which is in the possession of the American Antiquarian Society and has been microfilmed as part of Wright's American Fiction. Eighteenth-century spelling and punctuation have been retained, and any ambiguities in word usage have been clarified in the notes. In bringing this new edition to publication, some silent changes were required. The heading of each letter (e.g., LETTER I) has been standardized for contemporary readers. The periods that followed each letter heading, salutation, date, and signature have been eliminated, as have the italics in each salutation (e.g., *To* Miss EMILY HAMILTON). The first word of each letter (and each published poem) was capitalized; this practice has not been retained. Silent changes were also made in places where confusion might occur, such as in the use of single and double quotation marks.

The texts of the published poems are taken from the *Massachusetts Spy*. Several titles originally appeared as capitalized italics (e.g., *RESIGNATION*); these formats have been standardized. Two of the poems include introductory paragraphs that were published in italics; these paragraphs now appear in a standard font, as do the dates of the poems. Capitalization found in the original publication has been retained for proper nouns and abstract concepts (e.g., CONTENT).

The unpublished manuscripts taken from the collection of the American Antiquarian Society are newly transcribed and have been collated with the transcriptions done by John Barnard Bennett for his 1942 master's thesis. A number of corrections to Bennett's transcriptions appear in this new edition, providing what is intended to be an entirely accurate representation of Vickery's work; Bennett's thesis was also central to verifying and occasionally correcting new transcriptions. Vickery was in the habit of underlining poem titles in her manuscripts; that practice has not been retained. The extracts from the poem "Tribute to Merit" (found in appendix 1) originally appeared in italics; they now appear in standard font. The translation of Virgil in appendix 1 is the editor's.

List of Characters in *Emily Hamilton*

Emily Hamilton, the heroine
Mary Carter, Emily's friend
Eliza Anderson, Emily's friend
Sophia Ashley, Emily's friend
Nancy Penniman, Emily's friend
Charles Devas, suitor to Emily
(William?) Lambert, suitor to Emily
Mr. Sever, suitor to Mary
George Gray, engaged to Sophia Ashley
Laurence Cutler, suitor to Eliza
Edmund Selwyn, suitor to Eliza
Mr. Hamilton, Emily's father
Mrs. Lucinda Hamilton, Emily's mother
Colonel and Mrs. Audley, Mary's grandparents
Mrs. Chapin, Eliza's aunt
Mrs. Penniman, Nancy's mother
Old Mr. Gray, George Gray's uncle
Louisa Selwyn, Edmund's sister
Fanny Devas, Charles's sister
Amelia Ashley, Sophia's sister
Betsey Winslow, a victim of seduction
Sally Parkman, a servant
Edward Belmont, neighbor to the Hamiltons
Clara Belmont, Edward's wife
Miranda Belmont, Edward's sister
Harriot Belmont, Edward's daughter
Le Fabre, former suitor to Clara Belmont
Mr. Belknap, Clara's father
Mr. and Mrs. Innman, friends to Mary Carter's parents

Emily Hamilton
and Other Writings

EMILY HAMILTON

EMILY HAMILTON, A NOVEL

FOUNDED ON INCIDENTS IN REAL LIFE

By a YOUNG LADY of WORCESTER COUNTY

Introduction

The following little work being intended principally for the perusal of my own sex, I flatter myself that they will view the production of a young Authoress with the eye of candor. Many imperfections will undoubtedly be discovered, for which, my youth and a scanty education must be an apology. Novel reading, is frequently mentioned as being in the highest degree prejudicial to young minds, by giving them wrong ideas of the world, and setting their tastes so high as to occasion a disrelish for those scenes in which they are necessitated to take a part. The observation will, in many respects, hold good, and there have been instances of the ruin of many young persons, produced by the erroneous ideas of romantic felicity, imbibed from an early attachment to this kind of reading. Novels, however, ought not to be indiscriminately condemned, since many of them afford an innocent and instructive amusement, and being written in the best style furnish the young reader with elegant language and ideas. Those which carry us too far from real life, and fill the imagination with a thousand enchanting images which it is impossible ever to realize, conveying at the same time an idea of perfect earthly happiness, ought never to be read till the judgment is sufficiently mature to separate the truth from the fiction of the story. But those which are founded on interesting scenes in real life, may be calculated to afford moral instruction to the youthful mind, in the most pleasing manner.

Perhaps some of the observations contained in the following pages may be found useful; I feel conscious of not having written any thing intentionally, which could have a tendency to injure the minds or morals of those who may honor them with their perusal, and if my efforts to please should be rewarded with a smile of approbation from a candid and liberal public, I shall be happy in endeavoring to deserve a continuance of their favors.

EMILY HAMILTON

Letter I

To Miss EMILY HAMILTON

W——, May 18

My Dear Emily,

If you have heard of the death of my father, you are no stranger
to the sorrow which rends the breast of your Mary. Early in life
deprived of my dear maternal friend, my father was rendered still
more dear to me. Heaven has been pleased to take him also from
me, and my distress on this melancholy occasion can be better
imagined than described. Oh! Emily, may you never experience
such sensations as mine; the days pass tediously along, and the
night brings me no repose. Sweet sleep is banished by my sorrows,
and the smiles of the season, though all nature blooms, can
afford no charm to lull my cares, or sooth[1] my anxious mind. The
distracted situation of my father's affairs, I have every reason to
believe, hastened his dissolution. Mr. Innman exerted himself all
in his favor, but it was too late to retrieve his property, and his
anxiety at leaving me an unprotected orphan, had increased with
his disorder, till the arrival of my grand parents, who adopted me
for their child, and I now experience from them all the tenderness
and affection they may be supposed to bestow on the offspring
of an only, beloved daughter. They omit nothing in their power
to render my residence with them agreeable; and my gratitude
induces me to suppress my grief, and endeavor to appear cheerful.
I hope after your return from Boston, that your letters will be
more frequent. Have you forgotten me, or do the pleasures you

are engaged in, occupy your mind too incessantly to permit you to devote an hour to friendship? A line from you, would for a moment dispel my cares, and animate with a smile of satisfaction the countenance of your

MARY CARTER

Letter II

To Miss MARY CARTER

Boston, June 7

The mournful intelligence of your father's death, my dear Mary, preceded your letter. With all the sympathy and compassion which your situation can excite, or friendship inspire, I share your sorrows, and earnestly wish for the moment to arrive when I shall clasp you to my heart and give you all the consolation in my power. I cannot be sensible of your sufferings, having never been deprived of indulgent parents, but fancy paints your distress in lively colors, and my tears flow while I view the sorrowful picture. I rejoice that you are with your grand parents, and shall ever revere them for their tenderness to you.

Adversity, my dear friend, is common to mortals; each one possesses a share of the misfortunes, as well as the pleasures of life. Daily observation, as well as the experience of past ages, teaches us, that perfect felicity is not to be found on earth. Though our sorrows are multiplied, and distresses on every side await us, we ought ever to reflect, that the goodness of the Deity is equal to his power, and feel assured that whatever trials he may appoint for us, he will afford us his gracious assistance to endure them. Though the dark clouds of adversity may for a while surround you, indulge the pleasing hope that you may again be blessed with the cheering smiles of peace and content.

"The sun which now envelop'd seems,
    Again may cheer the gloom of care,
    And gild those clouds that veil his beams.
    Nor always must the tear be shed,
    Nor always heav'd the rending sigh,
    The wounded heart must cease to bleed,
    And sorrow's flowing fount run dry."[2]

You have every reason to believe that your parents have exchanged a life of care, perplexity and distress, for a happy immorality.

"Then why should you repine,
    While Faith, with lifted hand
    Points to your kindred in yon blissful skies."[3]

You have a consolation above many; though an orphan, you have venerable friends who will watch over your youth, and guard you from those dangers to which unprotected females, especially if young and beautiful, are ever exposed.

The heat of the weather increases so rapidly, that I shall very soon return to S——, and visit again those loved retreats, where we have passed so many happy hours. Eliza Anderson will return with me; she has written to you and often mentions you with esteem and friendship. May peace resume her wonted seat in the gentle bosom of my lovely friend. Yours with affection,

EMILY HAMILTON

Letter III

To Miss EMILY HAMILTON

W——, July 20

Your letter, my dear Emily, afforded great consolation, and the affectionate attention of my venerable friends have restored me to a degree of cheerfulness to which I have long been a stranger. The society here is perfectly agreeable—the ladies are friendly and social; their conversation is sentimental and elegant.—Last Thursday I passed an agreeable afternoon at Col. Warner's. With his daughter Melissa, I have contracted an intimate acquaintance. She is truly amiable, and we live as sisters. She had invited a large party, and I have not made a more agreeable visit since I left S——. Some gentlemen attended in the evening, and as the weather was remarkably cool for the season, they proposed dancing, which the ladies readily accepted. At the earnest solicitation of a Mr. Sever I danced once, and then retired. Though my cheerfulness is in a great measure restored, my heart is not yet light enough to permit me to join in what once formed my most pleasing amusements, with any degree of alacrity. My grand mamma gently reproved me for returning home so soon. "It is not by secluding yourself from company and amusement, my dear girl," she said, "that you must expect to mitigate your sorrow; cheerful and innocent pleasures will have a much better effect. I do not wish you to become dissipated; our pleasures are criminal, only when we indulge in them to excess. Innocent mirth, I am always desirous to promote in young people, and though I am too old to take a part in their amusements, I always share the pleasure they receive from them. I shall always be happy, Mary, to see you so, and it is my wish that you should join in every rational diversion our neighborhood affords." I expressed my sense of her goodness as well as I was able, but the recollection of the favors I am daily receiving from her, operated forcibly on my mind, and gratitude almost suppressed the power of utterance.

I received a letter from Mrs. Innman a few days since, with the melancholy intelligence that Sophia Ashley was in a confirmed consumption. I wish most ardently to see her, but it is not probable I ever shall. You will undoubtedly visit her, and I wish you to write as particular as you can concerning her. Mrs. Innman wrote that she was to have been married this fall, to a very deserving man, for whom she entertained the greatest affection. I have never seen him, but from what I have heard of his character, I am induced to think him worthy of her. The approach of death is seldom welcome, except to those whom misfortunes have rendered weary of life. But,

> "When scenes of promis'd joy are nigh,
> Youth presuming, beauty blooming,
> Oh! how dreadful 'tis to die."[4]

Sophia, the pride of her sex, must ere long be consigned to the silent mansions of the dead. But will not the consoling reflection, that

> "The fairest flowers that grace this earthly sod,
> Are cull'd to beautify the dame of God,"[5]

be sufficient to check, though not wholly suppress, those painful sensations which her surviving friends must experience when they are deprived of an object so much beloved, and so deserving of their affection.

Such is the disposition implanted in us by nature, that though we have every reason to believe our departed friends are happy, we cannot forbear to mourn. Though reason teaches us that we ought rather to rejoice at their felicity, than to lament the loss we sustain, by being deprived of their society, it is not frequent that we can acquire sufficient philosophy to conquer the selfish principle which nature has given us, and to rejoice in their happiness while ourselves are distressed. Adieu, my dear Emily; may angels guard your steps and peace and happiness be ever yours.

MARY CARTER

Letter IV

To Miss MARY CARTER

S——, August 15

I have just returned, my dear friend, from a visit to Sophia Ashley. You desired me to write particularly concerning her. She is extremely weak, and so emaciated, you would scarce know her. I never saw a more interesting object; her fine dark eyes are irradiated with more than usual lustre. Her complexion, naturally very fine, appears more dazzling white; a faint glow tinges her cheeks, as her disorder at times renders respiration difficult. She is evidently wasting rapidly, but expresses no anxiety at her declining state; she is patient, tranquil and resigned. She talked for some time with her usual cheerfulness, till in the course of the conversation Mr. Gray was mentioned.—A mournful expression instantly took place of the smile which had before animated her features. "Ah! Miss Hamilton," said she, "that name will ever be dear to me. My attachment is not lessened by my infirmity; could any earthly object make me wish for life, it would be him. I already feel the pang that will rend his breast when I am no more. But the dearest friends must part, and can our separation be more painful now, than after a succession of happy years spent in contributing to each others felicity?" I was going to reply, but Amelia entering the chamber with the intelligence that Mr. Gray had arrived, prevented me. He came up soon after; Sophia received him with a smile which his feelings would not permit him to return. She saw the distraction of his mind, and with forced cheerfulness inquired about the people at R——, and the amusements of the season. He answered her inquiries affectionately, and taking her hand asked her if she was able to ride, adding that he had just purchased a remarkably easy chaise, and as the weather was perfectly agreeable, he hoped the air would be beneficial to her. She appeared pleased with the proposal, and desiring me to excuse her for leaving me, said she would ride a few miles. At her return she was much better, and took tea with the family. Mr. Gray was delighted with the alteration, and obtained her promise to ride with him the following morning. I do not think it is probable that she will live many months, but it is possible that she may continue till winter. I wish it was in your power to have the satisfaction of seeing her once more, and I am not without a hope that you will come. Yours with sincere friendship,

EMILY HAMILTON

Letter V

To Miss MARY CARTER

S———, September 18

Since I wrote you last, my dear Mary, a great alteration has taken place in our family. On the first week in this month, my sister Catherine gave her hand to Mr. Perry, in presence of a large party, who were invited on the occasion. And last week Fanny gave her's to Mr. Delwyn. They are both gone to reside at P———. I expect they will be rather discontented in that remote place, as they have ever been accustomed to see a great deal of company. It is a fortunate circumstance, however, that they will live very near each other.—I should have gone with them, but my mother was too unwell to permit my having an idea of leaving her. If she regains her usual health, I shall visit them in the winter with Charles Devas, who is nearly related to Mr. Perry. Charles, you know, was always very attentive to me, and I have reason to believe his partiality increases.—I esteem him highly for his amiable qualities and engaging manners, but it is his friendship alone I wish for, as I am conscious I never shall experience any other regard towards him.

True friendship is the most noble, exalted and generous sentiment that ever actuated the human mind. But how few are there who are capable of enjoying it in its original purity. How few are to be found who do not mingle selfishness, avarice, pride and ambition, with this most delicate refinement of the soul. It is by this, that friendship becomes no more than

—————"A name,
A charm that lulls to sleep,
A shade, that follows wealth or fame,
But leaves the wretch to weep."[6]

How often do we see people while in prosperity, followed, courted, caressed and admired; friends surround them on every side, and every face salutes them with a flattering smile. But the moment the scene is changed, those "summer friends" forsake them, and by their altered behavior, the shafts of adversity are acuminated, and their situation rendered still more wretched. A real friend is one of the greatest blessings of life. How truly wretched must that person be, who has no one to whom he can give the endearing appellation of friend, no one, in whose generous breast he can confide his secrets, and repose his cares.—The world, in such a situation, must appear a wilderness, and mankind as savages, from whom he has every thing to dread, and nothing to hope. Who would wish for existence without a friend? Not all the wealth the Indies could afford would bring one real joy, unless we could share it with those for whom we felt a particular affection.

"Our joys when extended, will always increase,
Our griefs when divided, are hush'd into peace."[7]

You, my dear Mary, have often experienced those delightful sensations which arise from performing those delicate attentions of friendship, which mitigates the pangs of adversity, and "lends the brow of woe a smile."[8] I am interrupted, adieu my dear girl; I anticipate the receipt of a letter from you by the next post. Sincerely yours,

EMILY HAMILTON

Letter VI

To Miss EMILY HAMILTON

W——, September 30

It is past twelve o'clock, the family have retired to rest, but not feeling any inclination to sleep, I devote myself to the pleasing amusement of writing to my Emily. A walk by moonlight, you are sensible, was always highly gratifying to me. This evening I walked for some time, and at my return, seated myself a short distance from the house, beneath a venerable elm. The moon shone with more than usual lustre, all was serene and beautiful, no sound was heard but the cherup of the cricket and the soft sighing of the breeze. The time and place was suited for contemplation, the beauty of the scene diffused a soft calmness over my mind; I retraced all the innocent, sportive scenes of our childhood when, hand in hand, we rambled through fields and groves, free from care, and gay as the airy songsters that warbled on the surrounding branches. That sweet romantic recess, where we have passed so many happy hours, was present to my view. I was seated with you and Eliza Anderson on the sloping bank—I saw the willows waving over the stream which fell dashing from rock to rock with its usual murmuring sound—I heard the gentle accents of your voice, and should long have continued in this dream of felicity, if the sudden noise of a carriage had not roused me from my reverie.

I should have realized this delightful vision, had not my grand mamma been attacked with a severe illness. She is recovering slowly, but we all feared her disorder would have been fatal. I shall not think of leaving her at present; in the winter, perhaps, I shall have the happiness to behold once more, those friends who will ever be dear to my heart. I enclose a letter for Sophia Ashley, which I wish you to convey to her; perhaps it will be the last testimony of my friendship she will ever receive.

I had no idea that Catherine and Fanny would have been married this fall; I should admire to see them in their new situation. They have both the most flattering prospects of future felicity; long, very long may they realize them. I was present a few days since, at the wedding of a Miss Hunt. A small number of her most intimate acquaintance were invited, of whom, I had the honor of being considered as one. She behaved with the greatest propriety. The deportment of Mr. Howard was dignified, tender and respectful. Their clothes were elegant and well chosen. Those of the bride were such as showed the elegance of her taste. I was attended by Mr. Sever, whom I mentioned in a former letter. This gentleman has been remarkably attentive to me ever since I resided here. I esteem him for many amiable qualities, but I am conscious I never shall experience that attachment to him, which he expresses towards me. Many of his opinions differ extremely from mine; he is fond of company, parade and show; my taste, you are sensible, is quite the reverse, and at present there is no probability that either of us will embrace the opinion of the other. His estate is small, but you are too well acquainted with my heart to imagine I would refuse an amiable man, merely for his want of property. No, could I meet with a man whose temper, taste and disposition agreed with my own, though his fortune were scanty, it would be no objection. I would willingly share with him his little all, and by industry and economy strive to increase our store. Mr. Sever must alter greatly, before I venture to give him the encouragement he earnestly solicits. His manner of living is vastly too expensive for his income, and the round of pleasures he is constantly engaged in, preclude even a possibility of his increasing his estate by his own industry. Such a man as this it would be absolute madness to marry, for in such circumstances, where is the woman whose industry and frugality could keep pace with his profuseness? Being engaged in conversation with him, a few evenings since, I ventured to hint, with all possible delicacy, at his extravagant conduct. He replied that youth was the season for pleasure, and he wished to indulge himself as far as decency would permit, in all the diversions he could. If I would give him a hope that he should ever obtain me, he would endeavor to become sedate and sober. I told him that my favor depended wholly on his future deportment. Too much inclined to dullness, I must bid you adieu, and retire to rest.

MARY CARTER

Letter VII

To Miss MARY CARTER

S——, October 28

Another letter from my dearest Mary; sweet girl, though we are divided I have still the happiness of knowing that I am not absent from your mind. I often take the greatest pleasure in retracing former happy scenes; our friendship began with life, and I never have enjoyed myself more perfectly than in your society.—I made a visit yesterday to Sophia Ashley. Her strength decays rapidly, but she is perfectly calm and resigned. When I entered her chamber she was sitting in an easy chair; Young's Night Thoughts,[9] in which she had been reading, lay in her lap. Her beautiful eyes sparkled with pleasure; she smiled, and holding out her hand to me, told me she was happy to receive another visit from me. Her appearance affected me beyond expression; in spite of all my efforts to prevent it my tears began to flow. "Why do you weep, my dear Emily?" said she, "your tears cannot restore me; I am resigned to the will of heaven, and often look forward with rapture to the hour of my release. Then will my happiness begin; my soul will take her flight to those blissful regions, where pain and sorrow, and the evils and vicissitudes of this life are denied admittance. No unrepented crime hangs heavy on my heart; all within is peaceful and serene. My heart is filled with gratitude to that being who gave me existence, that he has enabled me to resign it cheerfully to his will, with the blessed hope of a happy immortality." "Ah! Sophia," said I, "this will be great consolation to your sorrowing friends." "And can they," she replied, "wish for greater? But a few short years, Miss Hamilton, and we shall meet, never more to endure the pangs of a separation. Till within a few days my mind has been anxious concerning my Gray. I was his by inclination and affection; the day for our union was fixed; next month our nuptials were to have been celebrated, but ere that period arrives, this form will be inanimate, and the heart which has so long been his own, will cease to beat. But that same gracious Being who has hitherto supported me, will support him, and enable him to bear our separation with fortitude." Here her voice faltered; she heaved a sigh and after two or three minutes silence continued, "I am sensible, Emily, that Mr. Gray will be afflicted, greatly afflicted when I die: Be it yours, my dear friend, to administer consolation to the unhappy mourner. Tell him his Sophia wishes him to rejoice that she is removed from a world where happiness will not admit of perfection; tell him to be prepared to meet her in heaven, there to enjoy with her a blissful eternity. It is my desire that he may submit without repining, to the divine will, and to reflect that affliction is ever accompanied with mercy."

"The ways of heaven are dark and intricate,
    Puzzled with mazes, and perplex'd with errors,

Our understanding traces them in vain,
Nor sees with how much art the windings run,
Nor where the regular confusion ends."[10]

The family now entered, and Sophia desired to rest. Her parents and sister are deeply affected, while she begs them to check their sorrow and be resigned to an event, which she is sensible will soon approach. I shall visit her again in a few days, and will write directly after my return as I know you will be anxious to hear from her. Ever yours,

EMILY HAMILTON

Letter VIII

To Miss MARY CARTER

S——, November 17

Sophia, the amiable, engaging Sophia is no more. This morning her sainted spirit took its flight to the blest mansions of eternal peace. I came here yesterday, and was with her when she expired. She sat in her chair, and opening her handkerchief said, "the moment of my release is fast approaching," and expired in a few minutes after without a groan or struggle. Oh! Mary, description cannot do justice to what I then suffered. Her cold, inanimate features still wear the expression which they borrowed from her spotless mind. Innocence, virtue and benignity, still shine on the countenance of my friend; still let me hang over this dear form, and recal to mind every engaging virtue, every endearing quality of her, whom I shall converse with no more. The whole family are in the deepest sorrow; her aged mother wrings her hands and weeps, while her father making a vain attempt to conceal the anguish of his heart, endeavors to sooth[11] her, and offers that consolation which alone can mitigate their sufferings, religious hope, and unshaken confidence in God. Amelia's grief has rendered her almost incapable of attending to any thing; to her the stroke is unusually severe. The unfortunate Gray has not yet arrived. Sophia appeared to be unusually well yesterday, and he went to B—— upon business. He is sent to, and I expect he will soon be here. Adieu, I must attend Amelia; in the evening, perhaps, I shall have another opportunity to write.

Gray has arrived, despair is painted on his countenance. He endeavored to speak, but his feelings at first were too painful.—He took my hand, and laying his on his heart, fixed his eyes on mine with such an expression of sadness, as pierced me to the soul. "Oh! show me the dear remains," was all he could utter. I went to the room with him, he gazed on the corpse with silent anguish, his tears were dried, he could scarce breathe. He sunk into a chair and a deep sigh at length relieved his laboring breast. He entreated me to leave him for a few moments. "I will endeavor," said he, "to calm my grief, that I may be able to meet the family, if you will grant me a few minutes indulgence in private." I withdrew into the adjoining room, and he came to me in half an hour after, comparatively tranquil. A settled melancholy appears in his countenance, but his deportment is admirable. It is late and I must retire with Amelia; dear girl, may she find that repose which she so greatly needs.

21st

I have just returned from paying the last sad tribute of affection to my departed friend. "The cold grave now contains all that I held most dear," said Gray just now, "I feel an aching void in my heart. That lovely form where all the graces shone is cold, is lifeless; those eyes, which so lately beamed with sense and goodness, are forever closed, and all their lustre extinguished. Oh! Miss Hamilton, ask your own feeling heart, if ever wretchedness surpassed mine? Happiness long anticipated, was within my reach; but ah! how suddenly am I plunged into an abyss of woe! never more shall I taste of peace." "Strive to calm your sorrows," said I; "believe me, Mr. Gray, time will soften your anguish; your Sophia bade me offer you consolation; she wished you to be resigned and to reflect that she was happier, far happier than she could possibly have been on earth."

"Ah!" he replied, "perhaps she now sees me; perhaps the tear of celestial pity trembles in her eye; if tears of pity can be shed in heaven, she sheds them for me. No more on the fine evenings of summer shall I ramble with her, no more hear the sound of her silver voice. Never shall I realize those delightful visions of felicity which we have both indulged. How often have our imaginations painted in glowing colors, scenes of happiness which we were never to taste. But perhaps I ought not to intrude my sorrows upon you; it is natural for misery to complain—Will you forgive me?" "Yes," I replied, "I will freely indulge you. When the heart is oppressed, it is luxury to disburden to a sympathizing friend." "I hope," said he, "that time will soften my grief, but ages can never erase the lovely girl from my heart." Amelia entered the room where we were sitting, and Mr. Gray soon after withdrew. "Mr. Gray bears his misfortune with more calmness than I expected," said Amelia; "he adored my sister, and I feared her death would deprive him of reason." "I am glad," I replied, "that he is so calm, but I fancy he feels more than he wishes to express."

My father now came to carry me home, and left the family with regret. Mrs. Ashley and Amelia entreated me to visit them as often as possible. The house of mourning, my dear Mary, is instructive. I would not exchange my present melancholy sensations, this sweet pensiveness which is far from being unpleasing, for all the giddy mirth I ever experienced. Sorrow softens and ennobles the heart, and makes it more capable of receiving virtuous impressions.— Heaven grant that I may improve by the scene I have so lately witnessed, and that I may leave the world with the same bright prospect before me, that enabled Sophia to welcome death as the messenger of peace and happiness. May angels guard your steps, and felicity, temporal and eternal be yours. Adieu,

EMILY HAMILTON

Letter IX

To Miss EMILY HAMILTON

W———, December 20

I have not till now, my dear Emily, had an opportunity to answer your letters. I saw Mr. Anderson before I received your letters, and he informed me that Sophia was no more.

> Too good the mis'ries of the world to share,
>> The hand of mercy snatch'd her from our sight;
> Releas'd from this abode of grief and care,
>> Her gentle spirit sought the realms of light.
> From the rich source whence endless blessings flow,
>> She now celestial happiness enjoys,
> And blest beyond what mortals ere can know,
>> Drinks the rich cup of bliss that never cloys.[12]

Amelia must feel her loss more than any of the family. I can truly sympathize with her. I can write but little, as the person by whom I shall send this is waiting.—Next month I expect to visit you; I anticipate the time with pleasure. Ever yours,

MARY CARTER

Letter X

To Miss MARY CARTER

S——, January 8

Your short letter, my dear Mary, came safe to hand. I shall expect you with impatience; I shall count the hours, which, rapid as they fly, will seem tedious till you arrive. Do prevail with your grand mamma to dispense with your company for a month or six weeks; nothing could oblige us more. Eliza Anderson begs that you will set out as soon as you receive this; she is quite impatient, she says, for an interview. "I suppose," said Eliza, "that she will have new clothes to make, or something to fix to attract the attention of our beaux, that will keep her employed a fortnight." You know Eliza's lively manners; she is always sprightly, and she has such a flow of spirits, she is ever animated and gay. A Mr. Cutler, has for some months past, paid particular attention to her. "What would you do," said I, "if Mary should engage the attention of Mr. Cutler?" "Do?" she replied, "why I would be revenged some way, but I'll take care that he shall not see her; I had rather she would stay at Connecticut all her days than engross his affection." "I infer from this," said I, "that you are really in love with him." "I never told you I was," she replied. "But you cannot deny it though, my dear Eliza." "I could if I would utter a falsehood, but I do not feel greatly disposed to commit a crime at present. I am going to be serious now; the weather is extremely fine for the season; I never saw it more pleasant in January.—But do tell me your opinion frankly, Emily; if I were always to talk serious, would not my friends be better pleased with me?" "They are pleased with you now," said I; "you are innocently gay, and have serious intervals no doubt." "Indeed I do," she replied; "I am not the thoughtless, giddy creature people take me to be; I often have whole hours of serious reflection when alone, but when I am in company, I cannot suppress my vivacity. It is natural, my gaiety was born with me, and I believe it will never forsake me." "I hope," said I, "that you never will meet with any misfortune to depress your spirits, and that you will ever enjoy an uninterrupted series of innocent pleasures, untainted by care or gloomy discontent." "It is from contentment alone," she replied, "that my vivacity flows. I am one of those beings who generally find something pleasing in every object they behold. I mean to have a charming time this evening; I shall make Fanny Davis a visit, and she wishes you to accompany me. My brother will go, and Laurence Cutler, and your Charles will form quite a social little party." I thanked her and told her that I should be engaged in writing to you this evening, and that, and some family matters which could not be dispensed with, would prevent my being one of the happy party. Cheerfulness, I think, is perfectly consistent with religion. Does not a person who is always easy and contented, who looks around him with admiration and delight, who is sensible to the beauties of nature, whose heart is always filled with gratitude for the blessings which a bountiful Creator is showering around him, contribute more to the honor of his Maker, than one who indulges a fretful, gloomy, morose disposition; who views all objects with disgust or indifference, and is angry at seeing others enjoy themselves? It is not by always gazing at the dark side of an object, that we must expect to gain satisfaction or content. In every enjoyment of life, some tincture of the bitter is always mingled with the most delicious sweets.—But shall we refuse to enjoy the sweet fragrance of the rose, because a thorn may happen to wound our fingers as we pluck it? Were we always regaled with luxuries, they would pall upon our appetites, and we should lose our relish for them; but after we have experienced a transient evil, we receive the good that follows it with increased pleasure. Cheerfulness is ever attendant on Content, and we cannot be wretched while blest with their smiles.

Come sweet Content, celestial maid,
In all thy heavenly charms array'd,
Reside within my breast.
To thee I tune my rural lyre,
Thy charms my infant muse inspire,
Oh! deign to make me blest.
'Tis thine, sweet power, to soften care,
To chase the gloomy fiend Despair,
And bid the fleeting hours,
More swiftly, sweetly pass away,
And as their changing joys decay,
Protract their pleasing powers.
Creation's beauties vainly glow,
In vain shall heaven their charms bestow
Without thy cheering aid.
In vain the blooming spring delights,
Or Autumn's lib'ral hand invites,
All, all their beauties fade.
'Tis thine to check the anxious sigh,
To wipe the tear from sorrow's eye,
And sooth[13] the aching heart.
Oh! then with me forever dwell,
Thou, in a palace or a cell
Canst happiness impart.[14]

Adieu, my dear Mary, I shall now expect you every hour.

EMILY HAMILTON

Letter XI

To Miss EMILY HAMILTON

W——, January 14

Next Monday, my dear Emily, I shall set out for S——. My heart
beats with impatience for the day to arrive.—I was present last
evening at an elegant ball; this is the first I have attended here,
though frequently solicited to go. The amusements here, are very
different from those at S——. Cards, so fashionable with you, form
no part of an evening diversion here, and I am really rejoiced at
it. A game at cards may at some times be pleasing, but they ought
never to be introduced into a company of sensible people. Cards,
by banishing rational conversation, too often exclude friendship,
and many times excite envy, if not malice. I have often with regret,
seen the countenances of my female friends redden with anger,
after being losers at several games in succession, and have many
times heard them use indecent, if not profane language, to express
their sentiments on the occasion. And by this, what was introduced to heighten the pleasure of the company is generally in the
end, a source of peevishness and discontent. I once heard a gentleman at S——, remark, that it was the surest way in the world to
judge of a lady's disposition, to see her engaged at a card table. If
she won without being extremely elated, or lost without suffering
her vivacity to be depressed, he should think her temper excellent.
Your own judgment will convince you whether his observation
will always hold good. Perhaps he did not reflect, that there might
be some art used in both instances.

I have often heard the men make this observation, that cards
preserved the characters of the absent. Since a lady could not be
supposed to attend to the game, and to scandal at the same time.
I hope there are not many who deserve this reproach. That there
are some who delight to injure absent characters, cannot be denied. But can it be possible that a lady of any delicacy or sensibility,

can wish to injure any one's reputation, especially one of her own sex? Can a lady hope to raise her own reputation by ruining that of another, or conceal her own faults, by industriously striving to prevent the frailties and errors of others from being buried in oblivion?—Would she not appear to infinitely greater advantage, by drawing the veil of candor and charity over their errors, and endeavoring to bring their good qualities into view? Let those who are so fond of expatiating on the follies of others, turn their attention to themselves, and they may find sufficient employment for their powers of reformation. Would each one as industriously strive to correct their own errors, as they do to correct those of others, they would in a short time discover the benefit which would result from it. We all have something to amend in our conduct, and we should undoubtedly be wiser and better if more of our time were employed in examining our hearts, and removing our own bad qualities. Did every one take this method, I am persuaded we should hear very little scandal. I shall conclude this with some lines which I read a few days since in an old magazine; I presume you will be as much pleased with them as I am.

> "Think not, my Emma, e'er to rise,
>   Nor hope to win by your bright eyes,
>   If slander you embrace.
> For know, that she who slander's friends,
>   Or hears them wrong'd and not defends,
>   Shall meet deserv'd disgrace.
> Lay not the basis of your fame
>   On ruins of another's name,
>   Nor envy merit's praise;
> Be virtue your unerring guide,
>   Gain one true friend, in her confide,
>   Till death winds up your days."[15]

ever yours,

MARY CARTER

Letter XII

To Miss EMILY HAMILTON

W——, February 6

I have only time, my dear Emily, to inform you of my safe return. The riding was very disagreeable, but fortunately, we met with no accident to retard us a moment. My grand parents received me with pleasure. How shall I repay their constant tenderness! All I can do is to retain them in grateful remembrance. Mr. Sever was the first to bid me welcome; he professed himself vastly glad to see me, and of consequence I was obliged to be entertained by him the whole evening. My respects to your parents and compliments to my acquaintance at S——. I shall expect a letter from you by the bearer of this, and I hope a longer one than I have time to write. Ever yours.

MARY CARTER

Letter XIII

To Miss MARY CARTER

S——, March 1

I am glad, Mary, that you wrote so soon after your journey. I felt anxious for your safety, as the roads were so bad, but your letter has put an end to my fears and restored my tranquility. If you had tarried with us a fortnight longer, the riding would have been more agreeable, and you would have been present at another ball. On Thursday we all went to Mr. Davis's; the hall was tolerably well filled, the music was excellent, and I never was more animated in my life. The evening glided away I knew not how; I had no idea that it was more than nine, when one of the ladies told me the clock had just struck eleven. I was sorry that the hour to retire had arrived, the company was so agreeable, the music and every thing so pleasing. Mr. Lambert, the young merchant, to whom you were introduced at Mr. Anderson's, was my partner. Though he has resided in this town but a few weeks, his amiable manners and lively conversation have procured him the esteem of all who are acquainted with him. He inquired if I had heard from you since you left us; I told him I had; he then inquired if your journey had been agreeable, &c. and concluded with saying, "If Miss Carter were here, she would be an additional ornament to our ball." I got home a little before twelve. Mr. Lambert requested permission to pass an hour with me the next evening, a request too agreeable to refuse. He came accordingly, and I must do him the justice to say, he appears to be a finished gentleman. Whether I am deceived by his appearance or not, I cannot determine. His character is very good here, and at N——, the place where he resided last. I am not apt to be very suspicious, yet I should like to know more concerning him. I must own I do not wish to hear any thing to his disadvantage; his manners and conversation are peculiarly elegant and pleasing. If he continues as agreeable as he appears at present, I think it probable I shall be quite pleased with his society. Adieu my dear Mary, and believe me sincerely yours.

EMILY HAMILTON

Letter XIV

To Miss EMILY HAMILTON

W——, April 2

Then you frankly own what I told you I suspected when at S——. I could easily discover your partiality for Lambert, and was pleased to see him so very attentive to you. I shall be quite disappointed if there is not a greater degree of intimacy between you, than you perhaps imagine. He is indeed a very agreeable man, and I am happy that it is in my power to give you some information respecting his family and character. Two circumstances which are highly necessary for you to be acquainted with before you engage your heart too far.

A gentleman from C——, was at our house a few days after my return from S——, and asked me several questions respecting Mr. Lambert. From this gentleman I obtained my information. His parents reside at C——, and are very wealthy, respectable people. Lambert went to reside with an uncle when he was fourteen years old, and at his uncle's death he became by his will, sole heir to his estate, which was between two and three thousand pounds. Col. Woodworth, with whom he resided at N——, was his guardian. His character is very good; the gentleman remarked that he was rather inclined to profuseness than the contrary, but he never suffered his expenses to exceed his income. That his disposition is excellent, is acknowledged by all; his natural and acquired abilities are such as to render him respectable. After this information, my dear Emily, from a person who has been acquainted with him for many years, I presume you will not hesitate a moment. I think you may safely venture to encourage his attention. No female ought to receive the addresses of a man with whom she is but slightly acquainted, till she makes an inquiry concerning his character. If she is deceived in her expectations, after she has received all possible information concerning him, she will at least have the consolation to reflect, that it was not owing to her own indiscretion. A man of sense would not have a very favorable opinion of a girl, who would, without inquiry, accept him without hesitation. He certainly would not have a very high opinion of her prudence, if he had of her virtue. Since the path of rectitude is so narrow, females especially, ought to be very cautious how they deviate from it.— One error has frequently been attended with remediless ruin. Men are allowed to trace their steps back again, but women never. "If once they fall, they fall to rise no more."[16] A melancholy instance of this truth has recently occurred but a few miles from us. A young girl of sixteen by the name of Matilda Capron, had been very much admired for two or three years, for her uncommon beauty, and her sprightly conversation gave pleasure to all who heard her. She was courted and caressed by all whose circumstances permitted them to consider themselves on an equality with her. She repulsed them all as considering herself too young to engage her affections to any one, but it was visible that she took pride in the innumerable conquests her beauty and wit had gained. Sometime last spring, a gentleman who was travelling for the benefit of the country air, as he was in a declining state, stopped at a tavern but a short distance from Mr. Capron's, intending to remain there a few weeks. In a day or two after, as he was walking out with his landlord's daughters, he saw Matilda. Charmed with her uncommon beauty, he inquired who she was, and requested the girls to call at her father's when they returned from their walk. They complied with his request, and invited Matilda to pass the next afternoon with them. She accepted the invitation, and was conducted home by the agreeable stranger. He soon found means to gain her esteem, and his visits to her became very frequent. A visible alteration took place in his health, which he imputed to her. "You" said he, "have restored me to health; I can never forget the obligation; it is in your power alone to make me completely happy.—Permit me to hope that I may pass the remainder of my days in endeavoring to make you so. I cannot live without you." She owned a return of his passion for her, and very indiscreetly consented, as her parents were very much opposed to their intimacy, to see him as often as he pleased, provided he would make his visits in a private manner. Nearly two months had passed in this way when a letter was brought to Matilda by a boy who belonged to the tavern. She opened it and found enclosed a fifty dollar bill, and on reading the letter she found that the man in whom she had placed the highest confidence, had left her. He assured her that he should never forget the favors she had conferred on him, and wished that she might be happy with some one who was at liberty to return her affection; adding that as he was already married, it was not in his power to fulfill the promises which he was now sincerely sorry he had made her. Matilda for the first time saw her error; she became melancholy and dejected; she shunned society, and would frequently pass whole days in her chamber. Her parents suspected the cause, and with the tenderest solicitude entreated her to make them acquainted with the causes of her dejection. But all their entreaties were vain; she still concealed the fatal secret till her situation became too obvious to remain longer unknown. Unable to bear her disgrace, or witness the silent reproaches she received from every eye, she walked to the place where she had been accustomed to meet her seducer, and with a ribband he had given her, suspended herself from the branch of a tree on which he had engraved his name and her own. She was found soon after by her father who was accidentally passing that way. It is not in the power of language to do justice to the sufferings of this afflicted family. After her funeral they found the story of her misfortunes which she had written and directed to her parents; from this it appeared, that she expected to go with him, and that he had engaged to carry her to Newhampshire,[17] and marry her privately. Young and inexperienced she listened to the deluding flattery of an artful libertine, and in the flower of youth and beauty, made her exit in the most horrid manner. Let her unfortunate story serve as a warning to all who may be acquainted with it, and teach every female to distrust the man who seeks to conceal his intentions from her parents. Honorable love will never seek concealment. Had Matilda possessed as much prudence as beauty, she might have been happy. Very little penetration would have sufficed to discover his intentions before she had proceeded far. But it is more than probable that her pride and vanity were gratified by the attentions of a man whose appearance was uncommonly splendid, and from this motive she had encouraged those attentions till it was too late to retract. You, my dear Emily, will drop the tear of pity for the sad fate of this lovely, unfortunate girl; we are all liable to err, and ought therefore to be constantly on our guard. Adieu my dear friend, may happiness be ever yours.

MARY CARTER

Letter XV

To Miss MARY CARTER

S——, May 9

The intelligence concerning Mr. Lambert, communicated in your friendly letter, pleased me extremely. He improves upon acquaintance, and I think him very amiable. My parents are pleased with his attentions, and he can easily perceive by their behavior to him, that he is a welcome visitant. I received a letter this morning from Nancy Penniman, in answer to one I sent her some time since, in which I invited her to leave the noise and bustle of Boston for awhile, and enjoy the beauties of nature with me in the country. She has accepted the invitation, and I expect her next week. It would add greatly to my felicity if you would come too. I hope you will pass at least one week with us.—Nancy has seen but little of you, but she has seen sufficient to make her admire you; come then, my dear girl, and secure her friendship. Eliza Anderson is going to Salem in a few weeks to reside with her Aunt Chapin; I shall regret her departure exceedingly, as she is the only person in the neighborhood with whom I have any intimacy.

I have been to P——, since I wrote to you last. Catherine and Fanny are in a better situation than I expected from what I had heard of the place. The prospect is rural and extensive; I was quite charmed with it. Charles Devas, who went with me, is quite in love with the place. It is not very thickly inhabited at present, but I believe in a few years it will far exceed S———. I must, though reluctantly, bid you adieu, as I have company coming in. Ever yours,

EMILY HAMILTON

Letter XVI

To Miss EMILY HAMILTON

W———, May 15

I am under the disagreeable necessity of telling my dear Emily, that it is not in my power to accept her kind invitation. My grand papa is gone to Albany, and will be absent for several weeks. My grand mamma is always solicitous to procure for me every pleasure in her power, but at present she is in a bad state of health, and is unwilling that I should leave her; but she earnestly requests that you will come here with Miss Penniman and Eliza Anderson, and pass a week or fortnight with us. She thinks a visit here would be more gratifying to Miss Penniman, than to have me at S———. If she is fond of rural scenes, she will find a great variety of them here. The society is perfectly agreeable, and adapted to your taste; nothing on my part shall be wanting to render your visit pleasing; I really anticipate a great deal of satisfaction in having you all here; do not disappoint me. It will delight my grand mamma too, she is never happier than when she has a circle of amiable young people in her parlour. Her conversation is always cheerful, interesting, amusing and instructive. Notwithstanding her age, she is always fond of seeing young people enjoy themselves; she has not forgotten that she was once young, but delights in recalling to remembrance, the pleasures and amusements of her early years. She is always contriving to encrease my enjoyments, and to render my residence here too pleasing to permit my forming a wish to quit it.

Mr. Sever still continues his attention and assiduities, but my esteem for him decreases daily. He appears to be more attached to me than ever; I am sorry for it. I cannot forbear treating him with kindness, but I cannot give him the encouragement he solicits. That I can never return the affection he professes is certain; to admit his visits is wrong, for is not that a kind of encouragement? There is no similarity in our tastes and dispositions, and can there be happiness in a married life, when each pursues a different object? In my last conversation with him, I thanked him for the polite attention which he had ever shown towards me, and frankly told him, that as I was sensible it would never be in his power to gain my affection, I could not justify myself in receiving his visits, and that I had not a doubt but he would meet with another person who would be sensible of his merit, and make him far happier than myself. He replied that he must submit to his fate, but since I had refused him to hope for my affection, he dared not to presume that I would give him my hand from pity, and let him endeavor by making it the whole study of his life, to render me happy, to gain my affection. I answered, that I never would give my hand without my heart, and that I could not think of continuing our intimacy any longer.—"Let me be allowed however," said he, "to make you one visit more, and if you still continue in a determination which will be fatal to my peace, I will not oppose it." I must own that I am distressed, but I have a satisfaction arising from the consciousness that he is sensible I never gave him that encouragement which might induce him to believe I ever intended a connexion with him. Adieu my dear Emily, I shall expect you with the greatest impatience.

MARY CARTER

To Miss MARY CARTER

S——, May 29

Miss Penniman has been here a week; she is in an ill state of health, but she is much better, she assures me, than when she left Boston. The weather has been remarkably fine ever since she arrived, and she flatters herself that the change of air, and the exercise of walking and riding, will produce a great alteration in her health. When she came, she was pale, languid, and almost exhausted, with the fatigue of her journey. She retired early, the next morning when she rose, she desired me to walk with her. The sun had just risen, a light mist hovered over the meadows, and the dew sparkled on the grass. She looked from the window and appeared delighted; "what a beautiful prospect" said she, "I have never before seen any thing so charming; will you walk out with me, Emily, I long to have a nearer view of those objects which appear so beautiful at a distance?" I walked with her into the garden, the morning air refreshed her. "Ah" said she, "how different from Boston. The delicious fragrance of the opening blossoms revives my spirits; I seem to inhale new health at every breath." The change of air has indeed made a visible alteration in her appearance; a delicate flush appears in her cheeks, and her strength increases daily. She is eager to recover her health that she may walk by moonlight, but sensible that the evening air is prejudicial to invalids, she has denied herself the indulgence. She did not expect to tarry but a month, but my parents are so much pleased with her, that my father, who will set out for Boston tomorrow, intends to solicit Mrs. Penniman to consent to her tarrying till October. By that time, it is probable her health will be quite established. I flatter myself that Mrs. Penniman's fondness for her amiable daughter will induce her to comply with this request. I have shown your letter to Nancy, she has accepted your invitation, and is delighted with the opportunity now presented her of seeing a part of Connecticut. I have also communicated your plan to Eliza, and she had determined to go, but contrary to her expectations, her Aunt sent for her yesterday, and tomorrow morning she is to set out for Salem.

I shall set out for W——, with Nancy, on Monday, in a chaise; Mr. Gray, who is going to Hartford, will accompany us on horse back, and I shall then have an opportunity to introduce to my Mary, one of the most deserving young men I was ever acquainted with. The melancholy which took possession of his mind, after the death of his Sophia, has in some measure subsided, but he has never yet been able to mention her name without tears. I have seldom seen him, and have not had any conversation with him for some time, till last week. He has been [on] several journeys to endeavor to dissipate his dejection by variety of company and objects, but he tells me he has little hope of succeeding, for while he is viewing a beautiful prospect, the idea that Sophia would also have been charmed with it, rushes upon his imagination, and bids him mourn anew. Could he find some amiable female, who resembled Sophia, in her person, manners and conversation, I believe it would have a greater tendency to soothe his sorrows than any thing else. I have often thought, Mary, that you were extremely like her, and have wished that he could see you, but never hinted my ideas to him. Who knows, my friend, but you may become the object of his affection? He is worthy of yours, if your heart is not already engaged, and should he, as I expect he will, find you engaging enough to transfer to you that affection which he had for Sophia, I am convinced that a more desirable union could not take place. Do not think me romantic, I am serious. Such an event may happen, though you perhaps will think it quite improbable. He is descended from a respectable family; his fortune is easy, and his character and morals unexceptionable. After you have seen him, and conversed with him, I shall talk with you upon the subject; till then adieu.—Yours with real friendship.

EMILY HAMILTON

Letter XVIII

To Miss ELIZA ANDERSON

W——, June 7

You see by the date of my letter, dear Eliza, that I am at the residence of our beloved Mary. I have now passed three days in this delightful village, and could I have your company, every wish would be gratified. It was really an unfortunate circumstance that your Aunt sent for you so soon; Mrs. Audley and Mary are very much disappointed, and Nancy laments the loss of your lively conversation extremely. Mrs. Audley far exceeds my expectations; the warmth of Mary's praises did not do justice to her character. I could scarce have believed that a woman who had lived seventy five years, and had experienced so great a variety of afflictions as she has, could have preserved all her natural sweetness of temper, and a large share of the sprightliness of youth. Sense, goodness, and benevolence, beam from her eyes, and smiles of ineffable sweetness animate a countenance, which still possesses many of the charms for which she was greatly celebrated in the more early part of her life. She is beloved by all who have the happiness to be acquainted with her. The poor, who are constantly relieved by her bounty, look up to her with affection and gratitude, and appear to consider her as something more than mortal. Their affectionate enquiries after her health, and the concern visible in their countenances, at her present feeble state, is at once a testimony of her worth and their regard for her. Mary is all attention to her, and never appears to greater advantage than when she is attending her aged benefactress. You would be delighted to see her assisting the old lady to dress. Mary is always employed on that occasion in preference to any other person; she endeavors to have her cap, handkerchief, &c. put on in the most becoming manner, and she always succeeds admirably. Col. Audley is now at Albany,

Mary is impatient for his return. She told me last night that she thought herself very happy in the protection of her grandparents. Other Orphans, she said, were frequently without friend or protector, while she was blest with every enjoyment she could reasonably desire. She is highly sensible of the privileges she enjoys, and truly grateful for them.

Mr. Gray accompanied us hither on his journey to Hartford, and in compliance with Mrs. Audley's request, tarried here the first night. I am very much deceived, if he does not already entertain a partiality for Mary. I believe he has not passed an evening more agreeably for some months. Mary engrossed almost his whole attention, and his look and manner, when he left us the next morning, convinced me that he would have received more pleasure from her company, than from his journey.—Mrs. Audley desired him to call upon her at his return; he promised that he would, and I have not a doubt of his fulfilling his engagement. After he was gone, I asked Mary if she was pleased with him? She replied that she thought him quite agreeable, but it would be necessary to see more of him before she could say a great deal in his favor. "You will undoubtedly see him again" said I "and you will find he improves upon acquaintance." Their manners and dispositions are similar, and should the union I wish for, take place, they will undoubtedly be happy with each other. We have had a large party of young ladies here this afternoon, many of them were beautiful, but all were pleasing. Their manners are elegant, and their conversation agreeable. We are all to assemble to morrow at Capt. Winslow's. I have never seen more amiable girls than his three daughters. The two eldest have fine complexions and easy shapes, but Catherine, the youngest, is really charming. She is just sixteen, every beauty adorns her face and form; her fine dark hair flows in graceful ringlets on her snowy neck, her cheeks glow with the blushes of health, and the expression of modesty and innocence in her sparkling black eyes, is quite enchanting. Her dress is peculiarly plain but graceful.

"Beauty, like hers, needs not foreign aid of ornament,
But is, when unadorn'd, adorn'd the most."[18]

It is past eleven, Mary and Nancy are begging me to close my letter with assuring you of the continuance of their esteem and friendship. "Come, Emily, do throw by your pen." "Yes, yes, you dear girls, only let me tell Eliza I shall never think of her but with sincere affection." Adieu dear Eliza; ever yours,

EMILY HAMILTON

Letter XIX

To Miss MARY CARTER

S——, June 29

Our little journey is at length completed, my dear Mary, and I am safe in my apartment. Nancy is tolerably well, but she is rather fatigued. Mama entertained a thousand fears for our safety during the thunderstorm. It commenced when we were within ten miles of home.—We heard the thunder at a distance, the thick clouds gathered rapidly, and every appearance indicated a violent tempest.—In an instant the rain began to pour, and we were nearly a mile distant from any kind of shelter. The thunder rolled over our heads, and the lightning flashed on all sides; Nancy almost fainting with terror entreated me to drive faster: When instantly a terrible flash of lightning with a tremendous clap of thunder, frightened our horse. He ran down the hill with the utmost fury, all my endeavors to stop him were vain, Nancy screamed, and I was apprehensive the chaise would overturn. I tremble even at the thought of past danger, for the moment we reached the bridge, the horse by some means extricated himself from the tackling, and as I still kept the reins, by his springing forward, I was thrown into the river. Nancy, who was left in the chaise, shrieked for help. In this deplorable situation perhaps I should soon have expired, had not Heaven sent a deliverer. The people at the tavern, which was not far distant, seeing the horse run by, went to stop him, and hearing the shrieks of Nancy, ran to our assistance; a gentleman who was with them plunged into the stream, and brought me out. I fainted in the arms of my deliverer, and did not recover my recollection till after I had been in the house some time. By the kind attention of Mrs. M——, I recovered so well that I was able to take tea with Nancy and the gentleman. He received my acknowledgements for his assistance, in a manner the most easy and elegant, assuring me that he should ever esteem that moment the most fortunate of his life. People thus thrown together by accident, generally feel a curiosity respecting each other. As the obliging stranger did not express a wish to be acquainted with our names, I suppressed the desire I had to know who he was; but his manners and conversation gave sufficient evidence of his being a worthy man. I must own it would give me satisfaction if I could discover his name. He does not appear to be more than twentytwo or three; his person is remarkably fine; I never saw a more elegant form or face. While we were drinking tea the sun threw his last rays upon the adjacent wood with more than usual splendor; the air was fresh, and the calm serenity of the scene inspired us with delight. We had the pleasure to find that our new friend was an enthusiastic admirer of the beauties of nature; his conversation on the subject was charming. Surely, Mary, this man must be vastly superior to those with whom we daily converse. The evening was delightful, the moon shone with resplendant lustre. Nancy and I retired early, intending to pursue our journey with the rising sun. We had not been in bed but a few minutes, before we heard Mrs. M——, in the next chamber, giving directions to the maid to prepare a bed for the gentleman below; he came up soon after they had withdrawn, and walking to the window, threw up the sash and exclaimed, "Ah! why cannot the beauty of this scene calm my agitated mind? All nature will soon be hushed to repose, all but those, who unhappy like me, know not how to extricate themselves. Oh! Clara, Oh! my father!" I was alarmed, and continued to listen with anxiety—he sighed deeply, "Mistaken parent! mountains of gold could not procure me an hour's repose.—But ah! 'tis past, let me strive to submit. Long have I felt disturbed, long have I known that my peace of mind was bartered for worldly wealth, but never till this fatal hour"—here he paused, and taking a flute, played a tune so exquisitely mournful, my tears flowed ere I was aware. After walking hastily across the chamber for some minutes, he resumed his complaint. "No chain can confine the freeborn mind. But why do I complain—must all my days be embittered by the recollection of one sweet hour—I will exert my reason, I will, if possible, tear from my heart every idea—lend me assistance Heaven—pardon my weakness—look down with compassion on a wretched man, doomed to suffer a seclusion from what might form the happiness of his life—Oh! tear the idol from my heart; let inclination and duty go hand in hand; enable me to sustain with fortitude, every trial, and assist me to overcome every temptation, however hard, however difficult." I was really uneasy, I whispered to Nancy and asked her what she thought? "Either that he is unhappy by the loss of a beloved object," said she, "or that he is on the point of marrying one he cannot love." "I fancy," I replied, "that his distress proceeds from both the causes you have mentioned, yet, who would have thought he was unhappy; his countenance did not betray the state of his heart, and yet I thought it was very expressive." "I thought so too," said Nancy, "but perhaps the recollection of his misfortunes may press more forcibly upon his mind when he is alone, from his putting a restraint upon his feelings when he is in company." I acknowledged the justice of her supposition, and was proceeding, when I heard him go to the window again. "Oh!

that thy mild beams, benignant planet, could diffuse a soft calmness over my mind; why is it not as calm, as tranquil as the scene I am viewing? How often, but with far different sensations, have I gazed on thee? How often have my thoughts ascended from thee, to thy great Author, while my soul overflowed with rapture? I have beheld the Creator in his works, and experienced the most refined pleasure. Ah! why did I not meet my fellow mind at a time when I might have been permitted?—O! madness, why do I indulge the idle?"—Some person now tapped at his door, he opened it, and was desired to permit a gentleman who had just arrived, to sleep in the same chamber, to which he politely consented. The new lodger entered, and I found by the short conversation which passed between them, that they were strangers to each other. As nothing more occurred to disturb us, Nancy was soon asleep. I was unusually wakeful; I felt as if interested in the sorrows of the stranger; his pathetic exclamations had affected me beyond expression, and I was concerned at his misfortunes, though I was not satisfied as to the cause, and I perplexed my mind with fruitless conjectures, till through weariness, sleep at length closed my eyes. We arose early, the first rays of light were scarce visible in the east. We opened the window and inhaled the pure air of the morning. We conversed for some time on the adventures of the preceding day and evening, till we found the gentlemen in the next chamber had risen. By their conversation it appeared they were going to A——, and consequently would not be company for us; we therefore determined to set out as soon as the chaise could be got ready.—We were joined in the parlour by our obliging friend, who inquired after my health with a degree of anxiety. After he received my answer, he told me he was going to A——, and asked if he should have the pleasure of travelling with us? I answered that we were going the other road. He was sorry, he said, that he was so soon to lose the pleasure of our conversation, and hoped that some fortunate circumstance would give him an opportunity to become acquainted with two young ladies, whom he should ever remember with respect and esteem. The other gentleman coming in and addressing himself to me, prevented my reply. As we were quite ready, we wished him good morning, and were handed to the chaise by our friend, who wished us health and happiness, and pressing my hand, assured me, while I thanked him for the obligation he had conferred upon me, that my satisfaction could not exceed his. He then bowed, and bid us adieu. Nancy thought she observed an air of melancholy on his countenance, but perhaps if she had not overheard his complaints, she would not have noticed it.—We reached home without any accident; Mr. Lambert made us an evening visit, and enquired very particularly concerning you. You will think this letter intolerable long and tedious: to prevent your being too much fatigued, I will conclude, with assuring you of the unalterable friendship of your

EMILY HAMILTON

Letter XX

To Miss MARY CARTER

S——, July 30

I had the pleasure of conversing with Mr. Gray, this morning, my dear Mary; he appears unusually cheerful, and I fancy you are the cause of this pleasing alteration. I inquired if his journey had been agreeable? "Perfectly so," was the reply. "Did you call upon Mrs. Audley at your return?" "I did, and was happy in having an opportunity to become more acquainted with her amiable grand daughter." "Mary," said I, "is a fine girl."—"She is indeed," he replied, "I was highly pleased with her." "Perhaps you found her engaging enough to induce you to make another visit at W——?" He smiled.

"Do you think, Miss Hamilton, if I should make another visit there, I should be a welcome guest?" "Your accomplishments, and the goodness of your character, Mr. Gray, I should suppose would procure you a welcome reception any where. Mrs. Audley is fond of agreeable company, and would undoubtedly be pleased with yours." "I will tell you, Miss Hamilton, that if I were sure of the old lady's approbation, it should be the study of my life, to gain and deserve the affection of the charming Mary." "She is worthy of you, Mr. Gray, and would undoubtedly make you happy." "Your intimacy with her induces me to ask this question, Do you believe her affections at present disengaged?" I laughed and assured him that I believed they were. "If my endeavors succeed," said he, "I shall think my attending you to W——, one of the happiest circumstances of my life." "Then I presume you have made some proposals to Mary?" "I have, and succeeded so far as to obtain permission to make her a visit." "May I ask when you shall go?" "Next week; I am impatient for the day to arrive: Will you favor me with a letter?" "Oh yes, is there any particular subject you wish me to write upon?" "If you have any influence with your friend, intreat her to crown my wishes by making me the happiest of men."—"Your own merit, Mr. Gray, is a better recommendation than any I could write." "You are pleased to flatter me, Miss Hamilton, but I am not so vain as not to think it very possible, nay, probable that she will reject me." "It is uncertain," said I, "what she will determine, but I am too well acquainted with the goodness of Mary's disposition, not to know that she would not long keep a worthy man in a state of anxiety and suspense, and she would also be far from encouraging a crowd of admirers, merely to gratify her vanity. This is unpardonable in any woman, and gives great reason to suspect her character." "Do you think, Miss Hamilton, that I have any reason to hope that she will determine in my favor?" "I do not wish to discourage you, Mr. Gray, but I believe you may possibly be rejected, and it is also possible that you will be successful; if the event terminates as I wish, you will be the husband of my friend. Mary's greatest objection, will be that of leaving her venerable friends." "If that is the greatest, it can easily be obviated. I will purchase an estate near Mr. Audley's; Col. Warner wishes to sell, and I have property sufficient, not only to purchase that, but to make considerable addition to it." He would have proceeded, but Nancy just then joined us, and the conversation turned upon general subjects.

I was rather disappointed at not receiving a letter from you by Mr. Gray; I shall expect one by the next post.

Mr. Lambert is coming towards the house; I will not go down, however, till I am called. There has been a great alteration in my sentiments with regard to him since I saw you. I wish I could be allowed to dismiss him; if my parents were not so fond of him, I should be happy. My mother was expatiating on some of his good qualities the other day as she was sitting alone with me, and observed that I did not appear so well pleased with him as formerly. I assured her, that I did not wish to receive his visits any longer, and that I was certain I never should have any higher regard for him, than for a common acquaintance. My father just then entering, overheard the last words, and asking who we were speaking of, Mamma told him what had been said. He desired me not to entertain any thoughts of dismissing him, and said he was very sorry I had so little judgment. He frowned and withdrew. For the first time in my life I received the frown of a parent; it cut me to the heart. My mother then advised me to admit his visits and to treat him with the same politeness and attention I had formerly done. I left her, and going to my chamber, tears relieved the oppression of my mind. Shall I own to you, Mary, you from whom no thought of mine was ever concealed, that the engaging stranger of whom I wrote in my last, has made an indelible impression upon my mind. Were Lambert like him, I would willingly comply with his and my parents wishes. With a man of good morals and good sense, I could be happy, if he did not possess a tenth part of Lambert's income. Lambert is not deficient in sense; his person you well know is pleasing, but with regard to his morals, I have doubts that must be satisfied before I proceed any further with him. Something was privately whispered me a few days since, which if true, will never be overlooked by me. Till this is cleared up, I shall remain unsatisfied. You must excuse me, Mary, if I do not gratify your curiosity respecting the abovementioned circumstance; at some future time you shall be made acquainted with it. I am summoned to attend Lambert. I hope his visit will be short.

For two long hours I have been obliged to listen to him with an appearance of satisfaction. Heaven knows it was only an appearance; I hate dissimulation, and yet I must practice it, or incur the displeasure of those whom I am in duty bound to obey. He came to beg the favor of attending me to a ball on Thursday, and to know if Nancy would allow his brother, who is in town on a visit, the honor to attend her. On Nancy's account only, I accepted the invitation; I knew she wished to go, and would be unwilling to, unless I went.—Present my respects to your grand mamma, and assure her that the remembrance of the hours I passed in listening to her charming conversation, will never be effaced from my mind. Ever yours,

EMILY HAMILTON

Letter XXI

To Miss EMILY HAMILTON

W——, August 22

You will pardon me for neglecting to write to you sooner, my dear Emily, when I tell you that my grand mamma has been extremely ill, and that my attention to her has prevented me from writing to any one. I suffered the greatest anxiety on your account when the thunder storm commenced, but happily you were carried in safety through every danger. You say the engaging stranger has made an indelible impression upon your mind. Beware, Emily, beware of giving a loose to your imagination; do not suffer yourself to think him so much superior to others; perhaps you may never see him again; you know nothing of his character or his heart; it is not impossible but that he is a villain.—"Surely," you will say "such a man cannot be a villain." But remember, my dear girl, first appearances are often deceitful; you say, if Lambert were like him, you should need no persuasion to listen to his addresses. Have you forgotten the praises you bestowed on him after you returned from the ball at Mr. Davis's? He had then been in town but a few weeks, and you wrote that even in that short time, he had gained the esteem of all the young people. You then admired him; since then he has declined in your esteem; And why? Because you imagine you have discovered a deficiency in his character. Perhaps it might be so with this stranger. If you had the same opportunity of acquaintance with him, you have had with Lambert, perhaps you would be equally disgusted with him. Lambert may have been slandered, or the report you have heard may be true; I think it is best to acquaint your parents with the causes of your dislike; surely they will not compel a beloved child, to act in opposition to her feelings, and sacrifice her own inclination, merely to gratify a man with whom they have no connexion, and to whom they are under no obligation.—If he is a man of sense, he will be better pleased with a dismission, than to be treated by you with coldness.—I was pleased with your conversation with Mr. Gray, and am charmed with his plan of purchasing Col. Warner's estate. He is really a worthy man, and I will tell you frankly, if my friends[19] are as much pleased with him as I am, I shall give him all the encouragement I can with propriety. His character is too well known and established, to admit a doubt of its goodness; his next visit will determine the event; if he appears as agreeable as he has hitherto, I shall accept his proposals; if not, I am at liberty to reject them.

My grand papa has been at home a week; he never returns from a journey without some token of his affection for me. He brought me some beautiful lutestring for a gown, and a small collection of books; among which were the Novel of Celestina, and the Wedding Ring.[20] The character of Miss Sidney, in the last mentioned, is truly amiable. Often have I wept at her sufferings, and admired her exalted mind, too noble to be depressed by them. I have sent it for your perusal.—My grand mamma has just sent for me to go down. Yours with sincere friendship,

MARY CARTER

Letter XXII

To Miss EMILY HAMILTON

Salem, August 28

The welcome testimony of your continued friendship, my dear Emily, came safe to hand. I expected a letter from Nancy, but was disappointed. How often does imagination seat me by your side! I see your lovely form, and listening to your gentle persuasive accents, seem to converse with you, till some interruption dissolves the pleasing vision. Often on fine moon light evenings, I look from my window and reflect that if I were at S——, I should be engaged in some agreeable walk with my Emily. How often at the close of day have we wandered to our favorite recess and enjoyed the calm prospect before us. The last time I was with you there, will never be forgotten.

> The sun was sunk, the evening sky serene,
> A light wind gently whisper'd through the wood,
> Fair Luna rising beautified the scene,
> Illum'd the grove, and glitter'd in the flood.[21]

When shall I again visit with you, that delightful retreat? How often in the fine evenings of summer have we sat upon the sloping bank—all was peaceful; no sound disturbed the silence that reigned around, but the soft murmur of the stream. Fond imagination delights to recur to those scenes of happiness, and smiling hope points to the joyful hour that will renew them. Nothing but the society of my much valued friends at S——, is wanting to make me happy here; I retain all my gaiety, however, and till that forsakes me I cannot be unhappy.

My aunt is an amiable woman, her conversation is always pleasing, and she possesses a sweetness of temper almost unequaled. I have made a more particular acquaintance with a Miss Selwyn here, than with any other young lady. She is very sensible, is a great reader, and her conversation is really charming. Her face is plain, but interesting; her merit procures her respect, and she needs only to be known to be admired. She has a brother who resembles her in all her accomplishments; they are often here, and an intimacy is begun, which, I hope, will terminate in a lasting friendship. Mr. Cutler made us a visit a few days since; my aunt was not very much pleased with him. I own I felt a degree of something like mortification, and a little symptom of resentment, when she told me after he was gone, that she hoped I was not in love with him.—"To me" said she, "he appears unworthy of your esteem; the man may be well enough, but unless I am greatly deceived, he is one of that most despicable order of beings, a male coquette." I made no reply, but was secretly vexed to find that a man whom I had long preferred to any other, should, by a woman of sense and penetration, be disliked and despised. His future behavior will show whether her suspicion is, or is not well founded. Adieu my Emily; write frequently, and believe that a greater satisfaction than reading your letters, is unknown to your

ELIZA ANDERSON

Letter XXIII

To Miss EMILY HAMILTON

W——, October 9

Your letter by Mr. Gray, my dear Emily, was highly interesting; your two lines of poetry were indeed significant, but I should have been better pleased if you had condescended to fill the paper.—I could not forbear laughing, though I must own I was rather provoked at you for disappointing me. Mr. Gray has solicited and obtained the consent of my friends to continue his visits, and has been very importunate with me; he begs that his happiness may not be long deferred.—I do not wish to put his constancy to a tedious trial, but if it were only for form's sake, he might wait a year at least. I shall be governed, however, wholly by my venerable friends; I can make them no other compensation for the benefits they are hourly conferring upon me, than to yield a willing obedience to their commands, and to acquiesce in their wishes. Mr. Gray has made a bargain with Col. Warner, and is to take possession of his estate next April; so that affair is settled to the satisfaction of all parties. We go on with amazing rapidity; I am ashamed when I think what a progress this man has made in my heart in so short a time. He has hurried me completely, and my friends are so anxious to see me happy, that it will be a wonder if I am not married before spring.—They scarce allow me time to reflect on the importance of the undertaking. I am rallied by all my acquaintance, for it is now generally considered that he is the accepted lover of your friend. Pray write by the next post, and tell me what you think of our proceedings. Ever yours,

MARY CARTER

Letter XXIV

To Miss MARY CARTER

S——, October 15

With pleasure, my dear Mary, I acknowledge the receipt of your two letters. I thank you for every friendly hint contained in the first. I will not suffer myself to be led astray by the delusions of fancy; it is more than probable that I never shall see the stranger again, and though the idea of him will never be eradicated from my mind, yet I trust it will never disturb my repose. First appearances, I am willing to allow, are often deceitful; I never, perhaps, shall have an opportunity of knowing whether I have been deceived in this man or not. To him, I owe my life, and he certainly has a claim to my gratitude, if no more. Lambert, as you say, may have been slandered; there is a possibility of it, but if he is innocent it will be known. We went to the ball, but how different were my feelings, from those of the first time I was attended by him. The company and music were the same, but Lambert and Emily were altered. I took very little satisfaction at the time, and should have still less to recount the adventures of the evening to you; I will pass them over in silence.

I am delighted with your frank communication, and the rapidity with which you go on. I have not seen Mr. Gray since I wrote that little billet to send by him.—I was dressing to go out, and had not time to enlarge, but the length of this shall make you amends. Marriage, indeed, requires time for reflection, but as your choice is fixed, you may safely trust to the wisdom and experience of your friends, and give them an instance of your affection for them, by suffering them to determine when the ceremony shall be performed.

When Mrs. Penniman consented that Nancy should remain here till this month, she obtained my father's promise that I should accompany her to Boston. Every thing is prepared for our journey, and next week Nancy will bid adieu to S——, and the friends her engaging manners have procured her while here. Mrs. Penniman is very desirous that I should spend the winter in town, but I am too fond of the country, and not sufficiently pleased with a city, to induce me to accept her invitation. I intend to stay a month, and I dare say I shall feel anxious to return to my native village long before that month has expired.

Mr. Lambert has just been here to take leave of Nancy, as she is going a journey. He did not know till now that I was to accompany her; he begged me to shorten my visit as much as possible, for every day would seem an age till my return. I told him gravely, that the length of my visit would depend on the pleasure I received in town; if I found every thing agreeable, I should probably pass the winter there, as Mrs. Penniman desired. "Mrs. Penniman must then receive me too," said he, "for I could not exist so long without you." To this I made no reply, but Nancy told him she hoped if he came to town he would favor her with a visit. He thanked her, and said it would be impossible to go to Boston, and deny himself the happiness of seeing her.

I shall certainly go to Salem if possible; I am quite anxious to see Eliza; since our separation she is dearer to me than ever.—I shall write to you from Boston, and shall depend upon your writing frequently to me, as I wish to be informed of every circumstance relating to your alliance with Mr. Gray. Nancy is writing her farewell to you; she has no expectation, I suppose, of seeing you again for many months. The pleasing alteration which has taken place in her health, will, I hope, induce Mrs. Penniman to consent to her passing the next summer with us. Yours with affection,

EMILY HAMILTON

Letter XXV

To Miss MARY CARTER

Boston, November 20

You are impatient I know, Mary, for an account of my journey, and the scenes which have occupied my attention since my arrival in this city. We had an excellent journey and were received by Mrs. Penniman with raptures. She viewed her daughter with heartfelt satisfaction. "Is this" she cried, "my Nancy, whom I sent into the country so pale, so thin and languid? I cannot, my dear child, be grateful enough to Heaven for the restoration of your health. Your glowing cheeks, your sparkling eyes, and the freshness of your form, give me unutterable delight." The glistening drops of sympathy flowed from the eyes of each; Mrs. Penniman embraced her amiable child, while her maternal heart overflowed with tenderness and gratitude. That evening passed in a manner the most agreeable. The next day was devoted to company: Nancy's friends and acquaintance came to congratulate her on her return, and to receive an account of her amusements and excursions in the country. They listened with attention, while Nancy, with a grace of manner peculiar to herself, informed them of every circumstance worth relating. She spoke of her visit to you in the most flattering terms, and of Mrs. Audley and her grand daughter, in such a manner as made all the company wish they had the same opportunity of becoming acquainted with people so amiable. They staid to supper, and one of the young ladies proposed that we should all meet the next day at her brother's house. He was delighted with the proposition, and said if the ladies would do his sister the favor to take tea with her the next afternoon, he would answer for the gentlemen's attendance in the evening, and if it was agreeable he would speak for some music, and have a private ball at his house. It was accordingly agreed upon, and after a little more conversation, the company retired highly gratified with the entertainment they had received. The next afternoon we went to Mr. Harlow's. His father, I was informed, died some years since, and left a large estate to him and his sister; she has constantly resided with him; they seem to be both actuated by one mind, and live in the most perfect harmony.—Mr. Harlow is soon to be married to a Miss Williams; her countenance is very interesting, and except Catherine Winslow, I never saw any female so completely beautiful. Her graceful manners and charming conversation, increased my esteem for her every moment. After tea the gentlemen arrived, made choice of their partners and commenced the ball—Mr. Morton was mine, and after we had ended the first figure, he led me to a seat, and taking one near me, began a conversation which would have been very pleasing had he mingled less flattery with it. The evening passed very agreeably, and an engagement was made before we separated that we should meet on Monday evening at Mr. Parker's. The next morning I walked out with Nancy to purchase some articles suitable for our appearance on Monday evening. From thence I went to a milliner's, and purchased a plain, but elegant and fashionable bonnet; it is really a little beauty.—She showed me some headdresses—they were loaded with finery; I cannot call it ornament. She produced one, however, that pleased me; four or five white roses were the only ornament I consented to have on it; she showed several trinkets, which she thought would be an addition to it, but I told her I was perfectly satisfied with it without any addition. She replied, smiling, "that my beauty was too great to escape notice, and that I needed not the glare of dress, to attract the attention of every eye." So much for flattery! I have been twice to the theatre, and received great satisfaction from the performances. On the last night I saw the amiable stranger; he was at a considerable distance from me; a lady sat with him to whom he appeared very attentive; from their manners I fancied she was his sister; I gazed at them for some time, and an involuntary sigh escaped me.

At the same moment his eyes were turned toward the place where I sat; they met mine, and gave me a sensation I dare not describe. O! Mary, forgive me when I tell you that notwithstanding every exertion I found I could not support myself, and telling Nancy I was ill, retired. Mr. Morton, who attended me, appeared very anxious as he led me to the carriage. During my ride home, I summoned all my resolution, and resolved to think no more of a man who I was sensible could never be any thing to me. The cause of my sudden indisposition I determined not to mention to Nancy, and I shall not attend the theatre again while I remain in town. Adieu, my friend; amid all the gaudy scenes which surround me, I feel the tenderest interest in your welfare. Ever yours,

EMILY HAMILTON

Letter XXVI

To Miss MARY CARTER

Salem, November 30

I left Boston the day before yesterday; I began to be fatigued with the round of amusements I was incessantly engaged in. Eliza shed tears of transport when she saw me; we embraced, and our tears flowed for some time before we could speak.—She led me to her aunt, and introduced me as one of her dearest friends; she gave me a welcome reception. This lady is agreeable, in the strictest sense of the word.—Eliza appears to enjoy herself perfectly here; the family is small, and the hours of Mrs. Chapin and Eliza are chiefly employed in reading and sewing. As the former is very much attached to books, one of them generally reads while the other is at work. Almost every evening they visit or receive company. The first evening after my arrival, Eliza sent for Miss Selwyn, who immediately came, accompanied by her brother. She expressed the greatest satisfaction at seeing me, and said she considered herself as being already acquainted with me, as I had so often been the subject of Eliza's conversation. I answered that from Eliza's description of her, she was entitled to my esteem, and that I hoped we should form a more perfect acquaintance. Mr. Selwyn appears to be extremely attached to Eliza; from his looks and behavior, it is very evident that a sensation more tender than friendship, leads him so often to Mrs. Chapin's. I hinted my suspicion to Eliza, and she frankly owned that she had suffered many anxious hours on his account. After Mr. Cutler had made his first visit to Eliza at Salem, Mr. Selwyn inquired of Mrs. Chapin, whether Eliza had any idea of a connexion with him?—On her replying that she believed she had, he sighed deeply, and said he had fondly encouraged the idea, that she would at some future day give him leave to endeavor to gain an interest in her heart. "As it is," said he, "I shall be silent; it may wound her sensibility to know how tenderly she is beloved when it is not in her power to return the affection." Mrs. Chapin does not esteem Mr. Cutler, and is very much opposed to his union with her niece. She endeavors to make Eliza think as she does, and by giving Cutler a dismission, to end the sufferings of Selwyn. But Eliza thinks her word too sacred to be trifled with, and while she owns herself sensible of all the good properties of Mr. Selwyn, she confesses that his rival still retains all her affection. She pities him while she sees him endeavoring to conceal his tenderness; she treats him with respect, and neither seeks nor shuns his society. She converses with him in the same manner she does with his sister, and solicitously avoids every thing that would discover to him her knowledge of his affection. Mr. Cutler is daily expected here; I hope he will arrive before I return to Boston, as I am anxious to hear from S———. I have long expected a letter from you, Mary;— if I do not find one at Mrs. Penniman's, when I return, I shall be quite disappointed. It is uncertain whether I shall tarry in Boston a month, or two months longer; the intelligence I receive from home will determine. But wherever I am, be assured of the unaltered friendship of your

EMILY HAMILTON

Letter XXVII

To Miss MARY CARTER

S——, December 15

Oh! Mary, I have a tale to unfold that will surprise you. You undoubtedly remember that I wrote you some time since, that with respect to Lambert I had doubts that must be satisfied before I proceeded any further with him. It had been privately told me that he had a connexion with a girl at B——. At first I disregarded the report, fancying it was only the effect of envy or malice; but from some circumstances I began to think there was a probability of its being true; and though I received his visits in compliance with my parents wishes, yet I carefully avoided giving him reason to think that I was ever likely to give my consent to be his. The day before I left Boston, I received a letter from my mother, in which was enclosed another from Sally, a girl who has lived with us several years. It contained the following:

> My dear Miss Emily, your presence is absolutely necessary
> here; what was long since suspected, has now proved to be
> true. My cousin yesterday introduced a little stranger into
> the world, and has given it the name of William Lambert.
> Of this circumstance, your parents are ignorant, and most
> of the people at S——, but it is not probable they will long

remain so. My aunt sent for me yesterday in the afternoon, and by your mamma's consent I went to see her. I found my cousin delirious; she raves and calls incessantly on Lambert's name; it would melt the most unfeeling heart to be a witness of her agonies. My aunt told me, that a few days since, Betsey informed her that Lambert had solemnly and repeatedly sworn within the last three months, that he would marry her the moment he could dissolve his engagement with you. That he paid his addresses to you before he saw her, is very evident. He engaged Betsey in a conversation with him very often, and having won her affection, persuaded her to consent to admit his visits privately. These visits were often repeated, till it became too late to retrieve the false step she had taken. Lambert has since deluded her with frequent promises of marriage, and has always found some plausible excuse for delaying it. The unhappy girl is now in the most deplorable situation imaginable; at some times she calls upon him with the utmost tenderness; at others she reproaches him with infidelity and cruelty. She has short intervals of reason; these she employs in weeping over her infant and bewailing the wretchedness of her situation, till a variety of cruel reflections crowding at once upon her mind, her senses leave her, and then she raves and weeps in a manner so affecting, that the most hardened wretch on earth could not refrain from tears.—Lambert is now absent on a journey, and is daily expected to return; my aunt flatters herself that if you were here, you might expostulate with him on the cruelty of his conduct. From the well known goodness of your heart, she is induced to hope that you will condescend to plead her injured daughter's cause; and by bringing the author of her misfortunes to a just sense of his errors, prevail with him to make all the reparation in his power. Till her fatal connexion with him, her character was unblemished. I know, Miss Emily, that you will shed a tear of compassion for the unfortunate girl; perhaps you may have more influence with Mr. Lambert than any other person. From your goodness and condescension, I flatter myself that you will return to S——as soon as possible after you receive this. Yours with real esteem, Sally Parkman.

Happily I was alone—unwilling that Mrs. Penniman or her daughter should know the real occasion of the resolution I now formed of returning immediately to S——, I read over my mother's letter again, in order to find something in that which would account for it. The following passage I thought would be sufficient for my excuse. "I flatter myself, my dear child, that I shall soon have the satisfaction of seeing you; if you can find more pleasure at Boston than at home, I am willing you should stay longer, but do not think me selfish, Emily, if I say I wait impatiently for your return." I carried the letter to Mrs. Penniman, and told her that I could not refuse the wishes of an affectionate parent. "And must we give you up then?" said Mrs. Penniman. "Surely" cried Nancy, "You have no idea of going yet?" I answered that I should ever entertain a just sense of their kindness, and the favors they had conferred on me, and that the remembrance of the many hours I had passed with them, would ever be dear to me. I told Mrs. Penniman, I hoped for the pleasure of another visit from Nancy in the spring, and that if I lived till another winter, I should undoubtedly visit them again, and that during our separation, I should write frequently to them, and hoped they would often favor me with returns. "But you do not intend to leave us this week, I hope," said Nancy. "I think," said I, "that I had better go tomorrow in the stage; if I wait till another week, you will be as unwilling to part with me as you are now." "I should be unwilling to part with you at any time," said Mrs. Penniman, "but if you really wish to return tomorrow, I will not make you uneasy by opposing your desire." "Since you evidently wish to go," said Nancy, "I cannot give you a better proof of my friendship than to assist you—but we shall indeed have reason to lament the loss of your company and conversation." The remainder of the day was passed in taking leave of my friends, and early the next morning I took a seat in the stage. I felt very disagreeably; the stage was filled with men whom I never saw before—not a female passenger among them. The gentleman who sat next me, inquired how far I was travelling, and having received my answer, told me he was going to the same place, and asked me if I knew George Gray? I told him I did. He then proceeded to tell me that he was Gray's uncle; that his nephew had lately written to him that he had purchased an estate in W——, and that he expected to be married to a young lady of that place in the spring. "He represents her as very amiable," said he; "Can you give me any information concerning her?" I told him she was my most intimate friend. "And is she then so very charming?"—I gave him your real character, and assured him that Mr. Gray could not have made a better choice. He appeared to be highly satisfied, and said that as he had always intended to make his nephew his heir, he had undertaken this journey on purpose to see his intended wife. So it is very probable you will receive a visit from the old gentleman. I shall pass over the remainder of my journey in silence, as nothing very particular occurred. My parents received me with tenderness and joy; how sweet the paternal embrace! I took the earliest opportunity to inquire of Sally respecting her cousin; she told me that her delirium had subsided, but her life was dispaired of.[22] Lambert, she said, had just come home, and that it was probable he would make me an early visit. In the evening my parents went to Mr. Anderson's, having been invited with a party of the neighbors, and soon after they had withdrawn, Lambert came. He flew to me, and taking my hand with pretended rapture, pressed it to his lips. I drew it from him, and reaching a chair, asked him to sit down. He looked surprised and mortified at my coldness, but seeming not to notice it, he expressed his satisfaction at seeing me, and said he had long been anxious for my return. "I do not know" said I, "why you should wish to see me; there are others to whom you ought to pay attention." "Others?" said he, "Is it possible for me to be attentive to others, while the image of so much beauty and goodness is forever present to my mind? Oh! Emily, my adored girl"—"If you please, Mr. Lambert, you may reserve your adoration for another occasion, and in the mean while, do me the favor to peruse this."—His surprise was now very evident when I handed him Sally's letter. He opened it, I watched his countenance; he blushed, and his hand trembled as he read. Having finished it, he threw it on the table and walked the room in great agitation. I suffered him to proceed with his reflections, which could not be very pleasing, for some time; at length I told him that I hoped he was sensible that our connexion was now forever ended. He sat down, and biting his lips, looked extremely confused. "Whatever engage-ment," said I, "you might think yourself under to me, I now release you from, and leave you at liberty to make good your promises, or to continue your cruelty to an artless, inexperienced girl, whose only error proceeded from loving you too well. She unfortunately listened to your delusions, and prizing your happiness above her own, has been undone by you." "Is there no way, Miss Hamilton, is there nothing I can do to restore myself to your favor; must I be forever banished from you?" "Can you think so meanly of me, Mr. Lambert, as to have an idea that I would listen to you after so flagrant a proof of your libertinism? No, believe me, Sir, I sincerely rejoice that I have discovered your real character, and I never will listen to any man who meanly triumphs in the ruin of my sex." "My example is not without precedent, Miss Hamilton: Why do you reflect with such severity on a common foible?" "If the crime of seduction is common, Sir, that does not render it less unpardonable. I shall deal very plainly with you, Sir, and laying aside reserve, I shall speak my real sentiments. It has ever been my opinion that the world has been too rigid, much too rigid, as respects the female sex. A woman's character is easily destroyed;—suspicion alone, often ruins a fair reputation. One false step forever blasts the fame of a woman; when she has once forfeited the title of virtuous, all is lost—no contrition, no repentant tears, can ever wash away the stain from her reputation. But the men are suffered to proceed in their licentiousness unpunished: Why should not the man, who destroys the peace and innocence of a fond, unthinking, unsuspecting girl, who perhaps placed the firmest reliance on his honor and his love, be considered with as much detestation and abhorrence, as the robber and assassin?—Why are there not as heavy punishments inflicted on them? Such men are the pests of society; families, as well as individuals, are robbed of their peace by them. Where is the heart so hard that will not bleed when the blooming innocent, the sole hope and support of her aged parents, is contaminated by a libertine? Unable to support her agonizing sensations, she droops, her beauty fades, the lustre of her eyes is extinguished, and a deathly paleness succeeds to the once blooming roses of her cheeks; the pangs of disappointed love, and the horror and remorse, ever attendant on conscious guilt, rend her heart; sweet peace has fled, never, never to return. Hope, cannot soothe her sorrows; if she looks toward the future, she must shrink dismayed at the gloomy prospect; nothing but disgrace, contempt, and reproaches await her. If she takes a retrospective view of past scenes, the hours of innocence, the contrast only serves to heighten her distress. Her parents with keenest anguish, behold their darling child, in whom they fondly placed their hopes of future happiness, declining in health, her honor gone, a prey to unutterable misery." "Oh! my God!" exclaimed Lambert, rising and walking hastily across the floor, "it is just I should suffer." "Does the picture I have drawn affect you," said I; "if you will go to Mr. Winslow's, you will find I have not done justice to the original. You will there see the fruit of your perfidy and villainy; you have rendered miserable, a whole family, which, till within a year past, has always been remarkable for its domestic felicity." "Heaven and earth!" he exclaimed; "you pierce my soul—but I deserve it all—I feel that I do." "Make then the only reparation in your power; marry her whom you have involved in such distress; protect her with tenderness from a world, all the contempt and scorn of which she will be forced to endure if you abandon her. Though you can never restore her mind to the serenity it once possessed, yet you may soften her affliction; though you cannot restore to her the sweet reflections of conscious innocence, yet much may be done. With the title of a wife, treat with the tenderness, affection and fidelity due to a wife; by this method of proceeding, you may, in some measure, heal the wounds which you have so deeply inflicted on her heart and the hearts of her distressed parents." "I will own," said he, "that I have an affection for her, but how can I marry her? Shall I not be laughed at, and despised by the whole world for marrying a girl in such circumstances? I shall be ridiculed by all my acquaintance, and be reproached with it to the latest hour of my life." "That you would be laughed at by a few inconsiderate fools, I am willing to acknowledge; but believe me, you would procure the esteem of the wise and the good: And can you submit to the stings and reproaches of a guilty conscience? Can you violate the most solemn oaths, by which, in the sight of heaven, you are bound to marry her, merely to avoid being laughed at, perhaps only for a few days, by a set of insignificant fops, whose opinions are not worth noticing or regarding? If all I have said cannot persuade you to do justice, think on the innocent infant; let that plead the cause of itself and its injured mother. Reflect on the peculiar severity of its fate; the disgrace of its birth will be ever remembered; and should it live to the age of manhood, think on the evils which will await him then; he will be reproached by the malignant and unfeeling, with a crime of which he was not guilty, and the infamous epithet which is ever bestowed on such unhappy beings, he must hear; his sensibility must be wounded, and he can never think on you but as his worst enemy." "I own," said Lambert, "that I have done wrong, and I confess I now repent my error; but you, Miss Hamilton, are not ignorant that our regard and respect for a woman vanishes, when we find her losing all respect for herself. It would have been well for Betsey, and for thousands of your sex, if they had not departed from their natural dignity. When a woman ceases to command our respect and esteem, she cannot reasonably hope to retain our love." "Very true, Sir, but if a man had any respect or esteem for a woman, he would not endeavor to degrade her, neither in his own opinion, nor the opinions of others. But all this is no apology for your cruelty; your sex are constantly using the meanest artifices, to delude those whose youth or inexperience prevent them from perceiving the fatal snare which is laid for them, till they are entangled in it. Every art is tried, every decep-tion practiced, and imprecations which might deceive suspicion itself, are used, and when too late, they find that the vows and promises, which they fondly believed to be binding, never meant any thing." "I flattered myself," said Lambert, "that this unhappy circumstance would have remained concealed, till I could have made you mine. That your parents were partial to me, I well knew, and I could easily discover also that I did not possess your affec-tion; but I had hope that I should at length prevail on you to consent to my wishes and those of your parents. I intended to have made ample provision for Betsey—that being above want, she might retire to some place where her misfortune was unknown, and render herself happy by a marriage with some worthy man." "Then you thought she had no delicacy left; if she is not worthy of you, she certainly is not worthy of any other man, and I believe she would think as I do." "I cannot submit to marry one so much below my rank in life, especially one whom I know has no more dignity of mind; at least I cannot submit to it at present. The child I intend to provide for, and place it where it can never have an opportunity of knowing who its parents were." "Then you will be guilty of more cruelty than I thought you capable of;—then it must never know the endearing name of parent, relation, or friend—a wretched outcast, it must ever remain ignorant of all it will be ever anxious to discover. Cruel, detestable resolution." "I would[23] go to Mr. Winslow's," said he, "and see her, if I were certain that I should not be laughed at by the whole world; I do not know but I might venture to marry her, but if I could obtain your forgiveness after making her all the compensation in my power without marrying her, it would give me infinitely more satisfaction. But since you have declared your sentiments so freely, I dare not hope that you will restore me to your favor, and allow me to hope that after I had sincerely repented of my errors you would allow me to call you mine." "This is the last conversation, Mr. Lambert, I shall ever consent to have with you, unless you marry Betsey, or some other person; as long as you remain unmarried, I shall never think of continuing my acquaintance with you; my resolution is unalterably fixed." "If Betsey should become my wife, would you condescend to visit her as a neighbor?" "I would, and I believe every body in the neighborhood would do the same. She is entitled to compassion; charity will teach us to overlook her error, as it is believed that it proceeded more from artless inexperience, than from vicious inclinations; she always sustained an unblemished reputation, and would still have sustained it, had you not been the most artful and the most cruel of your sex." "I am half resolved to have her, yet my pride will not suffer me to stoop so low." "If your pride was not too great to prevent you from committing a crime, I should not think it ought to be too great to prevent you from making atonement for it." He walked the room again for some time in silence; at length, he said he would consider of it. He then entreated me to forgive him for his design to deceive me, with respect to his connexion with Betsey. I assured him that I could easily forgive the wrong he had done me; he then begged leave to salute me, but I refused. He appeared rather dissatisfied, and took leave of me. My parents returned soon after, and asking where Lambert was, I produced Sally's letter, and repeated to them the conversation which had passed. They were extremely surprised, but expressed their approbation of what I had done. When I told them that I had consented to receive Lambert's visits only to please them, and that he had no share in my affection, my father took my hand, and assured me that in any future instance of the kind, he never wished me to sacrifice inclination to duty. To promote my happiness, he said, had always been his highest wish; he thought Lambert capable of making me happy, and therefore he had always been pleased with his attention. Write to me soon, my dear Mary; I am quite anxious to hear from you. Yours with real affection,

EMILY HAMILTON

Letter XXVIII

To Miss EMILY HAMILTON

W——, January 12

I wrote to you while you were at Boston, my dear Emily, but the letters were unfortunately forgotten, and returned to me last week. Your last surprized me; I had no idea that Lambert was such a wretch; I congratulate you on your happy escape; had you married him, you must have been wretched. I have ever been of your opinion, that the world has been too rigid with respect to our sex;

not that I would be understood as apologizing for their vices, but I have no doubt that there are many, very many, who, after their first error was past, would have returned to the path of virtue, had any pitying hand extended itself to their assistance. But instead of this, they have only met with reproaches and contempt; and being thus discouraged from endeavoring to appear again respectable, they have plunged still deeper into vice, till it has become impossible for them ever to reform. I have always wondered at those females, who seem most pleased when in company with those who are known by the appellations of "rakish fellows," "high bucks" &c. and seem by their behavior to approve of the conduct of those who drink deep, game, dress in taste, have expensive connexions, and indulge themselves in every fashionable excess, and at the same time treat with scornful coldness those who maintain an opposite character. If all females consulted their true interest,[24] rakes would be banished from their society, and consequently from the world; for if all women would resolve to be virtuous, and to support their natural dignity, few men would be vicious; and if they did not meet with the approbation of any woman, they would not go on in such a mad career of debauchery and vice. My heart has swelled with indignation, when I have seen a young lady listening with apparent complacency to the insipid conversation of one of those despicable beings. It seems to gratify the pride of some weak females to be admired by a rake, especially if his figure is pleasing. Those fellows are generally polite, tender and attentive, and they have such a smooth, artful, insinuating address, that they persuade those whom they flatter, to believe they are angels, while they are only endeavoring to sink them below the dregs of the creation. It is amazing to me, how any girl in her right senses, can listen to such men; they well know that these fine gentlemen are continually roving from fair to fair; that they vow eternal truth and constancy to each, and after a few interviews, leave them to lament their fate in solitude and wretchedness. Some girls, nay, almost all, who suffer themselves to be addressed by this kind of men, fondly imagine that their charms are irresistable; and each one has the vanity to believe that it is in her power to fix the affection of the dear creature who has made so much disturbance in the world; and finally have the glory of marrying and reforming a rake. It has been said, "that reformed rakes make the best husbands." I never could see the propriety of the assertion; might it not be said with equal justice, that if a certain description of females were reformed, they would make the best wives? I never would run the hazard of marrying a reformed rake, if such a being could be found; but I am rather inclined to think, that Phoenix like, there is only one in a century.

Mr. Gray has been here with his uncle; the old gentleman appears highly pleased with his nephew's intended wife, and you may depend upon it, I have not omitted any opportunity of shewing[25] the utmost respect toward him. He has oddities, however, which make him appear rather singular; but I am willing to make allowances for them. His generosity to Mr. Gray has been great; he has furnished him with a large sum of money, and has promised that he shall be his heir. Mr. Gray is importunate, and earnestly solicits that he may call me his, on the first week in March; I endeavor to have the ceremony deferred a month longer, at least; but his uncle and my friends are all on his side, and I have not much hope of prevailing. I wish you were here to plead my cause: Do you not think it would be foolish in me to let the man have his own way so soon? When I am married I expect to submit to his authority, but surely I ought to exercise my power as long as possible now. I shall wish for your company as much as a fortnight before the ceremony is performed; Will you oblige me by coming? I will send for you any day you will appoint.—Write soon, my dear Emily, and tell me when I may expect the pleasure of seeing you. Adieu, yours

MARY CARTER

Letter XXIX

To Miss MARY CARTER

S——, February 7

Yes, my dear Mary, you shall have my company; I am always happy in contributing to your satisfaction. I am impatient for the time to arrive, as I have long wished to converse with you; you may send for me the 18th of this month, if you please, and I will stay till a day or two after you are married. We are soon to have an addition to our neighborhood: Mr. Anderson has sold his farm to a Mr. Belmont, of Boston, who is to remove hither next month. I hope his lady is agreeable: My father admires Mr. Belmont; he was here while I was at Boston, several days, which gave him an opportunity of being considerably acquainted with him.

Mr. Anderson has purchased the estate which formerly belonged to your father, and Mr. Innman has removed to Springfield. Mrs. Innman made us a visit a few days before she went, and desired me to request you to write to her frequently; she intends in the course of the spring to make a visit at W——, as she is very anxious to see her aunt, and you in your new character. I have company coming in, and must bid you adieu. Ever yours,

EMILY HAMILTON

Letter XXX

To Miss ELIZA ANDERSON

W——, March 6

When I saw you last, my dear Eliza, I informed you that our friend Mary was soon to be married, but I did not then think how soon. Yesterday she gave her hand to Mr. Gray, in presence of her grand parents, old Mr. Gray, and myself. The dear girl could not consent to have the ceremony performed in a crowd, and at her request Col. Audley gave up the idea of a splendid wedding, and invited a large party to assemble at his house today. She was dressed in a plain white sattin; her fine dark hair was curled in ringlets, and she wore a small gauze cap, trimmed with white ribbands and roses, and a white waving plume, ornamented with spangles.—The embarrassment she experienced on the occasion, heightened the natural vermillion of her cheeks; her eyes shone with brighter lustre, and she appeared more charming than ever.

Mr. Gray was elegantly dressed, and his deportment was truly amiable and engaging. Old Mr. Gray is delighted with his new niece, and evinces his satisfaction a thousand times in a day. His manners are peculiarly odd, and his expressions different from those of most people. I conversed with him nearly an hour yesterday.—It appears that he is immensely rich, and Mr. Gray being his greatest favorite, he has determined to make him his heir. Mr. Gray had written to him an account of his connexions with Mary, and the old gentleman hastened to him with all possible expedition, that he might see the lady before he had gone too far.

He told me yesterday he came up with a full determination to "break off the match, for there was a young widow in his neighborhood that had a grand estate, free and clear of all incumbrances, and he knew she'd make George a darn'd good wife, and he intended to have hinted it to her as soon as she'd got her weeds[26] off; but the young dog had been too quick for him; and he believed Mary was the better woman of the two; and she was a dumb deal the best looking." "Your nephew Sir, has then been so fortunate as to please you, as well as himself." "Yes, I can't help loving the little tike for the soul on me; she's plaguy handsome, and a good natur'd little witch; I should not ha' lov'd more, an she'd ha' been my daughter." "She will doubtless think herself happy, Sir, in gaining your esteem; and will endeavor to secure it." "She has secur'd it. By jove, I'd knock any man down, that would darst to say one word against her in my hearing; though, faith, I don't believe she ever did any thing wrong since she was born. Now, look here young woman; did you ever know her to do any thing that wasn't right?" "Her conduct, Sir, has always been very prudent, and her character excellent."—"There now! I knew you'd say so, I knew you would, I knew she was clever and I know she'll make George a good wife too. I wonder where she is; she keeps mighty private to day, I suppose she's ashamed, cause she's gonter be married; poor little thing, she thinks its something dreadful to stand up fore a minister, I'll warrant ye now." Mary now entered the room where we were sitting, and desired me to go up stairs with her. "What, are you going to dress already my dear?" said the old gentleman. "No Sir," she replied, blushing. "Well, well, sit down a minute then, George is gone to walk with Mr. Audley, and I didn't care nothing about going out, and so I have been a talking here with Miss Emy about you, and now we shall call you Mrs. Gray in an hour or two—Oh! don't blush now don't—but I was going to say, that after you was married"——————Col. Audley and Mr. Gray now came in, and I retired with Mary—I related to her what the old gentleman had said about the widow, &c. and told Mary I thought she had been very fortunate in pleasing her new uncle. After the ceremony was over, Old Mr. Gray and Mr. Audley entertained us with stories; and the events of their youthful days. Mr. Ashley gave us an account of a couple whom he married a few years since; which made such an impression on my mind, that I believe I can relate it nearly in his own words. The subject was introduced by an inquiry of Mrs. Audley's concerning a lady with whom she had formerly a slight acquaintance, and in whose favor she had been greatly interested. She now resides at Hudson, Mr. Ashley was there a few weeks since, but did not see her. His friends then informed him, that she had every symptom of a rapid decline. "I can scarce believe" said he, "that she is still alive.—She has been very unfortunate, and has drank deep of the bitter cup of sorrow, but all her misfortunes have not been able to change the sweetness of her disposition; far from being depressed by sorrow she rises above it, and with the eye of faith, looks forward to those blissful regions of eternal felicity, where grief is unknown. I never knew a more amiable woman; the slight acquaintance you had with her, prevented you from knowing her real worth. She has always been a very religious person; strictly virtuous, and for sweetness of temper perhaps unequalled. She was always cheerful, and sometimes gay; she sung finely, and danced with uncommon gracefulness; these engaging qualities, and her uncommon beauty, procured her almost as many admirers as beholders. But to all her lovers, she was so unfortunate as to prefer the worthless Henderson. During their courtship, he was the most artful of men; constantly upon his guard, and never suffered an improper expression to escape his lips. His behavior was more serious and reserved than is common for a young man. He was handsome in his person, engaging in his address, and was capable of conversing with ease and elegance on every subject. But with all these flattering appearances, he was, at heart, a libertine. He concealed his real character so artfully from her, and from every one from whom she could receive information, that she beheld him as the only man it was possible for her to love, and as the only one with whom she could be happy. She married him with the most sanguine expectations of future happiness, but, judge what her sufferings must have been, when he threw off the mask, and discovered the most perfect villain that perhaps ever existed. In less than six weeks after their marriage, he came home from a tavern where he had passed the night in liquor; his clothes half torn off, and coming into the room with the most horrid oaths and imprecations, accused his innocent lady of committing crimes of which she had no idea; in the frenzy of his passion he turned her into the street; and bade her never to let him see her, nor hear of her more. A neighbor ran to her assistance and carried her to his house. She was so frightened and astonished at the terrible scene which had just passed, that she was delirious for several days; a violent fever ensued, and her life was despaired of. When Henderson recovered from his frantic fit and was informed of what he had done, he expressed the greatest sorrow, and vowed by his future behavior, to make reparation of his past offence. When her delirium had subsided, he went to her, and on his knees entreated forgiveness, making such promises of amendment and such professions of tender affection, as might have deceived suspicion. She forgave him and returned to his house; but ere a fortnight had elapsed he was again intoxicated, but offered no violence to her. Almost distracted with grief, she gently expostulated with him. Her tenderness seemed to move him to penitence, and while he was with her, he endeavored by every attention to calm her mind. He appeared for some time to be reforming; but happening to meet with an old bottle companion, he passed night after night at the tavern, treated his wife with the utmost cruelty every day, and again turned her out of the house—She endured all this with angelic patience; without uttering a complaint, and when her acquaintance mentioned Mr. Henderson's conduct to her, she would even apologize as much as possible for him. She was advised to part from her husband and go to her sisters; but she still loved him, and fondly hoped he would reform. He behaved well at times, for a month or two, and she was happy, he relapsed, and she was wretched. His conduct has for a year past, been worse than ever; and it is the opinion of every one that this is the cause of her decline. How bitter will be his reflections after her death! What can soothe his mind? Religion cannot, for he openly ridicules that, and every thing sacred. This has been a greater affliction to Mrs. Henderson, than his intemperance. Though his actions seem to have proved the contrary, he has ever been extremely attached to her. He has been frequently heard to say, that whenever Mrs.

Henderson died he would not live another hour; this resolution makes me tremble for the event. My friend has promised to write to me soon, and I expect a further account of her situation." "And I beg Sir," said Mrs. Audley, "that you will communicate to me the first intelligence you receive, for I shall be impatient to hear from her." He promised that he would, and after we had united in expressing our pity for Mrs. Henderson, and our wishes that he might not continue to be so blind to his own happiness, Mr. Ashley remarked that it was past ten o'clock, and took his leave. You, my dear Eliza, will shed the tear of pity for the sufferings of this amiable woman. How wretched must she be, to see the man to whom her heart is so fondly devoted, ruining his health, reputation and estate, by such an excess of vicious intemperance. Is it possible that love, that noble and exalted passion, can still dwell in the breast of a being so depraved? Surely, were he not deaf to the voice of reason, and a stranger to the fine emotions of pity and affection, his obdurate heart would melt at the woe he has occasioned; he would forsake the detestable course he is pursuing, when he sees that amiable woman, suffering all the pangs of grief and disappointment, her health declining, and her life nearly at an end. I am called to dinner, and must for the present bid you adieu. If I have time after the company we expect retires, I will finish my letter in the evening.

March 7

It was so late last night before the company retired, that I had more inclination to sleep, than write. They arrived between four and five o'clock, and after partaking of an elegant repast, at the request of Mr. Audley, they began to dance. The ball was opened by Mr. and Mrs. Gray, a Mr. Fenwick and your Emily. Country dances succeeded, and it was near twelve before the company retired. Mr. Fenwick is a very lively young gentleman, and is considered one of the principal beaus in W——. A young married lady whispered me, that she believed I should make a conquest of their little

favorite; "If you do you will be envied by half the ladies present."
I assured her I was far from wishing to give them any uneasiness,
and that I believed her suspicion groundless.—Mr. Fenwick, at
that moment, came to engage me as his partner for the next figure;
I was going to refuse, but he repeated his request so persuasively,
that I consented.—When we rose to dance, I observed that the lady
who stood next me, looked very much out of temper. She attracted
the notice of Mr. Fenwick, at the same instant; he spoke to her with
an air of gallantry, and asked her some questions in a low voice,
but she turned away her head with an air of indignation and contempt. "Is not this figure agreeable to you, Miss Phillips?" he asked.
"It is of no consequence to me," she replied, "what the figure is."
He was going to reply, but we were at that moment obliged to begin, and lost the remainder of the conversation.

When we were seated, I told Mrs. Gray what had passed; "I can
easily explain it," said she; "Miss Phillips has always been accustomed to receive the greatest attention from Mr. Fenwick, and she
is disgusted at the partiality he has shown for you this evening.
Only see, he is this moment seated by her, and endeavoring to obtain forgiveness. She is high spirited, and when once offended not
easily reconciled; she has always been taught to think herself handsome, and considers it as an affront offered to her beauty, if any
other lady meets with more attention than herself. She wishes to
engross the attention of every man in the company, and uses so
many ridiculous arts to display her charms, that she constantly de-
feats her own purpose, which frequently makes her ill humored."

Mr. Gray now solicited me to dance with him, and a Mr. Whitman requested the favor of dancing with the bride. Mr. Fenwick
had already called the dance with Miss Phillips, who appeared
rather more satisfied than before; but an expression of haughty resentment darted from her eyes as I passed her.

I think such behavior ridiculous; it gives her associates an
idea of her disposition, by no means favorable, and renders her

despicable to every man of sense.—Who, in his right senses, would marry a woman, who displayed such an irritable, jealous temper? If she showed so much resentment to a gallant, what might not a husband expect? I hope, for her own sake, that she will be led to consider of the consequences, and that she will obtain more command over her passions, or she will render herself very unhappy. Adieu Eliza; believe me with sincere friendship yours,

EMILY HAMILTON

Letter XXXI

To Miss EMILY HAMILTON

S———, March 15

My Dear Emily

I received your letter with pleasure—you wish to remain with your friend a fortnight longer. I am always happy when I can promote your satisfaction, and freely consent that you should stay. When the fortnight is expired, I will send for you, unless you previously inform me that Mr. and Mrs. Gray will accompany you home: It is but just that we should claim a visit from them, as they have such a lengthy one from you.

Mr. Lambert is gone to Newyork,[27] undoubtedly with the most painful reflections. Betsey Winslow is no more.—Lambert visited her soon after you went to W———, and requested her to accept a sum of money; alleging that it was not in his power to marry her, as he could not do it without dishonoring himself, beyond reparation—She heard him calmly, and without reply, he laid the money in her lap, and telling her that she might always command his assistance, was preparing to leave her: She clasped her infant to her breast, and without speaking flung the purse back to him indignantly and retired. He would have followed her, but she prevented him, and having vented her grief in some measure by tears, she conversed sometime with her mother, till painful reflections crowding upon her mind, a delirium took place, and a violent fever ensuing, she expired a few days after.

I cannot be thankful enough that my child's heart was free: Oh! Emily, had your affection been devoted to this man, you must have been unhappy.

Mr. Belmont, with his family, removed hither last week: Mrs. Belmont appears to be pretty and conversable: They have a young daughter who is really beautiful.—Mr. Belmont and your father begin to be very intimate; he is frequently here, and very busy with your father in concerting plans to ornament his new residence.— From his conversation one would imagine that he intends to transform his house and garden into a palace for some sylvan deity. He has visited that grove where you have often enjoyed so many happy hours with your young friends, and is charmed with it. He intends to make an alteration there, which will increase the natural fall of the water; and by removing the brush on the west side, render the prospect more beautiful and extensive.

Thus we are all of us pursuing some favorite scheme to render life happy, and strew our path with flowers. As we advance in years, life grows still more desirable, and we go on in the ardent pursuit of some favorite enjoyment, till death dissolves each pleasing tie that binds us to the earth. Adieu, my child, may angels guard your steps, and happiness without alloy be ever yours.

LUCINDA HAMILTON

Letter XXXII

To Miss LUCINDA HAMILTON

W——, March 25

Soon will the happy period arrive that will bring your Emily to the arms of the best of mothers. I shall set out for home on Monday, accompanied by Mr. Audley, as it would be inconvenient for Mr. and Mrs. Gray to leave home at present; in the summer they intend to make a visit to their friends in S——.

I am not sorry that Lambert has left the town, as I do not wish to be near such a wretch; I hope for his reformation, but I cannot say, that I do not wish him to suffer every pang a guilty conscience can inflict. It is well that I was not partial to him; but if I had been, this instance of his depravity, would have been sufficient to have enabled me to banish him from my heart forever. Never, never will your Emily suffer her heart to own an affection for a man who triumphs in the ruin of her sex. The bearer is waiting, and I have only time to add that I am your truly affectionate daughter,

EMILY HAMILTON

Letter XXXIII

To Miss MARY GRAY[28]

S——, April 6

I send a line by your grand papa, my friend, though I have nothing of importance to write. I went with mamma, last evening, to see Mrs. Belmont, and passed an hour or two very agreeably. Mrs. Anderson joined us, and we had quite a social time.

Mr. Belmont has been at Boston ever since I came home, and his lady is quite impatient for his return. She is already disgusted with the country, and is determined, if possible, to prevail on Mr. Belmont to remove to Boston again. I do not pretend to any skill in physiognomy, but if I am not deceived this lady has not the sweetest temper in the world. I do not know but she will appear more agreeable hereafter, but I do not think she will ever be any thing to me more than a common acquaintance. She has not the look of friendship. I received a letter from Eliza Anderson, yesterday, and enclose it for your perusal. Ever yours,

EMILY HAMILTON

Letter XXXIV

To Miss EMILY HAMILTON

Salem, April 2

I have received yours, my dear Emily, and cannot but regret that I was not present at Mary's wedding; but as she did not give me an invitation, I shall not congratulate her upon the occasion till I see her.

Mr. Cutler has made a very important discovery, and I confess I wonder that he had not made it long ago. He was at Boston about six weeks since, and discovered by the sparkling eyes and dimpled cheeks of Miss Maria Willson that it was not in the power of Eliza Anderson to make him happy, as he had long foolishly imagined. And he also discovered, that it was essential to his peace of mind, to impart his new way of thinking to the fair angel, who would undoubtedly condescend to bestow that happiness for which he so ardently sighed. He was all love, tenderness and submission; she agreed to accept him, and made him sole master of her fortune, which by the way, was more than three times as much as mine. However, it was not for riches that he admired her, nor the extreme beauty of her person, though he prized them both at their full value, they were nothing when compared to her seraphic mind. Her exalted virtue gave dignity to her eyes, and the purity of her soul, gave her personal attractions still greater force.

Such was the character he gave of her, to a friend in Boston, with whom I correspond, and I was informed of the proceeding, a few days before my perjured swain made his last visit at Salem. An explanation then took place, which terminated to the satisfaction of all parties. I received him with calmness and reserve, and without giving him the least idea that I had ever heard of his being attached to another person, told him that some particular occurrences had determined me to dissolve the connexion which had subsisted between us. He then mentioned that he had a partiality for another lady; but wondered how I could be informed of it: "Have you indeed?" said I, "well then, as you are provided for, you can have no objection to make." His miniature, which I had long worn, I handed to him, and begged him to present it to the lady to whom his heart was devoted, telling him that as I had returned that, I wished him to return mine; but he refused, and said that though he had given up the idea of possessing the original, he should not resign the picture, and refused to do either. I had indeed a sincere regard for Cutler; from a connexion with him, I anticipated happiness. By promoting his felicity I thought to encrease my own; but the delusion is vanished, and far from lamenting his inconstancy, I have learned to despise a heart so incapable of adhering to what was once its fondest hopes. Your Eliza will never rank with those soft hearted nymphs who wear the willow,

"And with their sighs encrease the passing gale."[29]

I informed my aunt of the circumstance, she was not sorry I know, that the connexion was broken; but she said something very soothing as if she thought I needed consolation. I could not forbear laughing, and asked her if she thought it really a misfortune to lose him. "Most people would consider it as such," she replied. "Why surely," said I "I am not in a dispairing[30] condition; I have youth"—"and beauty" said she, interrupting me, "to secure you the affection of twenty others." "Allowing this to be true, ma'am, I may reasonably hope that one out of the twenty will continue constant." "Oh! certainly, and perhaps Mr. Selwyn will be the one." "And perhaps some fair Carolinian, may have been attractive enough to make him forget me." "It is not impossible, but I am rather inclined to think the contrary; for I know he was extremely attached to you." "Let that be as it may," said I, "I am very easy." "I am glad you have such an easy temper Eliza." "I am glad too ma'am, for if I were so violently in love as some people have been, or pretended to be, I could not have obeyed my uncle's command of preserving your vivacity in his absence; it would have been your task under such afflictive circumstances, to have endeavored to restore mine." Louisa Selwyn came in, and my aunt told her the news; she could scarce believe it. "Ah!" said she, "it is well he altered his mind so soon; if you had been married it would have been much worse." "Oh yes," said I, "for I am now at liberty, and I never wish to retain the person, without the affection, of any man living." "There are others" said she, "who would be enraptured, could they have half the interest in your heart Cutler possessed." "That is encouraging," said I, "and I begin already to look forward with hope." "When do you expect your brother home, Miss Selwyn?" asked my aunt. "It is uncertain when he will come" she replied; "I had a letter from him yesterday, in which he informed me that he should come in June, or tarry till November. But I rather think he will come in June." "Perhaps" said my aunt, "he would be a candidate for Eliza's affection; there was always a great friendship subsisting between them"—"Undoubtedly," cried Louisa, "I'll write to Edmund, and hurry him home;" "you are extremely kind," said I, "but I am not in such a hurry to be married as to wish to have any one sent for; I believe I can wait patiently a few months." "Have you fixed a certain time of mourning then?" asked Louisa. "I ought to pay some respect to the memory of the departed," I replied, "or I should appear ungrateful." I have not passed an afternoon more gaily since I resided in Salem. I enclose a letter for my parents, and one for Mrs. Gray. I shall make a visit at S——, some time this summer. Yours with real friendship,

ELIZA ANDERSON

Letter XXXV

To Miss MARY GRAY

S——, April 20

Mary, I am more wretched than you can imagine. My mind has lost all the serenity it once possessed: Confused and bewildered in a maze of reflections the most painful—the light of day is odious—the night brings no repose, but fantastic imagination continually produces unpleasing images, and banishes sleep from my eyes.—One day last week, as I was sitting at my chamber window, I cast my eyes toward the road and observed a gentleman; I could not see his face, but it instantly occurred to me that I had seen him before. He advanced toward the house, and as he opened the gate, I had a view of his features, and instantly recognized the person who rescued me from drowning. A sensation wholly new to me, almost deprived me of breath; I retired hastily from the window, and threw myself upon the bed. My door was open, I heard him enter the parlour, my mother called him Belmont!—I heard no more. My senses forsook me, and the first object I saw was Sally, applying hartshorn to my temples. She had accidentally passed by my door, and seeing me, ran to my assistance. When I recovered, I had a faint idea that something had disturbed me, and collecting my

scattered senses, I remembered what had passed, and the dreadful
certainty, that the man whom I had long fancied superior to all his
sex, was no other than Mr. Belmont, returned upon me so forcibly,
that I was on the point of relapsing into the state of insensibility,
I had just quitted, but exerting all the reason I was then in possession of, I desired Sally to run down and get me some water. In the
short interval of her absence, I heard Mr. Belmont tell my mother,
he would call again in the evening. He went out—Oh! heaven support me—was all I could utter. I sunk back upon my pillow, and
heaven only knows the conflict which passed in my mind. Sally returned, and appearing anxious, asked if she should call my mother,
I told her no it was needless to alarm her, and that as I was better I would not detain her any longer. She withdrew and I begun to
devise a plan to avoid seeing him that evening. To see him before
I had acquired strength or reason to conceal those emotions the
sight of him had occasioned, I could by no means bear to think of.
He had been at Boston ever since my return from W——, till the
preceding evening I heard my father remark that he had just arrived. But little did I think that I should see in him the man whose
image was so strongly engraven on my mind. Oh! Mary, even to
you I never owned the real state of my heart, I had often blushed
in secret, that it was so much devoted to a stranger. It was involuntary, I was unguarded, his fine person, his humanity, his easy elegant manners, and the charms of his conversation, with the idea
of exalted merit, all conspired to win a heart which had till then
been free.—Gracious heaven! I have then been—distraction is in
the thought! I have loved a married man! To avoid seeing him that
evening, I thought would be happiness, compared to what I must
suffer from his presence. I went down to tea, but feared every moment that his name would be mentioned, or that I should see him.
Fortunately I escaped without either. I left the parlour, and ran
up stairs for a cloak, and coming down into the kitchen told Sally
I was going to Mr. Andersons. I trembled lest I should meet him,

and walked pretty fast till I passed his house. I heard a flute at a little distance, and listening attentively heard the same melancholy tune he played at M——'s tavern.—What I had overheard there came fresh to my remembrance, I shuddered; it was now evident that he was not united to the object of his wishes. A part of the mystery was now unfolded; time will perhaps develop the remainder. The evening I thought would never end: Mrs. Anderson as usual, was all life and spirits, but I had scarce any idea of what she said, my mind was so confused. I tarried till past ten, when I came home, my father told me he was very sorry I went out, for Mr. Belmont had been there and was quite disappointed at not seeing me, though he was too polite to suffer him to send for me. Heaven reward him for it, said I, mentally, and telling my father it was probable he would soon be there again, I took a candle and went to my chamber. I determined if possible to extricate myself from a passion, which could only be productive of guilt and wretchedness, if it were indulged; and knowing that the time would soon arrive that I should be necessitated to see him, and converse with him, I endeavored to acquire sufficient fortitude to enable me to disguise the real sentiments of my heart; sentiments, which I cannot own even to you, without blushing. When I arose in the morning he was walking in his garden, I went down and sat in the parlour, still dreading an interview. My situation was not unlike that of a thief, who conscious of guilt, imagines himself suspected by every beholder. In the afternoon I was sitting by the window and saw him come out of his house; now, thought I, the trying moment approaches, let me exert myself to meet him in a becoming manner. He opened the gate—I was on the point of flying, but I knew there was no one to receive him, my father had gone out, and mama complaining of the headache, had lain down—He entered—how my heart palpitated! He fixed his eyes upon my face for a moment, and coloring excessively, said, "Miss Hamilton I presume?" I bowed, and he continued, "I did not think when I saw you last,

Miss Hamilton, that I should so soon have the happiness of having you for a neighbor, and consequently an opportunity of becoming acquainted with a lady whose conversation interested me in her favor before I could be informed who she was."—I gathered courage while he was speaking, to be capable of answering, which was more than I at first expected. He enquired where my father was, and having told him, he said he would wait till he returned, and entered into conversation with me, with as much ease as if we had been long intimately acquainted.

When my father returned, he expressed a little surprise at hearing us converse in a manner so familiar. "This is not the first time Sir," said Mr. Belmont, "that I have had the pleasure of conversing with Miss Hamilton." "Not the first time? Why, I heard her say yesterday, she had never seen you." "This Sir," said I, "is the gentleman who gave me such timely assistance last summer; but for him, I should undoubtedly have perished. I did not then know to whom I was so much obliged." Tears started to my eyes, and they flowed from more than one cause. "I was agreeably surprised, Sir," said Mr. Belmont, "when I found that one of the ladies whom I had been so fortunate as to relieve, was your daughter." "And were you then," said my father, "so many hours with each other, and not know each other's names, and where each belonged? It is not common that people have so little curiosity." "Curiosity was not wanting on my part, Sir," replied Mr. Belmont, "but I had no way to gratify it, without asking a direct question, and that I thought would be rather too impertinent." "And the girls I suppose were as anxious to know who you were, but rather than trespass against the rules of politeness, you mutually agreed to remain in ignorance." Would to heaven, thought I—we had always remained so. My mother came down, and Mr. Belmont was prevailed on to stay and take coffee with us.

This intimacy gives me great uneasiness. To see and hear him every day will be my ruin;—were he less amiable, were he less engaging, I might be happy; but alas! the more I am acquainted with him, the more agreeable he appears. He is here every day; I do not see him if I can possibly avoid it. Sometimes he enquires after my health, and my parents send for me to go down; but little do they think how much their daughter suffers by complying.

> "Come, Peace of mind, delightful guest,
> Return and make thy downy nest,
> Once more in this sad heart."[31]

Oh! Mary, pity and forgive me; tell me what I shall do to obtain freedom and peace. Write soon to your

EMILY HAMILTON

Letter XXXVI

To Miss EMILY HAMILTON

W——, May 1

Your last communication, my dear Emily, at once surprises and grieves me. I scarce know what to say;—your own good sense will direct you. Your partiality for Mr. Belmont, cannot be called guilty, as it took place before you knew he was married. You are now endeavoring to overcome affection by reason, and you will undoubtedly succeed in time; but remember, my dear girl, matters of importance, are not often executed in a day. Be not dejected, all will be right;—I know your innocent heart too well, to imagine you capable of indulging this unhappy passion. I would neither anxiously seek, nor solicitously avoid his company; treat him as you would any other neighbor, and you need not fear discovery of your sentiments. We often by too great circumspection, discover the secret we are most desirous to conceal. The tell tale eyes, too often betray those secrets, the tongue conceals. I shall make you a visit in June, and hope to find you entirely easy. We still continue to live in as great felicity as this imperfect state of existence will admit of;—perfect happiness we have no right to expect in this life. Mr. Gray passes his happiest hours in my company, and I am always pleased when I can have his. The improvement and cultivation of his farm does not afford him many leisure hours, but those are devoted to reading, and chatting with me. I have frequent visits from my grand mamma. She is unusually well this summer, and I find constant satisfaction in her company and conversation. My family is quite large at present, and my domestic concerns will not admit of my writing so lengthy a letter as I could wish. Yours with real friendship.

MARY GRAY

Letter XXXVII

To Miss MARY GRAY

S——, May 17

Your letter, my friend, gave me pleasure: Time, I hope, will relieve me, but as yet, I cannot say I have experienced the salutary effects I hoped for. Mrs. Belmont professes the highest regard for me; she sends for me frequently, and I am obliged from politeness to pass considerable time with her. Her husband treats her with the greatest tenderness, and endeavors by the most delicate attention, to gratify all her wishes; but he has as yet been unsuccessful in every attempt to make her pleased or contented with her new residence. She frequently tells me that were it not for my society, she should be quite wretched. Mr. Belmont assures her, that she will soon be contented, and added that he would send for his sister, if that would afford her any satisfaction. She appeared pleased with the proposal, and said she believed she should enjoy herself better if Miranda were here. "Tomorrow," said he, "I will write to Miranda, and she will undoubtedly hasten to us. I flatter myself, Miss Hamilton, that you will be pleased with my sister; her manners resemble yours, and there is a similarity of taste and disposition existing between you, which I hope will be productive of friendship and mutual esteem."

Yesterday afternoon, Mamma and four or five of the neighboring ladies, went to visit Mrs. Belmont. After tea, as I was alone, I determined to take a solitary walk. I rambled a considerable distance from the house, and seated myself beneath a spreading tree. The sun threw his last rays upon the earth, and sinking below the horizon, tinged the light clouds which floated above, with a purple glow; the birds warbled their adieu to departing day, and by soft degrees, all was calm and still—The moon already gave her silver light; the mildness of the air, and the stillness which reigned around, calmed my mind. I rose and walked toward the grove, an indulgence I had rarely experienced this season, as I know Mr. Belmont frequently passes some time there almost every day.— I thought I might venture now, as they had company. I had scarce entered the path that leads to the recess, before I saw Belmont near me. I stopped, and was retiring, but he approached, and taking my hand, begged me to return; saying the beauty of the evening was too great to permit him to lose the pleasure of a walk: "I have been walking for some time," he added, "and was going to the recess which has so often charmed me. You, I perceive, were directing your steps to the same interesting spot: Will you allow me the pleasure of conducting you?" Disdaining to affect prudery, I suffered him to lead me to the farther side of the grove.—The trees are now so thick on that side that the rays of the sun scarce penetrate them; but the brush and some other obstructions being removed, the beauty of the prospect is greatly encreased on the other side, and the light of the moon is reflected from the water in a manner that has a very pleasing effect. We seated ourselves on the bank, while the stream gently murmuring flowed below. Never did the pale moon shine with more radience than at this hour, and Belmont's flute, conspired with the surrounding scenes, to fill the mind with sensations the most pleasing and sublime.—"Can there be any place," said he, "more charming than this retreat? All around us, is pleasing, beautiful. It has ever been wonderful to me, that any person could deny or dispute the existence of a Deity. When we behold the full moon in majestic splendor, surrounded by innumerable orbs of light, do not our thoughts naturally ascend to Him who formed them, and placed them all in such admirable order? Each flower that breathes its fragrance on the air, proclaims a great first cause. Who can examine their delicate texture, their beautiful and various forms, without admiration?" "It seems as if impossible," I answered, "that any one who contemplated the works of nature could be an atheist. Did they examine with attention the objects which surround them, surely the order, proportion, beauty and harmony of the whole, must strike conviction on their minds, and bid them acknowledge that a creation so amply filled with all that can delight the senses, or satisfy the wants of man, could not be the effect of chance." We conversed in this manner a while, and I at last ventured to mention that it was time to return.

During our walk, he told me that when Miranda arrived, I should have a constant companion in my rural excursions. He had often, he said, regretted that Mrs. Belmont's taste differed so much from his own—that he had often pointed out objects to her, which to him appeared captivating, that she had no delight in viewing. He attended me to the door and wishing me a good night left me. When I entered the parlour, I found my father preparing to set off immediately to Boston; his friend Mr. Boyd, was in imminent danger, and had sent for him to assist in making his will. He has a large estate and only two children and anxiously wishes my father to take the charge of their fortune till they become of age. He directed me to write to Miss Penniman immediately if I wished to, saying he should set out in an hour at farthest. I have not written to Nancy till now, since your marriage. Ah! were I as happy now as I was last summer. But why do I repine? I cannot alter my fate, and must submit with as much patience as possible, to bear the share of evil allotted me. The adventure of last evening has determined me not to indulge in another ramble, unless I am certain of not being accosted by any one. Adieu, dear Mary, continue your friendship, to the altered

EMILY HAMILTON

P.S. A letter I received from Eliza just now, I enclose for your perusal.

Letter XXXVIII

To Miss EMILY HAMILTON

Salem, May 15

I am still the same happy creature, that I always have been, Emily, and as fortunate as you please. Mr. Selwyn came home yesterday; Louisa I suppose informed him of all that had passed in his absence, and came with him to our house in a few hours after his arrival. He was to all appearance, very happy; he pressed my hand eagerly, while his eyes evinced the joy of his heart. "Then I may still call you Miss Anderson," said he, "you are not married yet I find." "Oh, no; and perhaps I shall not be, for fifteen or twenty years." "And could you live single so long and refuse the offers of those, who would esteem their lives happy, if devoted to your service?" "That would depend on circumstances that might occur in the mean time. If I found I could be happier in a single, than in a married state, would you not think it the height of folly, Mr. Selwyn, if I were to give up that happiness?" "Certainly.—But perhaps, Eliza, a man might be found with whom you would be happy, though I am conscious there are but few who could deserve you." "You are pleased to flatter me, Mr. Selwyn, but I am not yet so vain as to imagine myself in any degree superior to my sex." Louisa now left the room, and he continued—"It is not flattery, Eliza; the man who could obtain you, would be truly in an enviable situation. If you knew my heart, Eliza, you would believe me incapable of flattering one, whom I have adored in secret from my first acquaintance with her. Ah! Eliza, could you know what I have suffered, could you know the painful conflict—I saw you here, charming as an angel, could I forbear to love? You were engaged to another; honor forbid me to interfere, and I found I could not extricate myself from a passion so deeply rooted in my breast. I flew to Carolina, hoping by absence to cure the melancholy which had taken possession of my mind. But even there your lovely image was constantly before me; and when I obtained the repose of sleep, the virtuous Eliza was still present to my imagination. Unable to bear a longer separation from you, I returned, and shall I own my sensations were nearly approaching to happiness, when Louisa informed me you had disengaged yourself from Cutler forever. It was from that assurance only, that I dared to avow my affection for you; may I hope for your pity, Eliza, may I hope that you will listen to me?—If the most respectful, the most ardent love can merit a return"—"You are entitled to my esteem, Mr. Selwyn; as my friend I have long considered you, and"—"Will you, Eliza, make me happy, by consenting to receive me as a lover?"—I smiled assent. He pressed my hand to his lips, declaring he had received ample compensation for the anxiety he had suffered on my account. I blush, Emily, to read what I have written, yet what could I do? I was well assured of his sincerity; his generosity in forbearing to make me acquainted with his regard before he left Salem, made a lasting impression on my mind; pity and esteem, and perhaps a softer passion, made me determine in his favor. His well known worth, the goodness of his character, and our mutual friendship, plead his cause forcibly, and why should I keep him in suspense and needless anxiety. Louisa has guessed how our conversation terminated, and I am rallied by her and my aunt, but they shall not laugh me out of a good cause.—He avoided a declaration while he thought me engaged. This delicate method of proceeding, has given sufficient evidence that he preferred my happiness to his own, and would not give me the pain to reflect that any one was wretched or uneasy on my account. His constancy shall not go unrewarded; it shall be my endeavor to make him happy; he deserves my affection, and will undoubtedly secure it. Yours &c.

ELIZA ANDERSON

Letter XXXIX

To Mrs. MARY GRAY

S——, May 24

I still continue writing to you, my dear Mary, without waiting for your answers. Are you so deeply engaged in your domestic concerns, that you cannot afford one hour to enliven the spirits of your Emily? Every day almost, produces a new source of regret. Mr. Belmont set off for Boston with my father, and while he was absent I felt as if at liberty to make what excursions I pleased. I passed two evenings in the recess, and found the calm of solitude more soothing to my mind than I could have expected. The third evening I was seated near the entrance, watching the stream as it glided over the shining sands, and hearing a footstep, I rose hastily and perceived Lambert near me. "Angelic girl," he cried, advancing and seizing my hand, "how charming at this moment do you appear! sure nature never formed another half so lovely!" Surprized and provoked at this unexpected address, I would have withdrawn my hand, but he still continued to detain it, and throwing his arm around me, pressed me to his bosom. I pushed him from me with encreasing indignation. "I am at a loss," said I, "how to account for this familiarity; my conduct has never, in any instance that I can recollect, given licence for such behavior." "Your conduct, my angel, has ever been irreproachable, but who could behold an object so irresistably engaging without love?" And again, in spite of all my efforts to prevent him, he clasped me to his heart. "I am amazed at your insolence," said I, "and depend on it Sir, it shall not pass unnoticed." By a sudden exertion I released myself, and with hasty steps proceeded homewards. He followed, and entreated me to pardon him; but without deigning to reply, I went through the garden to the house, my cheeks glowing with anger and resentment. Charles Devas was waiting for me in the parlour; he had been at Newyork several months, and arrived here that afternoon. Lambert came with him;—Charles said that he had contracted immense debts since he had been in Newyork, by gaming, drinking, and other excesses, and had come to S——, for money to discharge them. I think it is highly probable that Lambert will, by his extravagance, soon make an end of his estate. It is a subject of regret, that a man of his talents should thus debase himself. He might have been an ornament to his sex, and to human nature. It is surprising, that he cannot be sensible of the injury he is doing himself. Devas observed that Lambert might have been as happy as any man living. I believe the observation just—he certainly had sufficient property to enable him to gratify every reasonable wish. His natural and acquired abilities are great, and rendered him a pleasing and agreeable companion. He will return to Newyork next week, and I rejoice that he is not to pass the summer at S——. It is late and I must retire.—Ever yours,

EMILY HAMILTON

To Mrs. MARY GRAY

S——, June 8

My father and Mr. Belmont, have returned. Mr. Belmont's sister came with them; she is a charming girl; Mr. Belmont paid me a high compliment by saying, I resembled her; I should be happy to possess half her engaging qualities. Yesterday, a party of young ladies were invited to pass the afternoon at Mr. Belmont's. I assembled with the rest, and was highly gratified by the entertainment. Mr. Belmont was absent till near sunset, when he returned, accompanied by the young gentlemen of the neighborhood and a musician. We danced until eleven and retired. I derive great satisfaction from the conversation of Miranda; she is easy, frank and engaging; her countenance demands esteem, and her manners secure it. She engaged me to walk with her this afternoon, and we endeavored to prevail on Mrs. Belmont to be of our party, but she refused. She has an unconquerable aversion to the country and all its amusements. I expressed my surprise to Miranda, while we were walking, that Mrs. Belmont should wish to be in Boston at this season of the year. "It is natural to us," she replied, "to wish for the company of those to whom we are most attached."—"It is indeed," I replied, "but is Mrs. Belmont more attached to her parents, than to her husband and child?" "No.—But to tell you a little secret Emily, between ourselves, there is one whom Clara prefers to the whole world, and was forced by the command of her father, to marry my brother. Of this circumstance Edward was ignorant till nearly a year after his marriage, and even then he came accidentally by his information, but in what manner he never would explain to me." "You surprise me, Miranda, is it from this then, that her dejection arises?" "It is, and from the consciousness that she can only esteem my brother, while his tenderness to her demands a grateful return.

Edward is unhappy; the match was made by my father and old Mr. Belknap, the father of Clara. She was commanded by her father to receive and encourage the addresses of Edward—Edward on the other hand was told, that Clara Belknap was the most desirable person in point of fortune, that he could ever have pretensions to, and was desired by my father to consider her as his future bride. In obedience to a parent's wishes, he made her several visits, and as she appeared very amiable, and quite willing to be his, they were hastily married. To common observers, they appear to be a happy couple, but to me, as I am well acquainted with their minds, the appearance is vastly different.—The deception she practised upon my brother, stings him to the soul—her conduct with Le Fabre—but I forget myself, I ought not to expose her."

"Was that the name of the person to whom she is attached?" "Yes, he is a Frenchman by birth—he received his education in England, and came to Boston a few years since. He saw Clara and loved her, and finding frequent opportunities to converse with her, their affection became mutual. Le Fabre's fortune being small, he proposed to wait some years before they married, or at least till he could accumulate sufficient property to support a family in the elegance to which she had been accustomed. He went a voyage to the Eastindies,[32] and on his return found Clara married." "But why," I asked, "did she not inform your brother of her situation in respect to Le Fabre?" "Her father had threatened to disinherit her if she did not marry Edward, and of the two evils, she thought she had chosen the least, as she could, by marrying him, not only possess all the elegancies of life, but have it in her power to continue her intimacy with Le Fabre, at his return." "Your conversation really surprises me," said I; "I had no idea that Mrs. Belmont married your brother from mercenary views." "As I have begun," said Miranda, "I may as well tell you the whole story, as to leave your curiosity on the rack. She had been married about three months when Le Fabre returned from the Indies; he heard of her marriage directly after he arrived in town, and went immediately to her to upbraid her inconstancy, and leave her forever. I was present; he came into the room where we were sitting—despair was painted on his countenance. The dreadful certainty that she was lost to him forever, overpowered his senses, and he sunk almost lifeless into a chair. In a few minutes he rose, and clasping his hands, exclaimed, 'Oh! my God! I came to upbraid you, to shew you my resentment, and to abandon you forever; but I strive in vain to tear you from my soul. Cruel woman! you knew I loved you, loved you more than life; you knew it was to procure ease and happiness for you, that I crossed the stormy seas, and exposed myself to a thousand dangers. Ungrateful! and even now could my death procure you happiness, I would this moment cheerfully resign my life. You have married Belmont—make him happy, and laugh at my sufferings; rejoice at my woes; sport with my misfortunes; do your utmost, and you shall still be loved, yes, adored by me, while I am doomed to drag the load of existence.'[33] Exhausted, he sat down, and Clara turning her swimming eyes upon me, entreated that I would leave them for a few moments. I complied, and retiring to a chamber, saw him leave the house about an hour after, with a countenance tolerably composed. Clara came to me, and begged me to conceal the late adventure from Edward; 'it may give him disagreeable reflections,' said she, 'and I would not for the world destroy the peace of a husband. Le Fabre will trouble me no more; we have taken an eternal leave of each other, and I never wish to renew our former intercourse. With your brother I expect to enjoy a long succession of happy hours.' Deceived by her conversation, I complied with her desire; but I found that she had private interviews with Le Fabre, frequently in the absence of my brother. He has of late, frequently lamented her behavior to me, and has told me that he had other causes of uneasiness that he could not reveal. 'I should have been happy,' said he, a few days since, 'had I resisted the wishes of my father: By paying a blind obedience to his will, I have rendered myself the most wretched of men. I find that wealth alone cannot procure but a small portion of happiness. The mind must be at ease if we expect felicity.' I endeavored to make him explain himself more perfectly, but he refused. 'You know,' said he, 'that I never refused to tell you any thing it was proper you should know.'" I was just ready to reply, but looking round, I saw Mr. Belmont advancing toward us with his hands full of fine strawberries; he presented them to us, and telling Miranda, Mrs. Belmont was waiting for her to take tea, he took a hand of each and we walked home; they wished me to accompany them, but I declined, as I wished to write to you.

I forbear to make any observations on what I have related to you; your own mind will furnish sufficient. I shall expect you daily: Mr. Gray ought to oblige us by a visit, as it was by my interference he became acquainted with you; and since I have been in some measure conducive to his happiness, he ought to bring you here, by way of compensation. I expect my sisters, with their husbands here next week, and am anxious to have you meet them, as it would greatly increase the satisfaction of all parties. Yours with unaltered friendship,

EMILY HAMILTON

Letter XLI

To Miss EMILY HAMILTON

W——, July 12

You will not accuse me of neglect, my dear Emily, when I have told you the occasion of my not writing to you sooner. My grand mamma has had a very severe illness—her life was despaired of for several days, but she is now slowly recovering. Mr. Gray has had a slow fever, and still continues very weak. You may imagine the painful task I have undergone would not allow me time to write.

I am pleased with the character of Mr. Belmont, but I fear you still find him too amiable for your repose. How perverse is fate! Had Mrs. Belmont been connected with Le Fabre, and you with Mr. Belmont, it appears that you might all have been happier. Many of the dispensations of providence at first view, appear capricious, but when taken into consideration, we find them to be conducive of our highest happiness.

> "In all his ways, confess the Almighty just,
> And where you can't unriddle, learn to trust."[34]

The Christian religion furnishes its believers with abundant consolation, in every affliction. Sensible that an allwise Creator will do them no injustice, they can look up to him as a father, a friend; and though they feel severely the blow that wounds their peace, yet they can say, "thy will be done." It is often essential to our peace, that our most ardent wishes should remain ungratified: What we cherish fondly one day, the experience of the next may learn us to abandon and despise.—Could we be allowed to choose our own fortune, or to direct the events of our lives ourselves, it is highly probable that we should be rendered miserable. Some good purpose of which we are at the time ignorant, is undoubtedly to be answered by every event we term unfortunate.

I have been induced by Mr. Gray, to defer our visit to you till the beginning of September. The weather is now so extremely warm as to render the journey uncomfortable, and it is probable it will be the month succeeding. Mr. Gray says you must excuse him till then, and he will convince you that he is not ungrateful for the favor you have conferred on him. He confesses that he can never repay the obligation, and begs that you will not consider him as unthankful, though he is at present under the necessity of refusing your invitation. I should be really happy to see your sisters, and hope I shall the next time they visit you. I return to you Eliza Anderson's letters—I cannot help wondering at Cutler's inconstancy, though upon reflection, it is nothing new nor strange for a man to alter his mind. I fancy Eliza will be happier with this new lover, and that she is more pleased with him, than she ever was with Cutler; but it is rather difficult to discover her real sentiments, unless she sits down with an intention to disclose them gravely: I enclose a letter for her and wish you to forward it. Ever yours,

MARY GRAY

Letter XLII

To Mrs. MARY GRAY

S——, July 20

My sisters made us a charming visit, and I cannot but regret their departure. I intended to have passed a month or two with them this summer, but the visit is now postponed. They were very desirous that I should pass the winter with them; but upon consideration I have determined to defer it till next summer, when, if my life and health continues, I hope to pass several months with them. I rode with them several miles accompanied by Charles Devas. Charles has been very assiduous to gain my affection ever since his return from Newyork. His amiable manners and exalted sense have secured my esteem; but unhappy that I am, I have no heart to give him—I am almost driven to distraction, when I reflect in what manner my affections are engaged. I have lost all my philosophy, all my fortitude. My mind has become weak, and I have sunk very low in my own opinion of late. Belmont can never be any thing to me: Devas is capable of making any woman happy; but never while I live, will I marry one man while my heart is devoted to another. From a hope that the amiable, the engaging qualities of Devas may bring me back to reason, I have been induced to admit his visits—my friends have no objections to him, indeed they cannot have any. I have indulged my imagination in figuring to myself that I am the wife of Devas—I see in him the husband, lover and friend; but in the midst of all the pleasing images my fancy forms, the idea of Belmont will intrude and fill my mind with the most painful reflections. Such is my singular situation, and can I be happy, while conscious guilt and remorse pray[35] upon my mind. I had a sweet hope that the time would arrive that I should again see the charming stranger, and fondly imagined that there was a possibility that I might one day be his. Thus I continued:

"Lost in the magic of that sweet employ,
To build gay scenes, and fashion future joy."[36]

The surprise that awakened me from the sweet allusion, stunned my senses, or surely I should have more reason left. Yours,

EMILY HAMILTON

Letter XLIII

To Mrs. MARY GRAY

S——, August 9

A new, and still more painful trial, than I have ever yet experienced, calls for all my fortitude and resolution to support it. Belmont's life is almost despared of. He had a lingering fever for some days, and being inattentive, and unconscious of danger, he deferred any application to a physician till three days, since, when his symptoms were truly alarming. I had not seen him for more than a week, till yesterday my mother went there and requested me to accompany her. He was asleep when we entered the chamber, but O! Mary, what language can describe my sufferings, while I gazed on his emaciated countenance. He awoke, and not observing we were near him, desired Mrs. Belmont to hand him some beverage; his parched lips, and the deep crimson of his cheeks, evinced the violence of his disorder. She mentioned that we had come to see him; he immediately turned his head, and enquiring after our health as usual, conversed for a few minutes with all his accustomed ease and elegance, and concluded by saying, he should undoubtedly be able to walk to our house in a few days. But, ah! he is ignorant of the opinions of those around him; his physician has informed Mrs. Belmont that in three days, or four at fartherest, he shall be able to form a decisive opinion. Mary, I cannot express the anguish of my mind when I reflect on his situation—He may not live but a few days, and should he die, distracting thought! What will support the wretched Emily? I blush at my weakness; surely Belmont would despise me, if he knew my folly.—to others in affliction, I have been capable of giving consolation, but now like a child I suffer myself to despair, to repine and weep. My health declines daily; I must impute the weakness of my mind in some measure to that: I was once firm, I did not suffer my spirits to be depressed, but now, instead of endeavoring to overcome my sorrows by reason and reflection, I yield to its pressure and almost sink beneath it. I promised Charles Devas that I would accompany him and Fanny, on a visit to their sister, Mrs. Hammond, to day. I must dress, and be seated in a company of sprightly people and be compelled to listen, or at least affect to listen, to subjects foreign to my heart. I must appear lively, and wear the smile of satisfaction on my countenance, though my heart is bursting with anguish. It is a painful task to learn the art of dissimulation, but for these few months past I have studied it so much, that I am nearly perfect in it.

Devas has just been here to inform me his sister would be ready in a few minutes. The chaise is coming; I will finish my letter at my return.

It was so late last evening before we returned I could not conveniently close my letter. The sun is just rising, and the air perfectly serene and clear. A fresh breeze blows from the northwest, and may it bring relief and ease to the suffering Belmont. I felt wretchedly during my ride yesterday, and from politeness alone, conversed with Devas and Fanny, who exerted themselves to entertain me. After we had dined, Mrs. Hammond informed us, that she expected a large party in the afternoon; my heart sunk at the information, but I resolved to appear cheerful, though it cost me never so much to disguise my real sentiments. The company arrived, and began to converse with great sprightliness. Mrs. Hammond requested the ladies to sing; after many apologies one of them entertained us with the following, which I recollect to have seen sometime since; the tune was soothing, and I listened to the lovely warbler with attention.

> "Time has not thinn'd my flowing hair,
> > Nor bent me with his iron band,
> Ah! why so soon the blossom tear,
> > Ere Autumn yet the fruit demand.
>
> Let me enjoy the pleasing day,
> > Ere many a year has o'er me roll'd,
> Still let me trifle life away,
> > And sing of love ere I grow old.
> The morn of life serenely rose,
> > And blush'd with beams too bright to last,
> For soon a lucid cloud of woes
> > The pleasing landscape overcast.
> Gay fortune with alluring guise,
> > Charm'd and deceived my dazzled view,

For while with friendship smil'd her eyes,
  Her hand the fatal poignard drew.
But, hush thy throbbing pulse despair,
  The sun which now envelop'd seems,
Again may cheer the gloom of care,
  And gild those clouds that veil his beams.
Nor always must the tear be shed,
  Nor always heav'd the rending sigh
The wounded heart must cease to bleed,
  And sorrows flowing fount run dry."[37]

Another of the young ladies sung a favorite air, and while she was singing, Devas, who had been walking with Mr. Hammond, entered the room. At our request Mr. Hammond sung the following elegant Masonic Ode, and was accompanied by Devas on a flute.

"Genius of Masonry descend,
  And with thee bring thy spotless train,
Constant our sacred rights defend,
  While we adore thy peaceful reign.
Bring with thee Virtue, brightest maid,
  Bring Love, bring Truth and Friendship here,
While social Mirth shall lend her aid,
  To smooth the wrinkled brow of care.

Come Charity, with goodness crown'd,
  Encircled in thy heavenly robe,
Diffuse thy blessings all around,
  To ev'ry corner of the globe.
See where she comes with power to bless,
  With open hand, and tender heart,
Which wounded is at man's distress,
  And bleeds for ev'ry human smart.

Envy may ev'ry ill devise,
And Falsehood be thy deadliest foe,
　　Thou Friendship still shall tow'ring rise,
And sink thine adversaries low.
　　Thy well built pile shall long endure,
Through rolling years preserve its prime,
　　Upon a rock it stands secure,
And braves the rude assaults of time.

Ye happy few, who here extend,
　　In perfect lines from east to west,
With fervent zeal the lodge defend,
　　And lock its secrets in each breast.
Since ye are met upon the square,
　　Bid love and friendship jointly reign,
Be peace and harmony your care,
　　Nor break the adamantine chain.

Observe the planets how they move,
　　And keep due order as they run,
Then imitate the stars above,
　　And shine resplendant as the sun.
That future Masons when they meet,
　　May all your glorious deeds reherse,[38]
And say their fathers were so great
　　That they adorned the universe."[39]

They were proceeding to sing another, but tea was served. After tea the gentlemen proposed dancing; I was sorry, not having the least inclination to dance myself, I felt as if too selfish to wish others to enjoy themselves. Mr. Hammond ran up stairs, and bringing down a violin, merrily offered to play as long as we would dance. The company instantly rose, and Devas led me to join the figure. I performed as "mechanically as a clock strikes;"[40] my imagination had fled to the suffering Belmont, and it was impossible for me to enjoy even a tolerable share of satisfaction. When I came home I found Sally waiting for me, and inquired if she had heard from Mr. Belmont. She replied that he was much better, and a hope was now entertained of his recovery.—Happy tidings! I am too much elated to suffer me to conceal the pleasure I experience. But what will my sorrow or my joy avail me? I will tear him from my heart, though I must ever esteem him; it is yet criminal to indulge an affection which can only be productive of misery. I will think of his perfections no more, but will endeavor to erase from my mind every idea that will tend to increase a partiality which is already too great. Ever yours,

EMILY HAMILTON

Letter XLIV

To Mrs. MARY GRAY

S——, August 19

With pleasure, my dear Mary, I hasten to inform you of the arrival of Eliza Anderson—she came home yesterday on a visit, accompanied by Mr. Selwyn—she sent for me immediately, and I flew to meet her; she is all life and gayety. Mr. Selwyn appears like a man who has happiness in view, and soon expects to be blest with the passion of it. All his behavior evinces the tenderness and delicacy of his attachment. They will remain here a fortnight, and I hope from the consideration of seeing them you will be induced to visit us within that time. Mr. Cutler, she tells me, still continues his attention to Miss Wilson, and from what she can learn, she expects they will be married in the fall. Mr. and Mrs. Anderson appear to be highly pleased with Mr. Selwyn, and I believe they think him vastly preferable to his predecessor. Mr. Belmont is recovering rapidly; he continues his visits to us, and passes several hours here every day. I write but short, hoping ere long to have the pleasure of conversing with you. Yours,

EMILY HAMILTON

Letter XLV

To Miss EMILY HAMILTON

W——, August 25

The desire of seeing Eliza and Mrs. Selwyn, has induced us to lay aside our engagements, and visit you sooner than we intended. On Monday we shall set out for S——, if nothing extraordinary occurs to prevent it. Old Mr. Gray will hand you this; he has been with us several weeks, and has appeared to enjoy himself perfectly. He is in a hurry to depart, as he wishes to reach B——, to night, and I must detain him no longer than to tell you I am yours with sincere esteem,

MARY GRAY

Letter XLVI

To Mrs. MARY GRAY

S——, September 19

I am almost alone, Mary; Eliza went away the day after you went, and in three days after, Miranda was sent for to go home. To lose so many agreeable people at once, is rather too much; I have now little company but my own reflections, and they are not very pleasing. The time has been when I could find more real enjoyment in solitude than in a crowd; but now I am most happy when I can fly, as it were, from myself. But as I told you, I begin to be quite partial to Devas, and I really wish I could be more so; I endeavor to set all his words and actions in the most pleasing light, and hope I shall succeed so far, as shortly to prefer his company to Mr. Belmont's. His uncle at Baltimore has sent for him and made him a very advantageous offer; it is as yet uncertain whether he will accept of it or not; I shall see him this evening, and he will undoubtedly acquaint me with his determination. I will lay aside my pen till this information is obtained, and then give you an account of it.

'Tis past 12 o'clock—Devas has just left me, and I will write till I have composed my mind sufficiently to retire to rest. He came a little after sunset, and sitting down by me with a pensive air, told me he had come to take his leave of me for some time. "My uncle," said he, "has made me a very advantageous proposal; I had determined to refuse his offer, and remain with you—but the hope of accumulating a handsome property in a few years, has induced me to leave you, though not without a hope that you will remember me, and that you will sometimes devote a few leisure moments to the man who must ever love you while his life remains. He took my hand and dropped a tear upon it as he pressed it to his lips. I was affected by his manner.—"Emily," he continued in a softened voice, "I have never yet disclosed to you the hope I have entertained of making you mine by the most endearing connexion, nor should I at this time have mentioned it, were I not under the cruel necessity of leaving you, or offending a beloved uncle to whom I am under a thousand obligations. I leave you free; I will not even ask you to engage yourself to me—your happiness will be mine, and should any other man fix his soul upon you, as I have, and should you find you could be happier with him than with me, I will not presume to say I should oppose the measures you might then adopt. But you may be assured it has ever been my highest wish to call you mine, and though you may never perhaps be sensible how great my affection is for you, yet you may be assured it can never admit of a change." I listened with attention—"your generosity," said I, "pleases me; the affection you profess I cannot doubt, when I reflect on the many instances of it you have shown me." I could not proceed, and continued silent with my eyes fixed on the floor. He took a picture from his pocketbook, and holding it toward me: "Will you Emily accept of this, and now and then look upon it and remember the original, who will then be far from you?" He sighed. "Since it is your wish," said I, "I will accept it, but I shall not need such a memorial to bring you to my remembrance. Your merit has secured my esteem, and I shall reflect often on the pleasing hours I have passed with you." I felt at the time, that I had said too much, but it was past, and I could not recall it. "You are all goodness, Emily, but I have yet another favor to request, a favor that I fear you will not grant:—I shall write frequently to you, and may I hope that you will sometimes condescend to soften and enliven the tedious hours of absence, by writing to me?" I hesitated, and was preparing to evade his request; but he continued, "do not refuse me this; it is all the consolation I can have while absent from you. Your letters, though never so short, would render me happy." I could not refuse him, and not without reluctance, however promised to answer some of his letters. The remainder of the evening passed in an interesting conversation. He bade me an affectionate farewell—his heart overflowed—I caught the infection of his sorrow, and wept involuntarily. "Notwithstanding the hopes you have allowed me to indulge of making me happy at my return," said he, "I feel a sad presentiment that I must never see you more; a dreadful something, for which I cannot account oppresses my mind." "May Heaven" I replied, "shield you from every danger, and grant you a safe return." I never knew till now how great my regard was for him; though my heart is now unaccountably divided, yet surely, I shall soon learn to devote my affection entirely to him. He has left me with the hope, that he shall in two years return, and make me his. His letters will contribute to increase my affection for the writer, and I may yet be happy. Ah! Mary, I still continue to erect castles, though convinced the employment is useless. Adieu,

EMILY HAMILTON

Letter XLVII

To Mrs. MARY GRAY

S——, October 20

The beauties of nature are rapidly declining—the weather is cold and rainy to day, and confines me to the house.—Notwithstanding the altered appearance of the surrounding scenery, I still find pleasure in walking and contemplating on the objects around me. The following beautiful picturesque ode, which I found a few days since among some loose papers, may perhaps please you.

> "'Tis past, no more the summer blooms!
> Ascending in the rear,
> Behold congenial Autumn comes,
> The Sabbath of the year!
> What time thy holy whispers breathe,
> The pensive evening shade beneath,
> And twilight consecrates the floods;
> While nature strips her garments gay,
> And wears the vesture of decay,
> Oft let me wander through the sounding wood.
> Ah! well known streams! Ah! wonted groves!
> Still pictur'd in my mind,

Ah! sacred scene of youthful loves,
Whose image lives behind!
While sad I ponder on the past,
The joys that must no longer last;
The wild flow'r strewn on Summer's bier,
The dying music of the grove,
And the last elegies of love,
Dissolve the soul, and draw the tender tear.
My steps were innocent and young,
The fairy path pursued,
And, wand'ring through the wild, I sung
My fancies to the wood.
I mourn'd the linnet lover's fate,
Or turtle from her murder'd mate,
Condemn'd the widow'd hours to wail;
Or while the mournful vision rose,
I sought to weep for imagin'd woes,
Nor real life believ'd a tragic tale.
Relentless power! whose fated stroke
O'er wretched man prevails!
Ha! love's eternal chain is broke,
And friendship's covenant fails!
Upbraiding forms! a moment's ease,
Oh memory! how shall I appease
The bleeding shade! the unlaid ghost!
What charm can bend the gushing eye!
What voice console the incessant sigh,
And everlasting longings for the last?
Yet not unwelcome waves the wood,
That hides me in its gloom,
While lost in melancholy mood,
I muse upon the tomb.

Their chequer'd leaves, the branches shed,
Whirling in eddies o'er my head,
And sadly sigh that winter's near;
The warning voice I heard behind,
That shakes the wood without a wind,
And solemn sounds the deathbell of the year.
Nor will I court Lethean strains,
The sorrowing sense to sleep,
Nor drink oblivion of the themes,
For which I've lov'd to weep.
Belated oft by murmuring rill,
While nightly o'er the hollow'd hill,
Aerial music seems to mourn;
I'll list to Autumn's closing strain,
Then woo the walks of youth again,
And pour my sorrows o'er the untimely urn."[41]

I have lately had a letter from Mrs. Penniman, and another from Nancy, with pressing entreaties that I would pass the winter with them.—Miranda Belmont has written likewise, and begs that I will pass one month at least with her. She is very intimate at Mrs. Penniman's of late, she tells me, though she never had any acquaintance with them till last summer. She had often seen Nancy in public, without knowing who she was; but happening accidentally to meet in the house of a friend, they formed an acquaintance, and now visit frequently. My parents are pleased with the idea of my passing a month or two with my Boston friends, and I expect to go the latter part of next month; if I do, I shall defer my visit to you until spring. But wherever I am, you may depend on the unalterable friendship of your

EMILY HAMILTON

Letter XLVIII

To Mrs. MARY GRAY

S———, November 17

I have just received a letter from Devas, my dear Mary, and will transcribe it for your perusal.

To Miss Hamilton
Baltimore, October 20

When I reflect, my dear Emily, on the distance which separates us, I am almost tempted to despair; but the soothing reflection that "distance only, cannot change the heart,"[42] bids me hope that I may yet be happy. I am engaged in a very lucrative employment, which I cheerfully perform, animated with the pleasing hope, that I shall soon be enabled to offer with my heart an ample fortune, and be capable of gratifying every wish of my adored Emily.

Many of the Baltimore ladies are beautiful, and I have seen one who resembled you in her person; but her mind falls too low to admit of a comparison with yours. It is a satisfaction, however, to see only a slight remembrance of those we are fondly attached to, and this may account for the satisfaction I have taken in the company of Miss Lloyd, though I was disappointed in her conversation. Alas! How often is a faultless face accompanied by weak intellects. With a female whose only ingenuity consisted in ornamenting her person, and uttering with studied politeness, a few common place sentences, calculated only to amuse a set of idle insignificant people, who meet only for fashion's sake, I could never be in love, even for an hour. Your beauty caught my eyes, but your virtues secured my heart. Love that is placed on beauty alone cannot be permanent; as that decays, so will the passion it created: But the charms of the understanding will remain, and by encreasing improvement, encrease and se-cure affection, though the once blooming cheek of the ob-ject beloved, should be covered with the paleness and wrin-kles of age. You, my amiable friend, have this consolation, that when you will cease to be admired for mere external charms, you have those of the mind which will never know decay, but by increasing improvement will shine with still brighter lustre. How happy will be the man who is destined to call you his own! How truly enviable will be his situation! To find in you an entertaining and instructive friend, blest with complacency, and constant good humor. "These are beauties that outlive all the charms of a fine face, and ren-der the decays of it invisible."[43] May I still presume that I shall be that happy man? I will indulge the hope, though it may prove illusive—it is too sweet to resign. I entreat you to write to me—I shall wait with anxious impatience for a letter; surely your gentle heart will not refuse that satisfac-tion to an absent friend. A line from you will give me more pleasure than any thing I can enjoy here.

I must bid you an unwilling adieu; may you enjoy un-interrupted felicity; I cannot expect it for myself while ab-sent from you. I look forward with impatience to the happy hour when you will condescend to reward with your love the constant affection of your

CHARLES DEVAS

I find that Devas has a larger share of my heart than ever, though every endeavor proves useless to prevent the idea of Belmont, from occupying a part in my affection. But I am firmly resolved to throw aside all my melancholy and dejection, and by entering with avidity into the sprightly scenes which await me, endeavor to discipate[44] all my discontent by mirth and gayety. I have tried re-tirement and reflection long enough to find that they avail me nothing, and now intend to mix with the gay multitude which will throng every place of public resort in Boston this winter, and try what that will do;—if it does not produce the desired effect, I can return home satisfied, at least with the consciousness of having performed my duty. You see I am resolved to be a lady of pleasure;—I shall communicate to you the success of every experiment, and depend upon knowing your opinion of it. Ever yours,

EMILY HAMILTON

Letter XLIX

To Mrs. MARY GRAY

Boston, December 6

You will see by the date, my dear friend, that I am in the very centre of fashionable enjoyment. I have been here but a week and have been twice to the theatre, and to a splendid ball. Two other evenings were passed in a variety of company and amusement. But I cannot say that I feel perfectly happy, notwithstanding the manner in which I have passed the time. I had hoped that by being absent from Belmont, I should forget him amidst all the hurry and dissipation of thought; but unfortunately I can go no where without being in his company. A few days before I came hither, Mr. and Mrs. Belmont were at my father's upon a visit; in the course of conversation I mentioned that I should go to Boston in a few days. Mr. Belmont immediately answered that he was going with Mrs. Belmont the next Monday, and begged me to accept a seat in his sleigh. Mrs. Belmont seconded the proposal, and my parents being fond of it, I was obliged to comply, though much against my inclination. We went immediately after our arrival in town, to Mr. Belmont's father's, and I met with the kindest reception from the family, but particularly from Miranda, who insisted upon my passing the first week with her. The next night we were conducted to the theatre by Mr. Belmont;—the Grecian Daughter,[45] was admirably performed, and drew tears from a great part of the audience. The entertainment concluded with the farce, called "The Deuce is in Him."[46] I was highly gratified by the performances and the music. As we were retiring, we were accosted by Nancy Penniman and Mr. Morton—a dispute instantly ensued: Nancy insisting upon my going home with her, and Miranda as resolutely upon the contrary. Mr. Belmont at length ended it, by saying he would not trust me to ride so far in the town that night, but I should go home with them, and he would carry me to Mrs. Penniman's himself in the morning. He performed his promise, but expressed some dissatisfaction at my being separated from them, but added that he hoped we should meet every evening. Mrs. Penniman was rejoiced to see me, and expressed her pleasure in very flattering terms, and entreated Mr. Belmont to make her a visit that evening, with his lady and sister. He promised he would, if he found them disengaged at his return. The day passed agreeably, and at the close of it, Mr. and Mrs. Belmont, Miranda, her lover Mr. Bently, and a large number of others whom Mrs. Penniman had invited, came to visit us. Cards passed away the time till supper, and it was very late before the company retired. The greater part of the next day was passed in preparing to make an elegant appearance in the ball room. I am always fond of neatness and simplicity, but on this occasion, I suffered myself to be governed by Nancy, and wore a greater profusion of ornaments than I wished to. The evening came, and I was attended by Mr. Williams, to the ball room, which I found nearly filled. I was hardly seated before I saw Mr. Belmont more elegant than ever, leading his wife, and followed by Miranda and Mr. Morton. They came instantly toward me, and expressed their satisfaction at meeting me so soon. Miranda sat next me, and in a whisper desired me to observe the gentleman who sat opposite to us, saying

it was Le Fabre. He is an agreeable figure, and though his countenance wears a melancholy expression, it is certainly very handsome. His eyes were rivited[47] on Mrs. Belmont while I observed
him, and he took the first opportunity that offered after the first
dance was ended, of conversing with her. Mr. Belmont left them
together, and solicited me to be his partner in the next dance. We
did not retire till near two, in consequence of which, I had a severe headache all the next day, and the opportunity it afforded me
of being alone, did not at all contribute to enliven my spirits. On
Sunday I went to church; I cannot say I dislike the mode of wor-
ship; but the situation of a stranger of another denomination, is
really awkward. Yesterday I went to the theatre again, and this evening am engaged at a card party. This is keeping it up: I am almost
tired of it, when I reflect that time spent in such a continued round
of amusement is no better than lost. I am called upon by Nancy
to begin to dress for the evening: Upon my word I am so hurried I
can scarce find time to reflect one moment; surely, love and every
thing else will be hurried out of my head, if not out of my heart at
this rate. Adieu dear Mary, I shall not be forgetful of you.

EMILY HAMILTON

Letter L

To Mrs. MARY GRAY

Boston, January 10

My time still passes in the same manner that it did when I wrote
to you last. Morning visits and evening engagements, occupy my
time so completely, that I have scarce a moment that I can call
my own. I am now with Miranda: Mr. Belmont and his lady went
home about a fortnight ago. Mrs. Belmont was earnestly desirous

to stay longer, but submitted to the judgement of her husband. I should exhaust your patience if I were to give you an account of every thing as it passes; suffice it to say, that I go to the theatre twice a week, to a ball once a week at least, and visit or receive company every day except the sabbath. I wrote a letter to Devas a few days since; the style was friendly, and I wrote nothing to discourage the hope I allowed him to entertain, though I forbore to give him any additional encouragement. I hope I shall one day be able to give him my heart with my hand. My time of writing is so short that I can only add I am sincerely yours.

EMILY HAMILTON

Letter LI

To Mrs. MARY GRAY

Boston, February 5

Though my time is not suffered to lag heavily along, for want of amusement, yet, at every interval of leisure, my heart springs forward with rapture to the happy moment that I shall return to my native vale. I am not very well this evening, having taken a cold, which has rendered me too hoarse to speak; I am therefore excused from going to the theatre this evening, and find myself much more agreeably entertained by writing to you. A letter was yesterday handed me from the postoffice, and casting my eye over the direction, I recognized the well known hand of Devas. I retired hastily to my chamber, and read as follows:

> Your letter, my amiable Emily, gave me more pleasure than I can express. My imagination often carries me to Boston, where I behold you among a crowd of rival beauties. I view

the sprightly group, and singling you from the number, gaze on that lovely face, till the cruel reflection that I am far, far from you, destroys the pleasing scene my fancy painted, and I unwillingly return to the duties of my station. My beneficent uncle has placed me in a situation far exceeding my expectations; he has placed me in a large store, filled with the most valuable productions of every clime, and bids me call half the profits arising from the sale my own. Though I should find my highest happiness in being near you, yet honor, duty and gratitude, forbid me to leave my generous uncle till two years are expired. I need not repeat that frequent letters from you would shorten the tedious hours of absence, while I could have the pleasure to reflect that you still held me in remembrance. I flatter myself that you will not neglect to give this satisfaction to one, whom, though you did not profess to love, you honored with your friendship and esteem. Adieu, my friend—may all the happiness attendant on virtuous minds be ever yours.

CHARLES DEVAS

Mary, this worthy man loves me, and shall I blush to confess to him, that his affection merits the return he wishes. Shall I refuse to accept the offered heart of the amiable Devas, merely because my affection is so foolishly divided. After I had promised to unite myself with him, at his return, I should consider myself as his wife, if I may be allowed the expression, and by indulging my imagination continually about him, I should lose even the shadow of an affection for any one else.

Nancy is coming up, and I must bid you adieu.

EMILY HAMILTON

Letter LII

To Mrs. MARY GRAY

S——, March 1

Never did my bosom glow with purer joy, than when I entered my father's house last evening. It was near sunset when I arrived; I found my parents and Mr. Belmont sitting in the parlour, without the least expectation of seeing me for a fortnight to come. They all came to receive me with the greatest joy. Belmont caught my hand, and pressing it eagerly between his, bade me welcome, while pleasure beamed from his eyes. How frail is the human heart! I set out from Boston with a full determination, never to spend a single thought upon the perfections of this man, and a single look destroyed all my good resolutions, and made me completely vexed that I had no more command over myself. I retired early, but in vain did I endeavor to obtain repose; reflection kept me waking, but no consideration shall tempt me to act ungenerously with regard to Devas. I will be just, though I suffer more than I have ever yet done, to extirpate the idea of Belmont from my heart. Ah! my dear parents, could you see the heart of your darling Emily, torn as it is by conflicting passions, how would your aged bosoms bleed to behold such a strange medley of love, hope, anxiety, distress and remorse. My constitution is naturally good, but I perceive the agitation of my mind and the long anxiety I have suffered, has sensibly impaired my health. I have reasoned with myself till I have been perplexed almost to distraction. I feel mortified at my weakness, but neither my pride nor my reason can teach me to banish entirely from my heart, a man, who, though he is the worthiest and most amiable of his sex, I wish I had never seen. Yours,

EMILY HAMILTON

Letter LIII

To Mrs. MARY GRAY

S——, March 30

Disappointed of the hope I had entertained of receiving a letter from you by the last post, I sit down to accuse you of neglect. The morning is delicious—the rising sun diffuses his enlivening rays—the air is serene and clear, and every appearance denotes the warmest day we have had this season.

> The robin sings, sweet stranger yet again
> Repeat thy grateful, joy inspiring strain.
> Ah! could this breast like thine with rapture glow,
> Could smiling nature dissipate my woe.
> I too with joy could greet the newborn day,
> Forget each care, and join thy pleasing lay.
> But ah! to this sad breast, returning spring
> Can no enliv'ning joy, no transport bring—
> For sick'ning fancy points to future woes,
> And o'er each scene a sable mantle throws.[48]

I have written to Devas; I think the letter must afford him satisfaction, and I mean to act consistently with that, let it cost me a greater conflict than I have ever yet endured. I believe I shall make you a visit soon, perhaps in the course of a fortnight or three weeks. I am quite anxious to see you, and shall undoubtedly find more pleasure at W——, than at any other place. The post is waiting. Sincerely yours,

EMILY HAMILTON

Letter LIV

To Mrs. MARY GRAY

S———, April 10

O heaven! What more shall I be called to endure! I scarce have power to write, from the variety of sensations which overwhelm and drive me to distraction. I have now evidence, unequivocal evidence, that the partiality which Belmont has ever shewn toward me, and which I imagined proceeded only from friendship, arises from love. Last evening I walked out, as the weather was remarkably fine: It was a clear starlight night, but I could not discover any object at a distance. You recollect that Mr. Belmont's orchard is separated from ours by a high wall—I was walking by the side of the wall, and heard some persons talking in a low voice: As I was alone, and at some distance from the house, I thought it would be most prudent to return. I had not proceeded many steps before I heard my name pronounced with uncommon emphasis. I started, as I knew the voice to be Belmont's. He continued, "This reflection robs me of repose; I have loved her from the first moment I beheld her; her attractions increase daily, and I find no satisfaction but in her company." I trembled:—"Is she then so very amiable?" asked the person who was with him.—"Yes," replied Belmont, "Emily Hamilton is every thing that is beautiful or engaging in woman." Almost breathless I hurried along by the side of the wall, knowing that would screen me from their observation till I could reach the garden. I went to my chamber and wept till my tears refused to flow any longer. The idea that I was beloved by him never entered my heart; and now the certainty of it renders me miserable. To day, after we had dined, Mr. Belmont came in, accompanied by a gentleman whom he introduced to me as his friend. I wished to fly, for the situation I was in was terrible to me. I knew Mr. Melvin came merely from curiosity; but I supported myself better than I could have expected and conversed with all the ease I could possibly assume. I shall come to you next week, for to stay here with the certainty that I possess his affection, while my own inclines so much toward him, would be the height of imprudence.—From W——, I shall return to S——, and tarry only a week, and then go to visit my sisters. I shall cherish my regard for Devas, and perhaps a long absence from Belmont may be productive of very beneficial consequences to him and myself.—Yours,

EMILY HAMILTON

Letter LV

To Mrs. MARY GRAY

S——, May 21

I had a very agreeable journey, my dear Mary, and found a letter from Charles Devas, at home. He wrote but short, but it was kind and affectionate, as usual. He is going a voyage to —— and expects to be absent from Baltimore several months. May heaven protect him from every danger, and grant him a safe return. I have not seen Mr. Belmont since I came home; he is gone to Albany, and is not expected back for three weeks. Before that time arrives I shall be at P——. My sisters have written and requested me to come by the week after next. I believe riding is serviceable to me, for I am much better as respects my health than I was when I left you. Mrs. Belmont presented her husband with a son, while I was at W——; it is a beautiful child and bears a striking resemblance to their little Harriot. Lambert, I hear, has by his extravagance, increased his debts greatly beyond his power to satisfy them, and is now imprisoned in Newyork. I cannot forbear heaving a sigh, when I reflect on what he once was, and what he now is. The contrast is shocking beyond description. It is astonishing to what lengths a man will go, who once enters the alluring path of vice.—Though the path may for a while be pleasing, and the gaudy objects by which he is surrounded, may allure him on, yet he soon finds the charms of the prospect to vanish before him, and present to his view a labyrinth of misery and wretchedness, without a clue to direct him. With the idea of extricating himself from the difficulties which on every side surround him, he plunges still deeper, and sinks into the abyss of wretchedness. My next letter I shall write from P——, where I hope to pass the summer, if not without care, at least with a tolerable share of content, whose smiles alone can make us prize life at its full value. Yours,

EMILY HAMILTON

Letter LVI

To Mrs. MARY GRAY

P——, June 20

This is retirement's favorite seat; all is stillness and serenity. I have seen no company, and have not made one visit since my arrival. The beauty of the place where we live pleases me extremely. A large stream flows through the meadows around the house, and the wild prospect appears more alluring to me, than all the gaudy splendor of a city.

> Here at the evening hour, alone, unseen,
> With pensive steps I tread the dewy green,
> And wander while the beam of morn
> Drinks the rich dew drop from the thorn.
> And oft I wander where the breeze
> Soft whispers through the waving trees;

'Mong craggy rocks that overhang the stream,
And while I view the wild romantic scene
Court sprightly fancy, ever gay,
To chase each anxious care away.[49]

I think I have a prospect of recovering my health, and my mind is
rather more at ease. I think often on Devas, and wait impatiently
for his return. I wrote to him before I came here, and suppose he
received the letter before he went to sea. I have received letters
from home and from Eliza Anderson. Eliza writes that she expects
to come home in October, and give her hand to Mr. Selwyn. She
is very desirous that I should be present on the occasion; I do not
think it probable, however, that I shall, for as my sisters wish me to
pass the winter with them, I know of no motive at present to induce me to return to S———. Catherine and Fanny live within call
of each other, a circumstance with which I am greatly delighted.
We pass all our afternoons and evenings together generally, unless
I am disposed to take a solitary ramble. They are entirely ignorant
of my situation, as respects Belmont; but I have informed them of
my connexion with Devas, and they impute my frequent pensiveness to his absence. I have not confirmed this conjecture, though
I did not choose to contradict it, as I did not wish them to make
any further inquiries. I anticipate a letter from you, my dear Mary,
with pleasure, and I beg you to fulfill your promise of writing frequently. Yours,

EMILY HAMILTON

Letter LVII

To Mrs. MARY GRAY

P——, July 17

I have just received letters from S——, my dear friend, and one enclosed from Mr. Gray: Permit me to congratulate you on the birth of your son.—May he prove a source of constant satisfaction and delight to you—may he live to be an ornament to human nature, and a blessing to society. I wish earnestly to see you, more earnestly perhaps than ever; but it is not probable I shall have that happiness for many months. Mamma writes that Mrs. Belmont is in a deep decline; her physicians have given it as their opinion, that the complicated disorders under which she suffers, will inevitably prove fatal to her. Mr. Belmont, she writes, is quite melancholy and dejected; he goes no where, and has almost wholly discontinued his visits at our house. The extreme heat of the weather perhaps may be one cause of Mrs. Belmont's declining so fast; she was very feeble when I came from S——, but I fancy if she survives the heat of this and the succeeding month, the autumnal air, and a journey may be very beneficial to her.—I have had a letter from Devas; he received mine a few minutes before he sailed, and wrote a hasty answer. He expresses a hope that he shall make a visit at S——, next spring, and appears to anticipate great happiness—he hinted toward the close, that if my consent and that of my friends could be obtained, it was his ardent wish to be united to me then, and carry me to Baltimore with him. This will require some consideration, but I cannot say that I should have any very weighty objections to make. I am fond of travelling, and a residence at Baltimore, for one or two years, would be pleasing. Every letter I receive from Devas confirms my resolution of sharing his fortune whatever it may be. I never can find a man more agreeable, except one whom I have no right to think of, and I have many more reasons to induce me to go to Baltimore with him, than I should choose to make many people acquainted with. However, I cannot at present know what will be for the best; I am willing to leave the events of my life to the disposal of Heaven. Were I allowed to choose my own lot, perhaps I should commit an irreparable error, and be more wretched than I should otherwise be. But whatever may be my situation in life, you may be assured of the continuation of my friendship and esteem for you. Adieu,

EMILY HAMILTON

Letter LVIII

To Mrs. MARY GRAY

P——, August 12

I receive letters from home very often, Mary, but none from you. Mamma's letter arrived yesterday, with the melancholy intelligence of Mrs. Belmont's death. She expired on the 4th instant, and left her family in great affliction. Her parents and brother, and Miranda, were present at the last mournful scene. She was calm and resigned, and retained her senses to the last moment. This must be a great satisfaction to her surviving friends. It is distressing to see a relative expire, even when we have obtained satisfaction from their last words, but more deeply distressing when they leave the world incapable of knowing the approach of the solemn hour. Mamma writes that Mr. Belmont appears deeply distressed, and passes most of his time alone; his reflections are undoubtedly painful, perhaps nearly as much so, as if their affection had been mutual. But it is a subject I am not fit to write upon. I am quite ill today; walked late last evening—the air was rather damp, and I took cold. I have had a severe headache for several hours, and feel quite incapable of writing at all. Yours with real affection,

EMILY HAMILTON

Letter LIX

To Miss EMILY HAMILTON

W——, September 3

After a long neglect of writing, my dear friend, I sit down with pleasure to answer your letters. My little son requires great attention, and my domestic concerns occupy almost my whole time. I fancy you will be highly pleased with Theodore; I have already imagined, with the fond partiality of a mother, that he has every attraction an infant can possess. His smiles, and sweet engaging innocence, give me a pleasure too great to permit me to describe it. Mr. Gray, with paternal affection, delights in expatiating on the charms of his son. When we are without company, he passes more time than usual in the house. I hope we shall not place our hopes too high, nor suffer our affection for the little innocent, to be too great.

Now is the time, Emily, to prove your constancy to Devas. You will find it rather difficult, I fancy, to give your consent to go to Baltimore with him next spring, but I hope you will not be induced to act ungenerously with him, though it may be some trouble to you to keep your thoughts from straying to what was once their most pleasing object. If Belmont really has a regard for you, it is not probable that he will conceal it many months, and should he, as I expect he will, make proposals to you, you will find it extremely difficult to decline them. You may perhaps think me rather hasty to introduce the subject so soon after Mrs. Belmont's death, but I am too much interested in every thing that concerns you, to defer it to a future time. Continue to write frequently, my dear girl, and do not indulge the idea of my neglecting you, if I do not answer your letters often, but believe you are never absent from the mind of your

MARY GRAY

Letter LX

To Mrs. MARY GRAY

S——, October 20

No, Mary, no earthly consideration shall induce me to break my promise to Devas. I know him too well, I know his affection for me to be too great, to suppose him capable of resigning me to another with any degree of fortitude—and should I have the offer you hint at, my consideration and regard for him, would compel me to refuse it. I have a sincere esteem for Belmont, and were I to indulge myself in that way of thinking, I should undoubtedly experience a return of affection for him, too powerful perhaps, to admit of its being easily overcome. Whatever partiality he might formerly entertain for me, will now perhaps, be obliterated. I think it is probable that he will marry again, but not very soon and there are others more deserving of his affection, and better calculated to take the charge of his family than I am.

I am very agreeably situated here, and shall not think of returning to S——very soon, though I am anxious to see my parents. Since I wrote to you last, I have visited at one or two of the neighboring houses with my sisters. The people appear friendly and social; their manners are different from those of the people at S——and W——, but I am quite pleased with them. A simplicity of manners, and natural politeness prevails here; all is peace, harmony, and good humor. The surrounding scenes still afford me pleasure though their appearance is altered. I feel as if retired from the world; and in the calm of solitude, enjoy myself much better than I hoped to when I came here. Time glides away with imperceptible rapidity, while I am pursuing the innocent amusements of reading and walking. My mind is calm, and my health tolerably good; though my spirits are not greatly elevated, they are not depressed—and there is so little variety to be found here, every thing is so still and quiet, that I seem to have attained another existence. Nothing of importance takes place from one week to another, and consequently I cannot have any thing very interesting to write. My letter is too dull and unvaried to admit of my enlarging it. Ever yours,

EMILY HAMILTON

Letter LXI

To Miss EMILY HAMILTON

S———, November 14

You have been so long absent from us, my dear Emily, that I wish for your return. Catherine and Fanny I suppose, expect you to pass the winter with them, and if it is your wish, I shall not oppose it. It would be a pleasure to me to have your company, but if you had rather defer your return till spring, I believe I shall make a visit at P———, with your father, as soon as the sleighing will permit.

Eliza Anderson was married to Mr. Selwyn, a few days since, and was very much disappointed by your not coming home to be present at the ceremony. She will return to Salem in a few days, where she is to reside.

Mr. Belmont will hand you this, and I believe you will think him greatly altered. Since the death of Mrs. Belmont he has been very melancholy; he has lost all the agreeable vivacity he formerly possessed, and shuns society as solicitously as he once sought it. He makes frequent inquiries concerning you, and this evening came to request me to write to you, saying he was going to D———, upon business, and would call at P———, to see you. Little Harriot passes half her time here; she is a sweet girl, but not fond of the woman whom Mr. Belmont employs as a housekeeper. She frequently complains to me that Miss Anna is cross to her, and I fancy the complaint is not without foundation. A woman who has the care of young children, ought to possess an even temper and a good disposition, or she will not easily obtain respect or esteem from them. Young minds are easily prejudiced either very much in favor of a person, or against her. I wish you to write by Mr. Belmont, when he returns, that I may know when to expect you, or whether it would be most agreeable to you, to remain at P——, till spring and receive a visit from us this winter. If the latter, I think it probable we shall come about the last of next month. Your affectionate parent,

LUCINDA HAMILTON

Letter LXII

To Mrs. MARY GRAY

P——, December 9

Mr. Belmont called upon me a few days since, my dear Mary, and brought me a letter from my mother. He is altered greatly in his appearance; dejection sits on his brow, and he appears like another person. I was sitting alone when he came, and had no notice of his arrival till I rose to open the door. He took my hand, and fixing his eyes eagerly upon my face, inquired after my health in a voice hardly audible. I was affected by his manner, and desired him to sit down. After a little conversation, he mentioned Mrs. Belmont, and said she had an earnest desire to see me before her death; but was deprived of the satisfaction. He conversed for some time about her, and mentioned that her death had made a great alteration in his family, as he had now no one in whom he could place much confidence. Catherine came in, and the conversation took a different

turn. In the course of the evening, he asked when I expected to return to S———. I told him it was improbable that I should return
before May. "Devas is expected home then," said he, "have you
heard from him of late?" "Not since July," I replied, "he is at sea I
suppose." He rose, and walked the room for some time in apparent
agitation. Every endeavor of my brother and Catherine, seemed
useless to enliven his spirits. He retired early, and the next morning bade me adieu with an air of melancholy, saying he should do
himself the pleasure of calling again in a few days for a letter to my
parents, if I would write. Four days have now passed since he was
here, and we expect him every hour. In spite of all my efforts, a regard more tender than mere friendship, arises in my heart for him,
but I will banish it. The sight of him has destroyed the calm serenity of my mind; but I hope to regain it when he is absent. I wish
for, yet dread the return of Devas. Strange that my mind can have
no more stability. Belmont is coming, I will endeavor to behold
him with indifference. Mary adieu. Yours,

EMILY HAMILTON

Letter LXIII

To Mrs. MARY GRAY

P———, January 13

Mary, the sorrows I am now called to endure depress my spirits more than usual; I have just had letters from S———. Devas, the
amiable, the worthy Devas, is no more. As he was returning from
——— a violent storm commenced while they were at sea, and continued for several days with unabating violence. The vessel leaked,
and the hands exhausted with labor and fatigue, were obliged to
take refuge in the boat, as their last resource: All were saved but the

hapless Devas; they were taken up next day by a vessel bound to Carolina. Dear, hapless youth—all his golden prospects faded before him; no more can he anticipate with delight, his return to his friends and his beloved Emily. In the morning of life, with the fairest prospect of happiness before him, he has found a watery grave. Perhaps his latest thoughts were full of love for me, and his last sigh arose with a prayer for my happiness. My tears flow too fast to permit me to proceed at present.

For the future fate of Devas, I have a well grounded hope, which precludes anxiety. The innocence of his life, and the purity of his sentiments and morals, and an assurance of his being a real christian, leave me no reason to doubt of his living in a state of happiness. The same goodness of heart, and amiableness of manners, which rendered him dear to me while living, now afford me the greatest consolation. I mourn indeed, but not like those who are without hope. Had he been of a different turn of mind, the sudden manner in which he left the world, would have been far more terrible and shocking.—Since we cannot know how soon, nor how suddenly we may be called from life, it is highly necessary that we should often reflect on that important, interesting period, and prepare to meet its approach without terror; yet the number is comparatively few of those, who could perceive the approach of death without distressing apprehensions. Religion is frequently considered, by the young and gay, as a gloomy thing, unfit to be introduced among sprightly people. They imagine it banishes amusement and gaiety, and renders those who feel its influence morose and unsocial. But their ideas are wrong. Religion, indeed, forbids vicious indulgencies, but it is not an enemy to any kind of innocent enjoyment. I recollect that a few months since, I was with a party of young ladies at Mr. Hall's; they were speaking of Augusta Evans, and mentioned that she had been to a ball, and in a few minutes after her return went to her chamber. A young lady who was at that time with her, followed soon after, and found her at prayer, and that it had made a deep impression upon her mind. "I have heard," said one of the ladies, "that Augusta constantly prays every day." "I hope," said I, "that she is not the only one who practices her duty." The lady blushed, and said she believed there were but few who practiced it in that way. "If she were so religious, I should not think she would go to balls," said Charlotte Hall. "She undoubtedly knows the difference between religion and superstition," I replied; "superstition would teach her, perhaps, that all diversions were criminal, and offensive to God; but religion does not forbid us to enjoy any of this world's pleasures, provided we enjoy them innocently and with moderation." "Well," replied Charlotte, "I shall begin to think better of religion if this is true, but I am sure our ministers never encourage pleasure." "They do not encourage levity and dissipation" I replied, "but they are not enemies to mirth at proper times. It would be highly improper to appear sad and disconsolate at a wedding, but still more so, to be gay and merry at a funeral; we may at all times be cheerful, and yet innocent." Other company coming in, put an end to the conversation at that time, but Charlotte has frequently renewed it since, when I have been with her. She has many times owned to me, that she could never think of death without horror, and always endeavored to prevent her thoughts from tending that way. She had always, she said, considered religion as improper in young people, and it always appeared to her that it must depress their spirits, and have a very disagreeable effect upon their minds. A little reflection, I should suppose, would have convinced her of the contrary; for can there be any thing on earth more pleasing, than to be able to look up to the Supreme Being with humble confidence, and consider him as a father, protector and friend. Why can we not with as much ease and confidence, request favors of him, as of an earthly friend, and return our grateful acknowledgments for those we have already received.

There are many people who pay such a scrupulous attention to the rules of politeness, as never to receive the smallest benefit from another, without returning thanks, who ridicule the idea of prayer or praise to the Almighty, notwithstanding he is continually showering innumerable blessings around them, and is the source from whence all their pleasures flow. This appears highly inconsistent, but though it is a disgrace to those who openly profane the sacred name which the christian reveres, we must own the truth of the assertion. True religion not only increases our pleasures, and opens to us continually new sources of enjoyment, but renders the pangs of adversity less distressing. It is a subject of regret that it is so little practiced; in this country especially, where we enjoy so many blessings, it is strange that our citizens should be unmindful of the power who protected them, and their rights, and placed them in possession of peace, liberty and independence, and has preserved them from the horrors of a war which has involved Europe in distress. No nation, perhaps, had ever more to induce them to be grateful and virtuous than this—yet we are too apt to forget the hand who bestows our felicity, while we enjoy it without interruption.—Adieu my dear Mary—write by the earliest opportunity to your

EMILY HAMILTON

Letter LXIV

To Mrs. MARY GRAY

P——, February 13

Since I wrote to you last, my dear Mary, I have been severely ill with a fever; my friends here were extremely anxious on my account, and would have sent for my parents, but I assured them I did not think myself dangerous, and was unwilling to give them an unnecessary alarm. For more than a week, I did not leave my bed; and even now I am too weak to sit up more than an hour at a time. I have written to my parents, and received an answer; they wish me to come home as soon as I am able to take the journey. I am to send them word as they mean to send for me; but I do not think I shall be able under a fortnight or three weeks. Mamma wrote that she had heard from Lambert; he had escaped from prison, and gone to Canada, and was now under sentence of death. She was ignorant of his crime. How dreadful! Little did any one imagine when Lambert first came to S——, that he would ever be sentenced to an ignominious death.—May heaven grant its mercy to the unhappy wretch. Though he has erred, yet he is entitled to our pity. All my compassion is awakened; the tears of sorrow overflow my eyes, when I reflect on his wretched fate. My bosom bleeds for him, and I half forget the injury he has done. May his example deter others from deviating from the path of rectitude. Mary, I am conscious your tears will flow with mine; a young man in the prime of life, blessed with a fine person, a good education, and great natural abilities, and yet come to such a dreadful end. My present feeble state will not admit of my enlarging as I could wish. Yours,

EMILY HAMILTON

Letter LXV

To Mrs. MARY GRAY

S——, April 20

I am once more in my dear native village, Mary, and feel a satisfaction I have long been a stranger to. My health increases daily, and I begin to look forward with pleasure. Mr. Belmont came to P——, a few days before I came away, and told me that he was going to

D——, and my parents wished me to return in the chaise with him, if I was able to perform the journey. I accordingly prepared my things while he was absent at D——, and came home with him. During our journey he paid me the greatest attention, and would frequently stop, that I might not be fatigued. The journey has been serviceable to me, and I am almost well. He mentioned Devas, and conversed in a manner that pleased me extremely concerning him. He acknowledged his worth, and said that he always thought him capable of making any woman happy. "Though it is painful," said he, "to be deprived of an object to whom we are tenderly attached, yet it is possible that we may afterwards be attached to another as tenderly, and enjoy as much happiness as we anticipated with the other." I do not know that I shall ever marry at all; Devas possessed a large share of my affection, and I think I could have been happy with him. I am determined never to give my hand to any man, unless I can give my heart, unoccupied by any former passion. Where there is a want of reciprocal affection, a married couple cannot be happy, even though they possess the best of tempers, and every convenience of life. If either of them are attached to another object, the anxiety of their minds will banish happiness and mutual confidence.—Happiness dwells with content, and there cannot be content when the mind is continually in pursuit of a favorite wish it can never obtain. Mrs. Belmont could not be happy, though most people thought her so. Blest with all that could render life agreeable, she was unhappy, because the object of her affection shared not those blessings with her. Belmont was equally unhappy. Miranda has often told me, that conscious of his not possessing the affection of his wife, he had not the satisfaction of considering himself as the husband of her choice; this proved a constant source of uneasiness to him, and poisoned all his enjoyments. How greatly are people deceived by external appearances: Mr. and Mrs. Belmont were considered by their acquaintance as the happiest couple existing; but to me, who knew more of them, they appeared in a quite different light. Neither wealth nor honor can confer real happiness; it is to be found only in the mind;—if the mind is not at ease, local enjoyments can afford but little pleasure. When my heart has been sinking with sorrow, the consciousness that I possessed an ample fortune, could not procure me an hour's repose. How often have I envied those, who surrounded with poverty, slept sweetly on their hard beds, after the fatigue and toil of a day passed in earning a subsistence.

The wealthy may find satisfaction in contributing to the support of the aged and infirm, and in relieving the necessities, and encouraging the younger poor. There is an exquisite felicity attendant on charity, which none but those who have hearts of sensibility can ever experience.

There is a poor family in this neighborhood, to whose support I have sometimes contributed;—it consists of a man, his wife and seven children. Mr. Patterson is above thirty, and his wife is about the same age. They were possessed of a small estate, and by indefatigable industry, were in such a way of living, as to bring up their children decently at least. But sickness and unavoidable misfortunes, reduced them so low that they were induced to part with their little farm; this was bought by my father, who still permits them to live upon it rent free. In imitation of his example, I have been induced to visit and relieve them occasionally; this is at once a source of gratification to me, and a benefit to them. I was conversing with Mrs. Patterson, a few days since; she was remarkably cheerful and lively, and behaved like a person perfectly at ease. I could not forbear wondering that a woman so poor, with such a family of children, none of whom are yet capable of doing any thing for their support, could be so merry, though I would not injure her feelings by expressing my admiration. In the course of conversation, she remarked, that she had nothing in the world to make her uneasy, for that the goodness of our family had removed every present difficulty, and that she hoped if Mr.

Patterson's health continued, they should soon be in a situation to live without being obliged to the charitable assistance of the neighbors, though she should ever remember their kindness with heartfelt gratitude. "I shall always have reason," said she, "to respect Mr. Belmont as long as I live—for while you were at P——, he gave us money, and sent us things we were in need of, very often. He charged me not to mention it, but I did not promise that I would not, for such generosity ought not to pass unnoticed. I told him that he always gave every thing in such a manner, and so much like you, that it seemed as if he was obliged to us for accepting it." I could only answer her with a blush, and soon after took leave of her.

By this time I presume you are tired of reading, and I conclude with telling you, as usual, that I am sincerely yours,

EMILY HAMILTON

Letter LXVI

To Mrs. MARY GRAY

S——, May 17

I was happy to hear from you by Mr. Ashley, my friend, though I was disappointed at not receiving a letter from you. He says you wish me to make you a visit; I should be happy to, but do not think I can conveniently till autumn. I have been from home so long that I dare not mention a word of going again for some time.

I was on a visit at Mr. Hunt's, on Monday afternoon, with the Miss Willis's[50] and Miss Duncan.—In the evening, Mr. Belmont and several other gentlemen came.—The evening passed delightfully; several beautiful songs were sung by the company, and the following by Mr. Belmont:

"The gentle Swan with graceful pride,
Her glossy plumage laves,
And sailing down the silver tide,
Divides the whisp'ring waves.
The silver tide that wand'ring flows,
Sweet to the bird must be,
But not so sweet, blithe Cupid knows,
As Delia is to me.

A parent bird in plaintive mood,
On yonder fruit tree sung,
And still the pendant nest she view'd,
That held her callow young.
Dear to the bird's maternal heart,
The genial brood must be,
But not so dear a thousandth part,
As Delia is to me.

The roses that my brow surround,
Were natives of the vale,
Scarce pluck'd and in a garland bound,
Before their hue grew pale.
My vital blood would thus be froze,
If luckless torn from thee,
For what the root is to the rose,
My Delia is to me.
Two doves I found, than new fall'n snow,

More white the beauteous pair,
The birds on Delia I'll bestow,
They're like her bosom fair.
May they of our connubial love,
A happy omen be,
And such fond bliss as turtles prove,
May Delia share with me."[51]

They sung the Indian Philosopher,[52] and desired Mr. Belmont to accompany them on his flute, with which he immediately complied. At the close of the evening, Mr. Belmont came to me, and said his chaise was at the door, and he wished me to allow him the pleasure of conducting me home. As we alighted, he pressed my hand, and said if it would be agreeable, he would call in the morning to inquire after my health. He came after breakfast, and we talked over the occurrences of the preceding evening. After he was gone, my father smiled, and walked round the room for some time, in his usual manner; at length turning to me, he said, "Emily, can you tell me how long Mr. Belmont intends to remain a widower?" I started, "No Sir," I replied, while my face glowed, "How is it possible I should know?" Mamma looked up, and seeing my confusion, "What answer did you expect to your question, Mr. Hamilton?" she asked with a half smile. "I did not expect one much different from that I had," he replied, "but I expect Emily will be capable of making one more satisfactory in a few months." He laughed and left the room. You know when my father is in the humor he never spares any one. I did not see him again till dinner time; as soon as we were seated, he looked upon me with a smile; "I think, I heard you observing last evening, Miss Hamilton"—"Pray Sir," said I, "do not"—"What Emily, do you blush at the repetition of a conversation you listened to with such apparent pleasure in the morning? Miss Duncan has a fine voice, Miss Hamilton, but it has not such an agreeable effect"—"Indeed Sir," said I blushing, "I cannot bear"—"Oh! you cannot bear to hear it from any one but Mr. Belmont, very well, I will call him in this afternoon."—"Dear Sir," said I, "I beg you not to laugh at me thus for nothing." "Well, I will say no more now, but when he comes again, I hope he will not wholly forget to speak to me."—However, I am resolved not to be laughed at for nothing—it is true Belmont did direct his conversation chiefly to me, a circumstance very unusual with him. He is now advancing toward the house, to afford more sport, I suppose, for my father.—Mamma has sent for me to go down and I must bid you adieu.

EMILY HAMILTON

Letter LXVII

To Mrs. MARY GRAY

S——, June 22

Since I wrote you last, my dear Mary, I have not had occasion to heave one sorrowing sigh. The attention of Belmont is truly delicate and respectful; it increases daily, and I need not say I am pleased with it. He is here frequently, and my father indulges himself, after his departure, in rallying me most unmercifully. I went some time since to visit Mrs. Anderson; she had no other company, and we had quite a pleasing conversation. While we were at coffee, Mr. Belmont came in; he did not know of my being there previously to his coming, I am persuaded, but Mrs. Anderson looked at me as if she placed his visit to my account. At her request, he took a seat at table with us, and appeared highly gratified at the opportunity of enjoying a friendly conversation. The satisfaction is much greater that we have with only two or three select friends, than we can possibly enjoy in a large party. During our walk home, he expressed his pleasure at finding me there, and added, "I find you so irresistably engaging, Emily, that I cannot deny myself the satisfaction of seeing you every day; I have sometimes fancied that you would think my frequent visits impertinent, or at least troublesome." What could I answer, Mary? I never was more confused, than when he continued—"May I be permitted to indulge the grateful idea, that you will receive my addresses, or is there some more fortunate person who has already engaged your heart?" I answered him with all the ease I could assume, and consented to receive a visit from him the next evening. When I entered the parlour, my father was reading, and I hoped to escape unnoticed, but I was disappointed, for he threw down his book, and began, "Why did not Mr. Belmont come in, Emily?" "I suppose he thought it unnecessary Sir." "When does he intend to make us a visit?" "It is probable he will come to morrow Sir, he usually comes every day."—"I do not know but I shall go to Boston, with your Mamma in a day or two—Do you think you could entertain him while we were absent, Emily?" "Perhaps he would not come while you were absent Sir, and there would be no occasion"—"Why do not you think, Emily, he would visit you then as well as now? You would certainly need his company more, and though very agreeable at any time, it must be peculiarly pleasing then"—smiling archly.—I looked very grave; "I have not the vanity, Sir, to suppose Mr. Belmont comes here so often on my account; he certainly came as often, and indeed oftener when Mrs. Belmont was living, and surely you cannot suppose he had any idea then"—"Come, come Emily, you cannot deny that he pays more attention to you, than any one in the family now, but when Mrs. Belmont was living, he was rather more attentive to me, and I cannot help remarking a change so obvious to every person who will take the pains to notice it." "I did not know Sir, that Mr. Belmont failed in respect to you." "His respect may be the same it ever was, but then he has a different way of showing it; perhaps he imagines, that by suffering my daughter to engross all his attention, he shall render himself so agreeable to me, that I shall not hesitate to give my consent to"—"Dear Sir, I beg that you will not thus"—"Emily, your confusion is a sufficient evidence that you believe me; however, I will not press the subject any farther to night. I think it is probable that I shall set out for Boston tomorrow, as I have had letters which require immediate attention; your mamma will accompany me, and as we shall be absent nine or ten days, it is possible Mr. Belmont may call upon you, and if he does, as my friend, I wish you to treat him with politeness at least." I was going out but he called me back and said, "If Mr. Belmont should make any serious proposals to you, I hope you will not be so blind to your own interest as to refuse them."

I ran up stairs, where I found Mamma preparing for her journey. She gave me a few directions concerning the family affairs, and concluded an affectionate speech, by saying, she should not long have me to manage our domestic concerns in her absence. I started, and desired her to explain herself. "Mr. Belmont," said she, "professes a great affection for you, and wishes to make you his wife. He mentioned his intention to your papa and to me, this afternoon. We could have no objection to make. Your understanding will convince you that you never can obtain a better partner for life, and I have reason to think he is the most agreeable man of your acquaintance, and I fancy you are too partial to him to reject his proposals. You are young, and the situation you will be in, respecting his family, requires consideration. But Harriot has an excellent disposition—she is fond of you, and will undoubtedly have as much affection for you, in a short time, as she had for her own mother. The little boy is too young to ever know a difference—and I know the goodness of your disposition too well, to permit me to entertain an idea of your ever being wanting in affection to them. A motherinlaw,[53] is indeed often found fault with, but if your own conscience does not reproach you, and you can secure the approbation and esteem of your husband, you need not fear the malice of the world." My father came up, and she said no more; but what she had said gave me sensible pleasure. They set off in the morning, at an early hour, and by being alone for the most part of the day, I had a fine opportunity for reflection. Mr. Belmont came in the evening, according to appointment, and we had a truly agreeable conversation. We were speaking of you, as being always very much engaged in your domestic concerns. "This I think, is an honor to Mrs. Gray," said he, "though some ladies would consider it as a disgrace." "I never thought it a disgrace," I replied, "for any woman, however large her fortune might be, to be well acquainted with all kinds of family work, and to take a part in it, for a transition from wealth to poverty is at all times possible." "It is indeed," said he, "and a woman who had always been accustomed to idleness and ease, would not if reduced to poverty, be capable of gaining a subsistance by ordinary means, but would be necessitated to eat the bread, of dependence. But to one who had in prosperity been industrious, the hand of adversity would be far less cruel, as she would have many resources, and the means of supporting herself with decency at least, and be infinitely more respected than one of an opposite character." I assented to the justice of this, and he continued, "It has ever been my wish, Miss Hamilton, since the death of Mrs. Belmont, to convince you of my esteem and affection for you, an affection which I have long indulged, and I will presume to say, not without hope of a return. Your happiness is far dearer to me than my own, it is in your power to make me completely happy, by consenting to become mine by the most endearing connexion in life. I should not thus early have disclosed my intention to you, but the situation of my family requires immediate attention. My children, Harriot especially, greatly need a kind maternal friend—they are in some measure neglected by the woman I have employed as my house keeper, and they cannot be supposed to entertain an affection for one of a temper so capricious as Miss Anne possesses. You I am confident would be the most proper person to whom I could entrust them; they are so very fond of you that they would find no difficulty in learning to consider you as their parent." The brilliant tear trembled in his eye, he pressed my hand and entreated me to forgive him if he had presumed too far. "You have indeed," said I, "called for my attention in an affair of a serious nature"—I could not proceed, and he continued, "It is indeed important—I do not wish you to enter into an engagement with me, till you have had sufficient time for reflection; of the consent of your friends I am assured, as I took the liberty to express my wishes to them, and they gave me infinite satisfaction by replying, that they had not the least objection, provided I could obtain your consent. That only is wanting to make me happy." I answered him with as much ease as possible, and he insensibly led me from one subject to another, till I found we had discussed almost every topic relative to my future situation, when I should become his wife, the mistress of his family, and a parent to his children. His tender solicitude concerning them gave me sincere pleasure. He assured me that he should ever be satisfied with my care and attention toward them, and he hoped their behavior to me would ever be such as to merit a continuance of it. Our conversation, the most pleasing I was ever engaged in, continued till past twelve, and even then he appeared unwilling to take his leave. Mary, all my affection is centered in him, to contribute to his felicity is my highest wish. Our dispositions are similar,[54] our love is mutual, and can we fail of being as happy as this life of imperfection will admit of? I shall write again soon, and hope my letter will rather have a tendency to enliven, than depress your spirits. Ever yours

EMILY HAMILTON

Letter LXVIII

To Mrs. MARY GRAY

S——, August 10

I can scarce persuade myself that all that passes is not a dream, I have so long been accustomed to sorrow and anxiety.—Last evening, I walked with Belmont; he came before sunset, and we went to the grove, once the witness of my sorrows, and unavailing efforts to eradicate his idea from my heart. We sat down on the bank; I reflected on the contrast, and tears of gratitude and joy, in spite of all my efforts to prevent them, flowed from my eyes. I wiped them hastily away. "What is the matter?" said Belmont with eagerness—"Nothing," said I—"Pardon me, Emily, if I say those tears can not proceed from nothing; am I not your friend? Tell me what sorrow"—"it is not sorrow," I replied smiling, "the remembrance of the many hours I have passed in this retreat will ever be dear to me, and some of them passed in the company of friends now absent, produce a recollection"—"I understand you perfectly, my Emily, but let us now bid adieu to care and every unpleasing reflection, and only look forward to the bright prospect now opening to our view. Since you have given me the hope of your becoming mine, why should the ceremony be delayed? Your mind is too dignified to permit you to pay an attention to too scrupulous forms. Why is it necessary to protract the days of courtship to a tedious length, when the choice of both parties is fixed?" "I do not wish to pay too much attention to forms," I replied, "yet I cannot consent at present, to pay no regard to them. I think the ceremony ought to be deferred"—"a month, and no longer,"—said Belmont, interrupting me. "And even that would seem an age, were it not absolutely necessary to wait till that time was expired." "You surprise me, Mr. Belmont, do you suppose I can possibly consent to such a hasty"—"Why not, Emily? Many important regulations in my family are neglected, and I entreat you for the sake of my children, that you will consent to an early day. Pardon me, if the situation of my family renders me more importunate than I ought to be; the whole study of my life shall be to promote your happiness and reward your goodness." He felt what he had said, the pearly drop of sensibility gave additional lustre to his beamy eyes, and he at length persuaded me to consent to be his in six weeks from that day. And can it be possible that I am so near what I once thought would be the summit of earthly felicity? Oh! Mary, have I not cause to be grateful to Heaven for the blessings which are showering around me? I have had a large share of sorrow, but I can now enjoy the consoling reflection, that I earnestly endeavored with all my power to free myself from the guilty passion which possessed my soul, and robbed me of repose. The pleasing certainty that I possess the undivided affection of Belmont, is an ample compensation for all I have suffered on his account.—But I forbear—you will think me too fond. I need not say that your presence and that of Mr. Gray would add greatly to my happiness—do leave your affairs if possible, Mary, I shall depend on your being present at the ceremony, even if you return to W——, the next day. I have company coming in, and must for the present bid you adieu.

EMILY HAMILTON

Letter LXIX

To Miss EMILY HAMILTON

W——, August 31

Having an opportunity to send directly to S——, I improve it to congratulate you on your approaching nuptials. Nothing but sickness will prevent us from attending, I shall therefore not enlarge, as I shall then have a personal interview which will be far more pleasing than a lengthy letter. I hoped to have had a visit from you, of a fortnight or three weeks, but now you will be deprived of the satisfaction of visiting your friends often. A wife ought to find her highest happiness at home, and you undoubtedly will find yours there. Where the affection of a married pair is mutual, they seldom wish to be absent from each other, or to be a great deal in mixed company. I find that I never enjoy myself so well as when, after a day passed in variety of company or amusement I retire with Mr. Gray to our little parlour and chat during the evening. I am quite domesticated, if I may use the expression, and little Theodore renders my hours of leisure and retirement still more delightful. Adieu my dear Emily, I hope soon to have the happiness of seeing you. Ever yours,

MARY GRAY

Letter LXX

To Mrs. MARY GRAY

S——, September 25

My dear Mary, the melancholy intelligence of Mr. Gray's illness, which I received from Mr. Howard, deprived me of the hope of seeing you. On Thursday I was united to the most amiable of men, and yet my interest in all that concerns you, clouded my joy. How solemn, how important is the undertaking I have engaged in! I feel anxious lest I should not answer the expectations of Belmont with regard to his children; though I feel the tenderest interest in their welfare and the greatest affection for them, I feel anxious. The conduct of a motherinlaw, is always inspected with a scrutinizing eye, and most of it called in question. If she corrects the vices of the children entrusted to her care, she is termed cruel—if she has children of her own she is charged with partiality, and it is difficult in such a situation to escape censure; but however I may err, it shall not be intentionally, and if I can please my Edward, and gain his approbation, why should I regard the censure of those who inspect the affairs of others while they neglect their own?

To oblige my father, I consented to have a large party at my wedding, and all our neighboring acquaintance were invited. To my great satisfaction, Mr. and Mrs. Selwyn arrived in town on a visit the preceding evening. Miranda had been here nearly a week, and could I have had your company it would have been a high gratification. Since our marriage, Mr. Belmont has given me a little history of his first connexion, I will relate it to you in his own words as nearly as I can remember them.

"Soon after I left college" said Mr. Belmont, "Miranda had a small party of her acquaintance to take tea with her, and my father observed to me a little before their arrival that a Miss Belknap was expected there and he wished me to make myself as agreeable to her as possible, adding that there was nothing so much wished for by him and her father, as to form a connexion between us. Her person and character, he said, were unexceptionable, and her fortune as large as any body's in Boston. I could not forbear smiling, but as I had never seen the lady, I resolved to remain silent upon the subject till I could form some acquaintance with her. When the company were assembled in the parlour, I joined them, and was introduced to Miss Belknap. I entered into conversation with her, and found her sensible, modest and unaffected. I was pleased with her—attended her home, and obtained leave to call upon her in the morning. She did not make any greater impression on my heart at the second interview, but as I fancied I should never find one more amiable, and as my father was so very desirous to see her mine, I began to be very attentive to her in all parties where we met, and frequently visited her at her father's, who took every decent opportunity of letting me know how much my attention pleased him. I had a sincere regard for her, but I had never experienced that degree of love which I then believed was only to be found in the imaginations of poets and novelists. But I fancied we should be as happy as if we had risqued[55] our lives to come together. In a short time after my marriage, I begun to fear that my happiness was not to be very great. I feared that the person of Clara was all I possessed, while her heart was devoted to another.—When I was with her, she was all gaiety and cheerfulness, but if I came into her apartment suddenly, I found her melancholy and dejected, but before I could have time to ask the cause, her countenance would brighten, and she would meet me with a smile. One day I found her weeping; 'Clara,' said I, 'what is the matter?' 'Nothing,' said she, wiping her eyes, and giving me a smile which was evidently forced. 'Do not deceive me,' I replied—'Will Clara weep, and refuse to let her Edward share her sorrows?' And throwing my arm round her, 'tell me,' said I, while I pressed her to my heart, 'Tell me if it is in my power to put an end to the grief which oppresses you.'—'Those novels, Mr. Belmont, which you gave me yesterday, are so affecting'—'What passage was you reading?' 'The departure of Willoughby, and the suspense and anxiety of Celestina.'[56] 'Then you wept for an imaginary evil?' Her father came in and prevented her reply: But every day produced some new source of regret;—often in the night she would murmur in her sleep, and call upon some name, which I could not perfectly understand.—Oh! heaven, thought I, if she has married me only in obedience to her parent's will, and against her own inclination, I must be wretched. Though I could place unlimited confidence in her virtue, I could not be happy while I believed she was sacrificing inclination to duty. My suspicions alas! were but too well founded: Why must gold, cursed gold, enslave the hearts of mortals, and render them callous and insensible to the softer feelings of nature! To paint the anguish of my mind at that time, would be impossible, when I found that the woman whom I had married, was engaged to Le Fabre, an amiable young Frenchman, whose only fault was want of property. I had often questioned Clara upon the subject of her dejection, and in the tenderest manner endeavored to discover the cause; but as she always appeared rather mortified and uneasy on the occasion, delicacy forbid any further attempt. In about three months after our marriage, I was at my father's, and conversing with him, when a servant came in and told him that

Mr. Belknap wished to speak to him, in the next room. My father attended accordingly, and desired me to wait his return, and from the dialogue which passed between them, I discovered too late, the cause of Clara's uneasiness. Mr. Belknap told my father that he should call at my house in a few hours, and desired him to accompany him. 'Clara,' said he, 'has found out by this time, I guess, that she is better off than if she had married that little devilish frog eater;[57] but she may thank me for it, for all the time when your son was at my house with her, I took care to sit where I could hear their conversation, and she knew it, and I swore to disinherit her if she refused him her hand.' 'That was wisely done,' said my father, 'that was wisely done—and I, on the other hand, kept myself well employed in telling Edward there was not such a fine girl upon earth, and I really believe he liked her pretty well. It is no matter whether married people love each other or not, if they only mind the main chance. I'll warrant they won't quarrel as long as they have money enough.' 'Aye, you was in the right,' said Mr. Belknap, 'but if the girl had been left to herself, she would have been Le Fabre's wife. You can't imagine, Mr. Belmont, what a plague that girl has been to me; for after I had done every thing for her, and she had agreed to marry Ned, she wrote a letter to that French idiot, full of love and constancy, and intreated him to hasten home and find some way to carry her off, that she might avoid this hated marriage;—only think, this hated marriage, with one of the handsomest and richest fellows in the country: Well, this letter I stopped while it was carrying to the post office, and forbid her the use of pen and ink; but not long afterwards, I found a letter which she had written to your son; in which she represented her love to Le Fabre, and begged Ned to refuse her, as she was sensible she never could feel that affection for him which he deserved, and that her heart was, and ever must be devoted to Le Fabre. I carried the letter to her, and tried to convince her of her folly, but all to no purpose; she was deaf to all I could say, and entreated upon her knees, that I would not insist upon her marrying at all; but I was too old and too wise to mind the tears of a foolish girl, and I'll warrant she thanks me for it now.' 'You did right,' said my father, and was proceeding, but I had overheard enough, and leaving the house in a rage, I cursed my fate, and the cruelty of old Belknap, and taking the first hack I saw, I ordered the coachman to drive to Menotomy, determined to avoid their visit that afternoon.

"The day which completed my twenty-second year, gave birth to my little Harriot, and I hoped that circumstance would induce Clara to lay aside all thoughts of Le Fabre, who had returned from sea about five months previous to this; but I soon found myself in an error—her dejection evidently increased, and I was not much better myself: Our hearts did not beat in unison, our tastes were different—she sighed for Le Fabre, and I sighed while I reflected that I was the occasion, though innocently, of her sufferings. It was evident that she preferred his company to mine;—I had reason to believe she had a sincere friendship for me, but friendship alone, in a wife, is too cold. Her fondness for company and amusement daily increased, and I could not prevent myself from believing that her anxiety to be present at every public amusement and party of pleasure, arose from the satisfaction she enjoyed in the conversation of Le Fabre, whom we always were sure to meet. From this persuasion, I resolved to remove into the country, and try if the quiet and tranquility to be met with there, would not restore my peace of mind. I did not like those frequent meetings between my wife and Le Fabre, for whenever they met they conversed with each other more than politeness and attention to the rest of the company would decently admit of, and I flattered [myself] that if Clara were removed from him, she might in some measure forget his attractions; yet how could I blame her—it is natural to us to seek the society of those for whom we have the highest regard. I had not hinted my plan of a country life to her, nor any other person, but I was fully determined that that year should be the last I would pass in Boston.

"The beauty of this place, and the romantic scenes which surround it, had always given me great pleasure as I passed this way; I was going to H———, on business, and I determined to call on Mr. Anderson, at my return, and take a nearer view of the farm, and if possible, make a bargain with him. Little did I imagine that journey would produce such events as have since transpired:—For the first time in my life, I was in love—in love with a person whose name and residence I was a stranger to. I had then the happiness to be instrumental in preserving your life, my Emily; when you fainted in my arms, your features, though overspread with the pale hue of death, gave me a sensation till then unknown. After your recovery I had a distinct view of your person—to me it appeared perfect, but your conversation soon convinced me that your extreme beauty was your least attraction. Unconscious of danger, I gazed upon your lovely face, and listened to your gentle, persuasive accents: Every action, every look conspired to charm me and without consideration or reflection, I resigned my heart. Night rapidly came on—you retired early with your friend, and the moment I was left alone, it occurred to me that I could never hope for peace. I hurried to my chamber, and should have passed the night in fruitless exclamations, had not the landlord intruded company upon me. I never closed my eyes—your all enchanting form stood before me—Clara and a thousand unpleasing reflections precluded all possibility of repose. Morning at length came—I went down stairs, and found you with your friend in readiness to depart: I attended you to the carriage, and bade you adieu with a heavy, aching heart.—Cheerless and sad, I pursued my journey; to what purpose, I exclaimed, have I met my fellow mind, but to pass the remainder of my existence in fruitless wishes;—I may never see her more, but were I at liberty to make her mine, I would make the tour of the universe, but I would find her. I had now some conception of what Clara had suffered, and all my compassion was awakened. I wished we could part, or that we had never seen each other. Honor, religion and duty compelled me to give up every idea of you, but I could not erase you from my mind.

"At my return I told Clara that I had bargained for Mr. Anderson's farm, and that I should remove thither the next spring. A flood of tears was the consequence of this information; I knew she dreaded a separation from Le Fabre, but I likewise knew it to be impossible that her sufferings could exceed mine. In the winter I saw you at the theatre, adorned with all the charms of beauty and innocence; you were with people to whom I was a stranger, and I could find no pretext for going to speak with you; I saw you retire hastily, and mentally exclaimed, why am I tortured with the sight of her, when I can neither discover who she is, nor reap any benefit from the discovery if I should make it!

"After I had removed into the country, I began to be very intimate with your father; you were then absent on a visit, but judge of my feelings on the day I first saw you at your father's. The satisfaction at finding you was overbalanced by my anxiety at being so near you, as I could not then hope to forget you. That heart must be marble, that would not receive an impression from so many charms. You encreased in my esteem daily—I found satisfaction in your company, but when you were absent I was pensive and abstracted.—Clara complained of my dullness, and I forced a smile; she complained for want of amusement, and we sent for company—you were generally of the party. I had often strayed to our favorite retreat, and indulged the visions of fancy, while her magic hand portrayed a thousand blissful scenes. On the evening I met you there by accident, I enjoyed great satisfaction. The moon shone with more than usual splendor—the falling of the water, the gentle whispers of the breeze, with the charms and elegant conversation of my adored Emily, conspired to render me happy, till the cruel reflection that you was not, never could be mine, gave me all the pangs of despair.—You knew not my love, I resolved you never should know it, for then I could enjoy the innocent pleasures arising from your company and conversation, but had you known the interest you possessed in my heart, motives of common prudence would have taught you to shun my society. Sometimes I had the vanity to imagine that you had a more than common regard for me; I even fancied that tenderness beamed from your eyes when they met mine, but I found I was deceived, and that you favored the addresses of Devas.—Immediately after the death of Mrs. Belmont, my whole mind was fixed upon you; I considered Devas as the most fortunate person on earth; I wished to have it in my power to make him happy another way, though I knew he would never give you up. But it has pleased Heaven to make me happy: I am blest beyond my most sanguine expectations—I anticipate with you a life of felicity."

Ah! Mary, his narrative recalled to my mind scenes of sorrow: But have I not received ample compensation for all?—

Since writing the above, I have received your letter, and rejoice with you that Mr. Gray is recovering. I anticipate your visit with pleasure—your presence will add to my satisfaction. Adieu my dear friend—believe me sincerely yours,

EMILY BELMONT

POEMS PUBLISHED IN THE

MASSACHUSETTS SPY

The following, written by a *Young Lady*, we hand to the Public with pleasure, and as the writer bids fair to be a favorite of the *Muses*, we wish to be indulged with such *Blossoms of Parnassus*,[1] as she may occasionally gather, to ornament our *Poetic Column*.

To the EDITORS of the MASSACHUSETTS SPY

GENTLEMEN,

The inclosed Lines are the effusions of a heart, filled with love for America, and gratitude to those who were instrumental in rescuing her from the oppression of British slavery; and conducting her in safety through all the horrors of a Revolutionary War, placed her in possession of Peace, Liberty, Independence and Happiness, unequalled on the Globe. Grieved at the indignities which have been repeatedly offered to the aged, the respectable ADAMS, these Lines were hastily composed immediately after the Letter of the contemptible Lyon[2] was published. Should you think them worthy to be inserted in your Paper, though I dare not think you will, a constant Reader will be gratified. But should this simple production be thrown aside, my youth and inexperience must be my excuse for venturing to offer it to the Public.

FIDELIA

LINES, Addressed to JOHN ADAMS, ESQ. late PRESIDENT of the UNITED STATES

Hail, ADAMS! hail, Columbia's³ fav'rite Sage!
Pride of thy country, glory of thy age;
No longer now by public cares oppress'd,
Long may'st thou live, by sweet retirement blest.
Long may thy virtues bless thy native plains,   5
Where heaven born Peace and Independence reigns.
To thee, thy grateful country still shall bring
An incense sweeter than the flow'rs of spring.
Yes, it shall bring that praise so justly due,
And with revolving years that praise renew,   10
Though base detractors every art employ,
The well earn'd meed by falsehood to destroy.
LYON and his confed'rates strive in vain
To bring reproach upon thy honor'd name,
Nor can their pois'nous breath attaint thy spotless fame. ⎫   15
Fame has for thee a deathless wreath prepar'd,   ⎬
Thy brilliant deeds shall meet their just reward;   ⎭
Thy name by all the great and good rever'd,
Shall by Columbia's Daughters be ador'd,
With that of thy copatriot WASHINGTON,   20
By whom such great, such glorious deeds were done.
Innumerable toils ye both endur'd,
Till Peace and Independence were secur'd.
And can Columbia e'er ungrateful prove?
Can she her friend, her saviors cease to love?   25
Forbid it Heaven! whene'er to this she's led,
May tenfold vengeance burst upon her head.
The pangs that rent her breast, what tongue can tell,
When her lov'd Hero bade the world farewell!⁴

And when at length thy glorious spirit flies,   30
To meet our WASHINGTON in yonder skies,
Ah: then again shall every patriot mourn,
And female tears bedew thy sacred urn.

FIDELIA

Taken from the *Massachusetts Spy*, April 15, 1801

BEAUTY

BEAUTY,[5] thou tyrant, whose despotic sway,
Enslaves thy thousands in one fatal day,
Listen for once to the pure voice of truth,
Thy radiant charms must all decay with youth;
And wrinkled age, triumphant in thy face,   5
Disperse thy bloom and banish ev'ry grace.
Those eyes which now bright Hesper's[6] beams outvie,
Of loveliest blue, transparent as the sky;
Those rosy cheeks, where health's fresh bloom appears,
Those lips, which all the ruby's crimson wears,   10
That snowy neck, now so divinely fair,
Shaded with ringlets of thy auburn hair,
All, all must yield to time's destroying hand,
And not one charm his dreadful rage withstand.
Then thy dim eyes shall trace thy form in vain,   15
For those bright graces which no more remain.
Ye fair, be wise, while yet tis in your power,
Improve each fleeting day, each passing hour;
Enrich your youthful minds with virtuous lore,
That will remain till time shall be no more.   20

FIDELIA

Taken from the *Massachusetts Spy*, May 6, 1801

FIDELIA begs leave to assure the Editors of the MASSACHU-
SETTS SPY, that she has not sufficient vanity to induce her to
imagine that any of her imperfect productions are capable of af-
fording an ornament to the poetic column, nor does she wish
them to exclude pieces of superior merit.

Leicester, May 9, 1801

Address to PIETY

Hail, PIETY! thou soft'ner of despair,
Thy presence mitigates corroding care;
When poignant anguish rends the troubled breast,
Thy heavenly influence sooths[7] our griefs to rest;
Without thee, what's all nature but a shade,   5
A worthless nothing, and for nothing made.
Without thee, every charm in nature flies,
No smiling prospect cheers our wand'ring eyes,
The rolling thunder, and the light'nings glare,
We shun amaz'd and stand absorb'd in fear.   10
When night with sable gloom involves the earth,
Imagination calls some spectre forth,
And tort'ring fancy wakens all her pow'rs,
To add fresh horror to the lonely hours,
To guilty minds this dread is only known,   15
These are the pangs felt by the bad alone;
For blest with thee, new charms adorn each scene,
Each verdant mead displays a brighter green,
Each blushing flower a sweeter odor yields,
And sheds fresh fragrance o'er the painted fields,   20
And when sublimely grand the thunders roll,
And forked light'nings flash from pole to pole,
With gratitude we reverence the power,
At whose command descends the enliv'ning show'r.

When solemn midnight in her dusky robe,   25
Extends her shadowy pinions o'er the globe,
No horrid visions agitate the breast,
But gentle slumber lulls our cares to rest.

FIDELIA

Taken from the *Massachusetts Spy*, May 13, 1801

Character of a Young Lady

SOPHIA is form'd with ev'ry grace,
A thousand charms adorn her face;
Her tresses brown in ringlets flow,
And shade her forehead white as snow;
Her speaking eyes are radiant blue,　　　　　　　　　5
Her dimpled cheeks of rosy hue,
Her smiling lips of crimson dye,
Her neck might with fair HELEN'S[8] vie,
Her shape is harmony and ease,
Her graceful manners always please,　　　　　　　　10
Her conversation, free from art,
Proclaims the goodness of her heart;
Such is her person—but her mind,
The seat of sentiments refin'd,
Is still more lovely: Virtue there,　　　　　　　　　15
At once protects the blooming fair,
Adds to the lustre of her eyes,
And ev'ry action dignifies:
With pitying tears her eyes o'erflow
Whene'er she hears the tale of woe;　　　　　　　　20
Her bosom bleeds at scenes of grief,
With haste she flies to give relief;
In ev'ry sorrow bears a part,
And soothes with care the wounded heart:
Though wrinkled age may steal her bloom,　　　　25
And each external grace consume,
Her mental charms will be the same,
And still her worth affection claim.

                                                        FIDELIA

Taken from the *Massachusetts Spy*, July 1, 1801

To FIDELIA [1]

Child of the muse, sweet minstrel, say,
Where mid fair *Leicester's* wild woods stray
Thy feet—or where, while blooms the spring,
Thy numbers through her green vales ring!
In fancy, lo, I see thee rove   5
The lovers consecrated grove;
And hear thee most melodiously
Chant thy sweet-hymn "to PIETY."

Child of the muse, Oh, where I say,
Deign'st thou to pass the hours of May?   10
Mid forests dim and meadows green,
I know thy angel form is seen,
With pensive steps and musing eye,
Tracing the works of DEITY!

And, while the scenes thy breast inspire,   15
Praise trembles on thy kindling lyre!
O never cease thy charming strain—
But strike thy well strung harp again.

THEODORUS

Taken from the *Massachusetts Spy*, June 10, 1801

To THEODORUS

Son of Apollo,[9] dost thou praise
FIDELIA'S simple, artless lays?
Could I like THEODORUS strike the lyre,
Or catch one spark of his poetic fire,
    Then should my numbers graceful flow,   5
    And bid the heart with rapture glow.

Yes, they should charm the list'ning ear,
Suppress each sigh and check each tear;
And while Diana's[10] beams illum'd the night,   10
And stars unnumber'd shed their gentler light,
    My song should echo through the vale,
    And float upon the ambient gale.

Fortune on me has never smil'd,
But sweet CONTENT each care beguil'd—
Oft at the evening hour, alone, unseen,   15
With pensive steps I tread the dewy green,
    And wander while the beam of morn
    Drinks the rich dewdrop from the thorn.

And oft I wander where the breeze
Soft whispers through the waving trees,   20
'Mong craggy rocks that overhang the stream,
And while I view the wild romantic scene,
    Lo! sprightly *Fancy*, ever gay,
    Chases each anxious care away.

Thus tranquil have my moments pass'd,   25
But ah! perhaps too sweet to last:—
May happiness, sweet POET, e'er be thine,
Though all the pangs of adverse fate be mine;
May constant pleasure dress each scene,
And sorrow never intervene.   30

FIDELIA

Leicester, June 18, 1801

Taken from the *Massachusetts Spy*, July 1, 1801

Resignation

Though earth were to its centre shook,
And lofty oaks to splinters broke,
      Torn from the mountain's side;
Though thunders roll'd from east to west,
And clouds in flaming fire were drest,   5
      In GOD I'd still confide.

The shock would in a moment cease,
The raging winds would be at peace,
      And silence reign abroad;
The raging clouds would cease to clash,   10
And vivid light'ning cease to flash,
      At his commanding word.

                     FIDELIA

Taken from the *Massachusetts Spy*, July 8, 1801

To the Memory of Miss H. who departed this life on the 6th of July, after a short illness

MARY to me a fragrant vi'let gave,
    Fresh from the turf she pluck'd the blooming flower;
Alas! not all my care nor art could save,
    It faded, languish'd, wither'd ere an hour.

In vain I lav'd it in the pearly dew,   5
    In vain I strove its su[n]ken leaves to raise,
Fast from the stem the vital moisture flew,
    I mark'd the sad decay with pitying gaze.

Sighing, I cried, is this thy cruel lot?
    Is this the end of all thy sweets and bloom?   10
And must thou thus neglected and forgot,
    Receive, in beauty's pride, an early doom?

See now the maid with ev'ry beauty form'd,
    See the mild radiance of her beaming eye,
Her dimpled cheeks with blooming health adorn'd,   15
    Her lips the rose bud's freshness far outvie:

But ah! should sorrow or disease invade,
    Thus would the lustre of her eyes decay,
Those cheeks so blooming now, would quickly fade,
    And ev'ry charm and grace be torn away.   20

RELIEF[11] was fair as when the rosy morn
    First opens to the view her cheering beam;
But yet her mind surpass'd her lovely form,
    Her worth and graceful manners gain'd esteem.

Sudden she droop'd as when the blushing flower,   25
    Scorch'd by the ardent sun's meridian ray,

Sinks to the earth and no enliv'ning shower
    Again restores it to the light of day.

In vain the parent's fondest hopes arose,
    Sudden the winged arrow sped its flight,   30
With bursting hearts they see her eyelids close,
    No more her charms inspire them with delight.

With anxious eyes they watch'd her parting breath,
    With anguish strove their darling child to save,
They saw her struggling in the clasp of death,   35
    Those hopes were lost which heaven so lately gave.

Too good the mis'ries of the world to share,
    The hand of mercy snatch'd her from your sight,
Releas'd from this abode of grief and care,
    Her gentle spirit sought the realms of light.   40

From the rich source whence endless blessings flow,
    She now celestial happiness enjoys,
And blest beyond what mortals e'er can know,
    Drinks the rich cup of bliss which never cloys.

Let this consoling thought your grief suspend,   45
    Let resignation check the flowing tear,
May blest religion all her comforts lend,
    And len'ent mercy heal the wound severe.

FIDELIA
Leicester, July 22, 1801

Taken from the *Massachusetts Spy*, August 19, 1801

To FIDELIA [2]

Where hangs that harp, whose mellow strains,
Late flow'd melodious o'er the plains,
Bourne on wings of softest gales,
That sport amid the flow'ry vales?
By cold misfortune's damps unstrung,   5
On the lone willow is it hung?
What cause so long withholds the lay
That so delights—sweet chantress, say?

O thou bright power, forever kind
To the wild sallies of the mind;   10
Guardian of genius' sacred fire,
Protector of the silver lyre,
Where'er thou dwell'st, whoe'er thou art,
Shield the fair minstrel from the dart
Of adverse fate, and richly bless   15
Her passing hours with happiness.
And while the muse each gift bestows,
And verse in golden current flows;
While fancy's treasures, bright and fair,
Inventions rich, and beauties rare,   20
Bid the world deck her brow with wreathes,
Such as fame for genius weaves;
May fortune bring her presents too
From the deep caverns of Peru,[12]
And be the maxim heard no more,   25
That a *rich* muse is always *poor*.

Then shall FIDELIA, blithe and gay,
As is the lark, that sings in May,
Rove, while the ruby lips of morn
Sip "the rich dewdrop from the thorn,"[13]   30

The hallow'd grove, or green sward dale,
And with soft music freight the gale.
While ev'ry swain with ravish'd ear
Shall, listning, drop his scythe to hear,
And virgins, bright in youthful pride,   35
That range the meadow's blooming side—
To cull the flowers, so gaily dress'd,
That sweetly wave on Flora's[14] breast,
Enraptur'd with the charming song,
That floats the echoing vales along,   40
To weave rich garlands shall combine
FIDELIA'S temples to entwine,
And, nurturing each with fondest care,
Shall bid them bloom immortal there.
          The muse such tributes e'er shall bring   45
To maidens, who so sweetly sing.

                                        THEODORUS
                                        August 12

Taken from the *Massachusetts Spy*, September 2, 1801

To THEODORUS

While thy soft numbers "freight the gale,"[15]
In vain shall grief this heart assail;
Thou bidst it still enraptured glow,
Unmindful of each cause for woe.
With gratitude to thee I bend,   5
And hail thee by the name of FRIEND.
Should it please heav'n my hours to bless,
May I deserve the happiness.
I never sigh'd for fame nor wealth,
I only ask *Content* and *Health*;   10
Their smiles a purer joy afford,
Than both the Indies' shining hoard.
To fame my wishes ne'er aspir'd,
I ever wish'd to live retir'd,
With heav'n born peace and friendship blest,   15
Where no ambitious cares molest.
        Where dost thou ramble, while the morn
Sprinkles with pearl the dewy lawn?
Say to what grove thou tend'st thy way,
To shun the sultry glare of day?   20
Where dost thou strike the silver lyre,
While thy high thoughts to heav'n aspire?[16]
While pensive ev'ning's peaceful shade,
In pleasing gloom involves the glade;
While all is silent, all is still,   25
Save the soft murmur of the rill,
Dost thou then turn thy beamy eyes,
To the bright glories of the skies,
There in his works the Author[17] view,
And chant thy hymns of praise anew?   30
Wher'er thou dwell'st be peace thy guest,

Nor cruel sorrow reach thy breast.
Thou, THEODORUS, hast a mind,
Noble, enlighten'd and refin'd;
Religion thou hast dar'd to own,   35
Bright form, alas, too much unknown!
With Fancy's eye I see thee trace
Each charm of smiling Nature's face;
And while her beauties strike thy eyes,
I see thee pause to moralize.   40
Then thy rich numbers soft and clear
Improve the heart and charm the ear.
Such gifts were ne'er bestow'd on me;
Vain is the wish to equal thee.
Oh! still thy dulcet strains prolong,   45
Nor cease to charm th' applauding throng.

FIDELIA
Leicester, September, 1801

Taken from the *Massachusetts Spy*, October 14, 1801

Evening Reflections

How sweet the gentle power of Eve!
While moon beams on the waters play;
Let me each scene of folly leave,
And near yon waving willows stray.

There seated by the murm'ring stream,   5
Enjoy the beauties of the night,
Enraptur'd view the peaceful scene,
Whose charms th' attentive mind delight.

Half hid by silver'd fleecy clouds,
The moon emits a fainter ray;   10
But fast as they her lustre shroud,
By gentlest gales are borne away.

Hither let Pleasure's vot'ries come,
View Nature in her simple dress,
And own the gilt illumin'd dome   15
Could never half those charms possess.

Here sweet Simplicity resides,
"Makes ev'ry artless scene her own,"[18]
Here blest with Peace the moments glide,
And mad Ambition is unknown.   20

Oh! ye who pass the hours of night,
In revelry and mad excess,
Ye ne'er have tasted true delight,
Ye search in vain for Happiness.

For know, the fair celestial maid,   25
Disdains to mingle with your train;
But in her heavenly charms array'd,
She seeks the calm sequester'd plain.

Then cease to kneel at Bacchus'[19] shrine,
The lustre of the stars surpass   30
The brilliance of the richest wine,
That sparkles in the flowing glass.

Oh! cease to spend the prime of life,
In gambling, drinking, strife and noise;
Think on the solitary wife,   35
Whose peace your wild excess destroys.

She's left perhaps with ev'ry pang
Of want and misery to mourn;
Around her hungry children hang,
And weeping wish their sire's return.   40

Thus pass the painful hours of night,
Her aching bosom fraught with grief;
At length perhaps at morning light,
You come, but not to her relief.

Stripp'd by a mercenary horde   45
Of cheating gamblers, you return!
Once smiling plenty crown'd your board,
But now your famish'd infants mourn.

Will not your hearts at this relent?
Can you unmov'd behold such woe?   50
A weeping wife, a fortune spent,
And children whom your crimes undo.

'Tis past, you cannot now retract,
A gloomy dungeon ends your course;
Those pangs your partner's bosom rack'd,   55
Return on you with all their force.

No more for you the rising morn
Is usher'd in with heartfelt joys;

Your hearts with late remorse are torn,
Reflection sad your peace destroys.   60

Such is of vice the dreadful end;
Then haste to leave the guilty course;
An ear to whisp'ring Conscience lend,
And shun the tortures of Remorse.

FIDELIA
Leicester, September 16

Taken from the *Massachusetts Spy*, October 28, 1801

[While fair FIDELIA, favorite of the *Nine*]

While fair FIDELIA, favorite of the *Nine*,[20]
      Charms with her heaven taught song, each feeling heart;
While THEODORUS with his lays divine,
      Doth bright APOLLO'S[21] influence impart;

While ANNA's[22] harp attun'd to Fancy's praise,   5
      Bids through the glowing veins each accent thrill;
While even Envy crowns her with the bays,
      And owns how deep she's quaff'd th' *Aonian*[23] till;

While DELLA CRUSCA, favoring Fancy's foe,
      Disclaims that power which animates his lines,   10
Fraught with imagination's warmest glow,
      Disowns the fire which in his numbers shines;

Say, can a youth one feeble plaudit gain,
      On whom the *Muses* never deign'd to smile,
Who courts their influence but to fly from pain,   15
      And tear imbitter'd moments to beguile.

Yet "Fortune" smil'd propitious "on his birth,"
      Gay Pleasure's sunshine beam'd upon his mind;
Soon Sorrow's clouds bedim'd[24] the "Day" of mirth,
      For Fate was cruel—LAURA was unkind!!!   20

A prey to fell despair and poignant pain—
      My throbbing heart at LAURA'S name takes fire!
Victim of hapless *Love*, I cease my strain—
      And "on the willow hang"[25] my trembling lyre.

                        EUGENE
                        October 27

Taken from the *Massachusetts Spy*, November 11, 1801

To EUGENE

Yes, cease, EUGENE, thy plaintive "strain,"
     To sprightly sounds awake thy lyre;
Let *Reason* banish lovesick pain,
     And *Fancy* gayer thoughts inspire.

Leave the "unkind," the haughty maid,   5
     Tear from thy heart each fond idea,
No longer let the midnight shade,
     Witness thy "tears"—thy constancy.

If on thy birth gay "fortune smil'd,"
     And sportive "pleasure" cheer'd the day,   10
No more remain affliction's child,
     But "chase desponding care away."

"Court" the mild "influence" of the Muse,
     And banish LAURA from thy breast;
Then shall celestial peace diffuse   15
     Her calmness o'er thy "throbbing" breast.

No longer strive her smiles to gain—
     Her cold indiff'rence to remove;
But let resentment and disdain
     Supply the place of slighted love.   20

And may some blooming maid be thine,
     Adorn'd with each engaging charm,
A faultless form, a soul divine,
     A heart with love and virtue warm.

And may the lightwing'd rosy hours
In swift succession pass away;
Thy path be strewn with sweetest flowers,
Nor "sorrow's clouds" bedim thy "day."

FIDELIA
November 13, 1801

Taken from the *Massachusetts Spy*, December 9, 1801

To FIDELIA [3]

And can this verse, so simply dress'd,
Dispel one care that haunts thy breast?
Say, can these numbers e'er impart
One real joy to cheer thy heart?
Then shall the muse with nobler fire,   5
And bolder fingers sweep the lyre,
To loftier strains shall wake the string,
Till in each vale the wild notes ring.

Rare is the muse amid the throng,
Who sing[s] our native vales among,   10
Who knows in numbers smooth and chaste,
With true simplicity and taste,
To tune to genuine song the lyre,
And feel the ancient poet's fire.
Rare is the bard, whose nervous lays   15
Resound religion's sacred praise;
Too rare, whose sweetly warbling muse
The *real good of man* pursues,
The charms of virtue recommends,
And decks with glory virtue's friends;   20
Robes truth in garb, so fair, so new,
So simple and enchanting too,
That all its angel form caress,
And emulate its artless dress.

But sure th' inventive muse, with ease,   25
Might mend mankind as well as please;
And while she rov'd the field, or waste,
For gems of thought, or flowers of taste,
The moral theme might decorate,
And mould the manners of the state.   30

Shall beauty's fading charms be sung,
The theme of every tuneful tongue,
While virtue's charms, divinely bright,
As is the radiant source of light,
Awake no string, no breast inspire,   35
Enkindle no poetic fire?
Shall love's soft tie, that frailly binds,
In shortliv'd transports, kindred minds,
Be hymn'd in many a rapt'rous strain,
While pure religion's holy chain,   40
Which, kindly linking earth and sky,
Connects our race with DEITY,
Awakes no mortal harp to join
The glowing Seraph's song divine?
No:—Thou, FIDELIA, yet shall sing   45
Their praise; on more than mortal string
Shall their transcendent joys resound,
And man shall venerate the sound.

      Thy lays are of the noblest kind,
As beauty, simple, yet refin'd.   50
To me no bright ey'd muses bring
Rich draught from the Pierian spring,[26]
No flowers Parnassian[27] cull for me,
Their care is all bestow'd on thee.

      Then still, sweet Daughter of the Muse,   55
The heavenly gift with wisdom use;
And let thy loud ton'd harp be strung
To renovate the moral song.

THEODORUS
November 4, 1801

Taken from the *Massachusetts Spy*, December 16, 1801

To THEODORUS

Ah, surely to thee are the Muses attentive,
      On thee all their care and affection bestow,
Or why is thy genius so fertile—inventive,
      Or why do thy numbers so elegant flow?

Inspir'd by Religion, and blest by the Muse,   5
      Thy strains are melodious, elegant, free,
And still o'er this breast a soft calmness diffuse,
      While my wishes aspire to be equal with thee.

While *Luna* dispenses her silvery rays,
      And the mild beaming stars their sweet radiance lend, 10
At the bright azure concave inraptur'd I gaze,
      Where elegance, order and harmony blend,[28]

Their graces attractive. Meanwhile the clear stream,
      With borrow'd rays sparkling, melodiously flows,
And still as it passes a tremulous gleam,   15
      On the willow deck'd margin incessant bestows.

From those scenes to their Author[29] my fancy aspires,
      Who commanded those orbs in such order to move,
And while I reflect earthly glory retires,
      And my thoughts to the regions of happiness rove. 20

The rain falls in torrents, and loud the wind rages,
      The songsters, late tuneful, have flown from the spray,
No more their soft music attention engages,
      But Spring shall restore them all joyful and gay.

Again shall the lily, the vi'let and rose,   25
      Be restor'd, and exhale their delicious perfume,
Again shall creation its beauties disclose,
      And each tree, though now leafless, be smiling in bloom.

Then why should we mortals presume to repine
      At evil—and still of misfortunes complain?   30
Let us rather rejoice in a being divine,
      Who will end all our sorrows—relieve ev'ry pain.

Though the clouds of adversity hover around,
      And envy and malice conspire to depress,
Let our spirits revive at the heart cheering sound,   35
      "When the innocent suffer, their wrongs I redress."[30]

Let our hearts be unbiass'd by earthly affairs,
      Let us learn the world's malice and scorn to dispise,
Then celestial Content shall dispel all our cares,
      And fair Hope, ever smiling, shall point to the skies.   40

FIDELIA
January 10, 1802

Taken from the *Massachusetts Spy*, March 3, 1802

To CONTENT

Come, sweet CONTENT, celestial maid,
In all thy heavenly charms array'd,
     Reside within my breast:
To thee FIDELIA tunes her lyre,
Thy charms her infant muse inspire,   5
     Oh! deign to make her blest.

'Tis thine, sweet power, to soften care,
To chase away the fiend despair,
     And bid the fleeting hours
More sweetly, swiftly pass away,   10
And as their changing joys decay,
     Protract their pleasing powers.

Creation's beauties vainly glow,
In vain shall heaven their charms bestow,
     Without thy cheering aid;   15
In vain the blooming Spring delights,
Or Autumn's lib'ral hand invites—
     All, all their beauties fade.

'Tis thine to check the anxious sigh,
To wipe the tear from sorrow's eye,   20
     And soothe the aching heart;
O! then with me forever dwell,
Grace with thy charms my humble cell,
     And happiness impart.

                    FIDELIA

Taken from the *Massachusetts Spy*, March 24, 1802

Lines, Occasioned by the Death of Miss E****

Could spotless honor and unsullied truth,
Protract the hours of health, or bloom of youth,
Could virtue, innocence, or beauty save,
From the cold mansions of the silent grave,
ELIZA,[31] blooming still, had flourish'd here,   5
And weeping friends escap'd a pang severe.

But ah! in vain shall FRIENDSHIP mourn,
        Or shed the tears of sorrow o'er her grave,
In vain the heart with keenest grief is torn,
        Can this restore the form it could not save?   10

The soul releas'd from earth, with rapture flies
To the bright seats of bliss in yonder skies;
Seraphic hosts with purest joy convey
The sainted spirit to the realms of day,
To dwell in bliss eternal near the throne,   15
Where vice and misery are alike unknown.

Then check the tender flowing tear,
        With Spring's first vi'lets dress her tomb,
And still with each revolving year,
        The emblematic flowers shall bloom.   20

She bloom'd in innocence like these,
        Their silken leaves like her decay,
Each flower the blast of death receives,
        Was she less fair, less frail than they?

Each Spring, their beauties they resume,   25
        They shed their fragrance o'er the lawn,
ELIZA, still more fair shall bloom,
        When resurrection's glorious morn—

.

Shall reunite the long divided friends,
    Through vast eternity to part no more;   30
That morn auspicious human misery ends,
    And all the pangs and cares of life are o'er.

FIDELIA
Leicester, 1802

Taken from the *Massachusetts Spy*, May 19, 1802

Summer

All nature smiles in vernal beauty bright,
Each scene is form'd for rapture and delight;
Here, in this sweet, sequester'd, calm retreat,
Remote from all that's vain, or proudly great;
Here let me pass, serenely pass my days,   5
With sweet content, and philosophic ease;
Here let me rove beside the murm'ring rill,
Or climb the bowery summit of the hill;
While Luna mild, dispenses silvery light,
And sparkling stars add beauty to the night: 10
Tall maples towering rise, in lofty pride,
And bending elms adorn the meadow's side.
Here the lank willows on the margin wave,
And in the stream their glossy foliage lave.
Groves, lawns, and flowery meads delight the eye,   15
And every scene charms with variety.
To hail the morn a thousand warblers rise,
When the first rays of light illume the skies.
Your joyful notes, sweet birds, my breast inspires,
My bosom glows, and palefac'd care retires.   20
Ah! still delight with your enchanting song,
And still your sweetly charming notes prolong;
Each smiling morn attune your gentle lays,
To your all bountiful Creator's praise.
Your orisons, the infidel reprove,   25
Who scoffs, regardless of a Savior's love.
Shall every bird that wings its flight in air,
A song of rapture, and of praise prepare,
While man, unmindful of the blessings given,
Scarce casts a look of gratitude to heaven?   30
Shall man alone, with "thankless pride repine,

Amid the stores"[32] which all around him shine?
No: Sure the bounteous gift his heart must warm
With grateful joy, while fields of waving corn,
Promise a golden harvest to reward   35
His toils, and crown his hospitable board.
He must, with joy, adore the bounteous power
Who sends the sunshine, and refreshing shower;
Protects his labors from the tempest's ire,
The swelling torrent, and the whirlwind dire.   40
Parent of nature, from whose bounteous hand,
Flows every blessing which our wants demand,
Teach us to merit more thy constant love,
Teach us those blessings rightly to improve;
And by increasing virtue to secure   45
That bliss which virtue only can ensure.

FIDELIA
July, 1802

Taken from the *Massachusetts Spy*, August 4, 1802

[Where the high spreading branches exclude Phœbus' beams]

Where the high spreading branches exclude Phœbus'[33] beams,
With smiling content I will carelessly stray;
Or sit on the margin of yon winding stream,
Enjoying the charms of the sweet summer day.

I never will sigh for the bubbles[34] of earth,   5
From them I can never true happiness find,
I regard not the honors of fortune and birth,
They're nothing, compar'd with a calm easy mind.

Let Envy and Malice unitedly rail,
They shall find I can look with contempt on such foes,   10
When weary they'll cease from the slanderous tale,
Their arts are too mean to disturb my repose.

Here blest I will ramble in this rural vale,
No follies henceforward my mind shall perplex,
My thoughts shall be free as the swift passing gale,   15
Nor pride, nor ambition be suffer'd to vex.

FIDELIA
Leicester, August 28, 1802

Taken from the *Massachusetts Spy*, September 8, 1802

Sonnet to FIDELIA

As when some lonely bird of liquid throat,
      That lives the deep and silent woods among,
Who, now and then, tunes her harmonious note,
      And cheers the hour with a melodious song:

So thou, enchanting Daughter of the Nine,[35]   5
      In this degenerate day of Poesy,
Pour'st o'er Columbia's[36] clime thy lays divine,
      And charm'st the soul to rapt'rous ecstasy.

Thy pleas'd admirers still thy verse shall read,
      Whilst thy soft numbers all their glow retain,   10
Till thy *young fame* shall o'er the world be spread,
      And thou shalt rival e'en PHILENIA'S[37] matchless strain.

O touch again thy gently sounding lyre—
Be mine the task to read, and to admire.

FREDERIC
Worcester, September 1802

Taken from the *Massachusetts Spy*, September 22, 1802

To FREDERIC

Ah no! PHILENIA'S name unrivall'd stands
    Amid the vot'ries of the tuneful nine,
The just applause her heavenly strain demands,
    Can ne'er be merited by lays like mine.

For her, the wilds, beyond the "parent flood,"   5
    Disclose a thousand varying scenes to view,
Where heroes crimson'd o'er the plain with blood
    Of slaughter'd chiefs, victims to vengeance due.

She sings the "virtues" of the savage mind,
    Where grateful friendship glows with "nature's" charms, 10
When great Ouabi,[38] matchless chief, resign'd
    His lov'd Azakia to Celario's arms.

To her, Apollo[39] gave the "golden lyre,"
    On her the muses ev'ry gift bestow'd;
Her bosom, frought[40] with genius' heavenly fire,   15
    With all the warmth of inspiration glow'd.

To dissipate the "sombre cloud" of grief
    That oft bedims the sunshine of my mind,
I court the muse, she brings that sweet relief
    Which in the giddy crowd I seldom find.   20

Thy gen'rous praise my gratitude demands,
    Thy gentle numbers cannot fail to charm;
Then touch the "sounding lyre"[41] with skillful hands,
    And let thy lays each feeling bosom warm.

FIDELIA
Leicester, September 1802

Taken from the *Massachusetts Spy*, October 20, 1802

UNPUBLISHED MANUSCRIPTS

Ode for the New year. Jan. 1st, 1784.

Hail sacred truth! first power divine,
Sure guide thro' time's dark maze,
I kneel at thy immortal shrine,
And Candour gaurd[1] these lays.

Ye nations round attend the strains,   5
The raptur'd muse triumphant sings
America's imperial reign,
Enthron'd above the frowns, above the smiles of kings.

For why have Albion's[2] martial bands,
Urg'd slaughter on with crimson'd hands;   10
Or bid their thunder's awful roar,
Attempt to shake Columbia's[3] shore;
How weak their arms, how vain their schemes,
Like playful fancy's idle dreams;
Whilst this was wrote in heaven's bright page,   15
Repel their hosts, oppose their rage,
Ye sons arouse, and watch your father's clay,
Nor basely give the hallow'd dust away.
Bold as the chieftain laurell crown'd,
See the rude peasant pant for fame,   20
He hurls his country's vengeance round,
And deals Bellona's[4] hottest flame,
Such were the troops by Warren[5] led,
When glory hov'ring o'er his head,
The hero rapt, in freedom's radiant car,   25
Where joining gods he pour'd vindictive war.
Swell ivery[6] note, burst peals of praise,
Great Washington demands the lays,
The father, friend, of human kind,
By the Almighty sire design'd;   30

To lend Columbia filial aid
Amidst embattled havock's field,
To lead her safe through slavery's shade,
The warriour, patriot, savior, shield.
Nor can the bard forget the brave,   35
Reclin'd on honor's blooming grave,
Who still exist in every breast,
By freedom's feelings e're[7] possest.

For eight long years of dubious strife,
The free born soul, contemning life,   40
Has heard the trumpets hoarse alarms,
Or wak'd to combat's din of arms;
But now fell war's terrific form,
Is chang'd for concord's softer air,
The world is friendship's fav'rite care;   45
No longer foes on hostile ground,
Bid desolation, burn around,
Or wing the battle's deathful storm.
See white rob'd peace, from heav'n descend,
In love's celestial garb array'd;   50
The powers of war unite as friends,
And sheathe the faulchion's reeking blade.
Arts, commerce, wealth, adorn her train,
Content & plenty lead each hour,
Learning asserts her ancient reign,   55
And Harvard hails the gracious power
Whilst science deck'd in robes of light
Bursts from the veil of honor's night
Calls Franklin forth, to him resigns the throne
And yeilds[8] the sceptre once ador'd her own.   60

Of empire lasting age to age,
So Freedom's godlike troops repair,

From sanguin'd plains, to private shades,
A Civic crown enwreaths their heads,
Nor crest plum'd victory blazes there.   65
Whilst other kingdoms pass away,
By fatal luxury's baneful sway;
Or sink in foul corruption's tide,
Oer whelm'd[9] by grandeur's haughty pride,
Columbia's congress form'd in virtue's cause,   70
Gaurd[10] equal rights, by Majesty of laws.

Hear then the truths, their high decree
Imparts to ev'ry state,
The voice of heaven, of liberty,
To form the good & great.   75
Rear'd at Jehovah's dread command,
The scourge of Britain's guilty land,
Avoid the crimes her annals show,
Be virtue, freedom's fame below.
Absorb the views of partial good   80
In energetic, social[11] love,
No hostile step shall dare intrude,
Or pluck the olive from the dove.

This be your chiefest, heartfelt joy,
To comfort, succour human kind,   85
Your nerves, your strength, for this employ,
And loose the wretch whom fetters bind.

So shall you rise to empire's noblest height,
Whilst other nations rush with sudden flight
To ruin'd grandeur's silent gloom;   90
Rock rooted deep, the queen of worlds remain
Till God's last fiat breaks the eternal chains,
And all creation sleeps in nature's tomb.

[Letter to Adeline Hartwell]

My Dear Adeline,[12]

I cannot express the Satisfaction your letter gives me; I am happy in hearing that you are so agreeably situated. May you long enjoy the happiness you anticipate. I hoped to have seen you here this fall, but as it is for your interest to remain at S——, I submit to the disappointment without repining. We never were at so great a distance from each other, before, but

> "Distance only, cannot change the heart."[13]

I am often borne on Fancy's sportive wing to the residence of my Adeline; I see her lovely form, I hear her well known voice, and seem to converse with her, till some interruption dissolves the pleasing vision. It is a great consolation to me that we can write to each other, we can do this, though

> "Alps rise between us, and whole oceans roll."[14]

I am unable to give you any information respecting the state of health Mrs Anderson is in at present; when I heard last from her, she had every symptom of a rapid decline,[15] I can scarce believe that she is still alive. She has been very unfortunate, and has drank deep at the bitter cup[16] of sorrow, but all her misfortunes have not been able to change the sweetness of her disposition. So far from being depressed by sorrow, she rises above it, and with the eye of faith looks forward to those blissful regions of eternal felicity where grief will never enter. I never knew a more amiable woman, the slight acquaintance you had with her, prevented you from knowing her real worth. She has always been a very religious[17] person, strictly virtuous, and for sweetness of temper perhaps un-equalled. She was always cheerful, and sometimes gay. She sung finely, and danced with ease—These engaging qualities, and her uncommon beauty, procured her almost as many admirers as be-holders. But to all her lovers, she was so unfortunate as to pre-fer the worthless Anderson.—During their courtship he was[18] the most artful of men, he was constantly upon his gaurd,[19] & never suffered an improper expression to escape his lips; his behaviour was more serious and reserved than is common for a young man. He was handsome in his person, engaging in his address,[20] sensi-ble and polite; he had a liberal education, and was capable of con-versing, with ease and elegance, on every subject; but with all those flattering appearances he was, at heart, A Libertine. He concealed his real character so artfully from her, and from every one, from whom she could receive[21] any information, that she beheld him as the only man it was possible for her to love, and as the only man with whom she could be happy. She married him with the most sanguine expectations of happiness—But judge, My dear Adeline, what her sufferings must have been, when he threw of[22] the mask, and discovered the most perfect villain, that, perhaps ever existed. In less than Six weeks after their marriage he came home from a tavern, (where he had spent the night) about four o'clock in the morning, in liquor, his cloaths[23] half torn off; and coming into the room, with the most horrid oaths and imprecations, accused his innocent lady of committing crimes of which she had no idea; in the frenzy of his passion he turned her into the street, and bade her never let him see, nor hear from her more. A neighbour ran to her assistance and carried her to his house; she was so frightened and astonished at the terrible scene which had just passed, that she was delirious for several days, a violent fever ensued, & her life was de-spaired of. When Anderson recovered from his frantic fit, he was informed of what he had done, he expressed great sorrow, and vowed by his future behaviour to make repartion[24] for his past offences. When her delirium had subsided, he went to her, and on his knees entreated her to forgive him, and made such promises of amendment as might have deceived suspicion itself—She forgave him, and returned to his house; a week had not elapsed before he was again in liquor, but he offered no violence to her; She was almost distracted with grief, She gently[25] expostulated with him— her tender distress seemed to move him to penitence, and while he was with her he endeavoured by every attention to calm her mind. He seemed for a fortnight to be reforming, but happening to meet with an old bottle companion, he spent night after night at the tavern, treated his wife with the utmost cruelty every day, and again turned her out of the house—She bore all this with angelic patience, She never uttered a complaint, and when her acquaintance talked to her about Mr Anderson's conduct, she would even apologize as much as she possibly could for him.—She had no parents, a Sister and three cousins were her only surviving relations, and they resided at a great distance. She was advised to part from her husband and to[26] go to her sister; but she still loved him, and fondly hoped he would reform—He behaved well at times, for a month or two, and she was happy, he relapsed, and she was wretched. He has for a year past been worse than ever, and it is the opinion of every one that his behaviour was the cause of her decline—How bitter will his reflections be after death! what can sooth[27] his mind? Religion cannot, for he has none; he openly ridicules that, and every thing that is sacred; this has been a greater affliction to Mrs Anderson than his intemperance—He really loves her and always has, though his actions seem to have proved the contrary— I fear he will plunge still deeper into vice, after her death, than he has yet done.—It has often been remarked that an habitual drunkard was never reformed by meeting with trouble—Mr Anderson has often been heard to say, that when his wife died he would not long survive her—I tremble for the event. I will communicate the first intelligence, I have from Mrs Anderson, to you as soon as possible.—Write often, for you may be assured that the perusal of your letters, is one of my chief pleasures—adieu my beloved Adeline, believe me to be your sincere friend,

Fidelia Maria
Leicester July 29th 1799

Written after reading some very elegant extracts from Campbell's pleasures of hope.[28]

Address to Hope.

Oh! thou whose pleasures Campbell sings sublime,
And cheats, with numbers soft, the ling'ring time,
Bid my dull hours thus sweetly, swiftly glide;
And as I wander near the river side,
Or where yon grove extends its pleasing shade,   5
A sweet retreat for contemplation made;
Or seated on yon hill, from whence the eye
Surveys at once a rich variety
Of ample fields with smiling verdure crown'd,
And woodlands shades whose branches sweep the ground;   10
And verdant meadows where the high rank grass
Waves to the gentle breezes as they pass.
Or as I wander thus at closing day,
Do thou be near to chase my cares away.
The setting sun has with his splendor ting'd   15
The evening sky. The clouds with purple fring'd,
And streak'd with red of ev'ry diff'rent hue,
Present a brilliant prospect to the view;
Fast as the sun declines, their colours fade,
And all their lustre softens in to shade.   20
Confusion ceases, and the cares of day
In peaceful silence now dissolve away.
Thus let thy influence within my breast,
Dispell my cares, and charm my griefs to rest.

Fidelia
July 1800[29]

A tale for those who deal in the marvelous

As two fair sisters sat alone one night,
Expecting soon to see some fearful sight;
Their palpitating hearts with terror fill'd,
And life's warm current was with horror chill'd.
'Bless me'! cries Fanny starting from her chair,   5
'I'm sure I heard a dreadful noise out there!
I can see nothing, it's as dark as pitch,
Nancy, I really think it was a witch,
Or else some spirit sent to haunt us here,
I'm scar'd to death, what shall we do? oh dear!'   10
'What did you hear?' said Nancy looking wild;
'I thought I heard the groaning of a child
As if it was a dying. Lord of grace!
There was a light flash'd right across my face!
Didn't you see it'? 'No, I'd shut my eyes.'   15
'Hark! mercy on us! there is something sighs.
I wish with all my heart we had a light,
I won't be left alone another night.
Aunt Hannah said when she was all alone
One night when uncle John was gone from home,   20
That something went thump, thump, and scar'd her so,
She had not hardly strength to stand or go.
He said the pigs were fighting in the sty,
But twasn't that no more than 'twas a fly.
Twas just a month before their Billy dy'd,   25
And uncle laugh'd because she sat & cry'd
And thought it was a warning, but he's found
Such things don't come for nothing i'll be bound.'
Says Nancy, 'come, let's go and make a light
With shavings, come we'll run with all our might.   30
There, now the fire burns clear we'll look about,

And if we hear the noise we'll both run out.'
'There, there it groans again!' 'yes, I heard that,'
'Why Fanny, only look, it's our old cat'!
She's fast asleep out here upon the wool,   35
And snores and groans'—'Why, mercy! what a fool
Twas to be so frighten'd at a cat!
Well, I am glad it's nothing worse than that;
I've heard so many things about the sights
That folks have seen when all alone a nights,[30]   40
And dreadful noises that they always heard,
Somtimes[31] an hour before the ghost appear'd,
That I was terrified almost to death,
I couldn't hardly draw my nat'ral breath.
Next time I hear a noise I mean to go   45
Right there, and find out what it is, I know'.
Aye, go fair maid, and I will warrant that
To prove as harmless as a sleeping Cat.

Fidelia

1800

[Why was I born devoid of evry charm]

Why was I born devoid of evry[32] charm
To gain thy friendship, or thy bosom warm?
Why was not beauty, elegance and worth,
With all the graces present at my birth?

Then had I never sigh'd in vain for you,   5
My pillow ne'er'd been steep'd in briny dew,
But mutual friendship in our breasts had burn'd,
And each fond sigh, had been with sigh return'd.
                                              Anne.

[Ask rather, why the fates ordain'd it so]

Ask rather, why the fates ordain'd it so
That thy warm bosom felt the fervid glow
Of purest love, for a falsehearted youth,
Who sought thy ruin. Sacrificing truth

And ev'ry virtue for accursed gold.   5
To gain a paltry sum, his honor sold,
And left thee, fond, despairing maid to weep,
And with affliction's tears thy pillow steep.

Arouse, indignant,[33] spurn him from thy breast,
Nor let his broken vows destroy thy rest.   10
Let just resentment in thy bosom burn,
And Peace shall to her wonted seat return.

Fidelia
1800

To Adelaide—

Fav'rite of the tuneful Nine,[34]
Strike again thy Silver Lyre;
Every power to please is thine,
Sing, and let us still admire.
Point out Nature's numerous beauties,   5
They instruct the attentive mind,
(If among thy various duties
Thou cans't leisure moments find.)
Ramble where the stream meanders,
Through the meadow or the grove,   10
In every scene behold the wonders
Wrought by Nature's God of love!
Veiw[35] the vast "expanse of heaven,"[36]
See the stars unnumber'd roll,
He who has their brightness given,   15
By his power supports the whole.
When the early blush of Morning
Paints with richest glow the east,
Flow'rs and plants the scene adorning
Smile in gayest colors drest.   20
Warbling birds with airy rapture
Sing their sweetest songs of praise
To their glorious Benefactor
While they charm us with their lays.

[Letter to Isaiah Thomas Junior]

Leicester February 13th 1802

Sir,

Your very obliging letter entitles you to my sincere thanks. The flattering compliments you have bestowed on my trifling production are greater, I am conscious, than they deserve. Had I known Mr Greenwood would have mentioned my name as the authoress of the Novel, I believe I never should have ventured to have had it thus exposed. It is, and ever has been, my wish to remain unknown. To his friendship, I consider myself in many respects greatly indebted, and in his Judgment I place some confidence. On supposition the little work above alluded to ever should appear in print, I shall never consent to have my name or that of Fidelia appear to it. The novel is written in letters and founded principally on facts, some of which I have heard from persons with whom I am connected. I have been careful not to write any thing that could have a tendency to injure the minds of the young and inexperienced. I have written the whole of it at hours of leisure, and the greater part after the family had retired to rest. I am quite ignorant of the manner of disposing of copy rights, and a faint hope that I might possibly gain something by it induced me to mention it in confidence to Mr Greenwood.

I will transcribe it as soon as possible for your perusal, should it be thought unfit for publication, I shall rest satisfied with the desision of your superior Judgment, and repose sufficient confidence in your honor to believe my name will never be exposed on the occasion.

Yours with respect,
S.V.

[Journal]

Monday December 18th 1815—

Began this Evening to instruct Harriot in Arithmetic.—Attended
to Eliza's improvement in writing—Taught Amanda for the first
time to make strait[37] marks with a pen—
Could the dear creatures know the interest I feel in all that concerns them, and my anxious wishes for their improvement and future usefulness, it would be a sufficient stimulus to their ambition—Taught them the probable reason of the twinkling of the
stars—All such information is communicated and received with
delight—It makes me happy to find one hour I can spare for the
improvement of my children—

T. 19th Harriot compleated eleven skains[38] of her first spinning,
which has employed her five days, excepting the time she has
been hindered by doing some nescessary work about house—
Attended to their writing half an hour this evening—Earnestly
wish I could devote more time to them—

W. 20th Harriot & Eliza attended to writing made some
improvement—

T. 21st Mrs Hall here in the evening—H. & E. visited Lucy &
carried their knitting—People have been searching for Mr
Green—Considerable alarm has been excited for his safety as
he took nothing with him but his razor, and left his affairs in
such a situation as made it reasonable to suppose he never intended to have any farther concern with them—

F. 22nd After all the children had retired, devoted an hour to Arithmetic—Taught H. to understand the meaning of simple Addition, why to carry 10 Xc.—ended the evening instruction with a sum in subtraction—Wish her perfectly to understand the meaning of terms as she proceeds, or the study will be found destitute of pleasure—Mr Green not yet found—

Appendix 1

Tribute to Merit

Federal Galaxy (Brattleboro, Vermont), August 24, 1801

At a period in the annals of literature, when puerile affectation and meretricious ornament are usurping the legitimate honors of genius, it is pleasing to a pupil of the school of Addison and Pope, to notice some instances of correct taste in our own country. Amongst the *nugæ canoræ*,[1] the trifling sing song, which abounds in foreign and American publications, the productions of FIDELIA and THEODORUS, in the Massachusetts SPY, are as a cool spring in the arid deserts of Arabia, or the solitary blue and yellow flower in the gloomy region of Nova Zembia. The paper which presents to the public these elegant effusions of sentiment and fancy, was, to the writer of this notice, in infancy, almost the only source of information, on subjects political or literary. With the SPY in his hand, he has often left the garden or the hay field, at the close of day, like the Italian cowboy,

"The high wood all under to wilder forlorn."[2]

The beautiful poetry which he now occasionally reads in that valuable paper, recalls by natural association of ideas, the remembrance of some of the most pleasing scenes of his infancy.

"Seat of my earliest years!
Still busy fancy loves with fairy touch
To paint its faded scenes."[3]

The lays of Fidelia are as superior to the turgid song of Della Crusca,[4] as they are to that *low* poetry which now abounds in European publications, under the name of *ballads*, in which simplicity is made much too simple. Fidelia is in the school of Pope: A modern ballad monger would correct that great poet as follows:

> Deepens the murmur of the falling floods,
> And breathes a browner horror o'er the woods.
>
> POPE's Eloisa[5]

CORRECTED.

> Makes the great flood fall harder down,
> And the woods look more dreadful brown.

In a word, the man of taste will bestow the same praise on the song of the rural Poetess of Leicester, that Menalcas does on that of Mopsus, in the fifth Ecologue of Virgil.——

> Tale tuum carmen nobis, divine poeta,
> Quale soper fessis in gramine; quale per æstum
> Dulcis aquæ saliente sitim restinguere rivo.[6]

Mr. Thomas is desired to copy the above into the Spy.

Appendix 2

[Review of *Emily Hamilton*]

Monthly Anthology and Boston Review, May 1805

Emily Hamilton, a novel. Founded on incidents in real life.
By a young Lady of Worcester county. Worcester.
Isaiah Thomas, jun. pp. 249.

This volume was sent to us, as the production of "a country girl, about eighteen years of age, residing in an obscure town, and by her *needle* maintaining her aged parents." Either of these circumstances would have interested us in its favour, but we could not view them thus combined without an earnest wish for the success of the author. We do not recollect any American female, except Mrs. Rowson,[1] who has written a novel which can be read with any pleasure; and we are not disposed to encourage the exertions of females to become known as authors, unless convinced that the amusement and instruction which they can furnish will extend beyond the circle of their own partial friends. Considering however the age at which it was written, and the peculiar embarrassments of the author, the novel before us is deserving of commendation. The style evidently displays the youth of the author, though more simple and correct, than that in which young ladies generally write. The sentiments are common, but just; and though the incidents are neither very numerous nor interesting, they evince considerable ingenuity.

Notes

Emily Hamilton

1. Soothe.
2. Unidentified.
3. Unidentified.
4. Unidentified.
5. Unidentified.
6. Oliver Goldsmith (1728?–74), "The Hermit," lines 73–76. The full stanza reads:

> And what is friendship but a name,
> A charm that lulls to sleep;
> A shade that follows wealth or fame,
> But leaves the wretch to weep?

7. A popular song in the eighteenth century, variously titled "A Song on Friendship," "On Friendship," "Friendship," "The World, My Dear Myra," and "The World." Its authorship has been attributed to several different individuals. The full verse reads:

> How much to be priz'd and esteem'd is a friend,
> On whom we may always with safety depend?
> Our joys, when extended, will always increase,
> And griefs, when divided, are hush'd into peace. (9–12)

These lines are taken from *A Select Collection of English Songs*, compiled by Joseph Ritson and published in 1783.

8. Anna Matilda (Hannah Cowley, 1743–1809), "To Fancy." It was printed in the *Connecticut Gazette* on October 14, 1801, claiming to be "*From*

Thomas's Massachusetts Spy." The issue of the *Spy* in which it appeared is undetermined.

9. Edward Young (1683–1765), *The Complaint; or, Night Thoughts on Life, Death and Immortality* was published in nine parts between 1742 and 1745. It is Young's most famous poem, for which William Blake did a series of illustrations in 1797. Among other things, it reflects on death and the brevity of life.

10. Joseph Addison (1672–1719), *Cato*, act 1, scene 1, lines 49–54. Vickery omits line 52. Addison's lines read:

> The ways of heav'n are dark and intricate,
> Puzzled in mazes and perplext with errors;
> Our understanding traces 'em in vain,
> Lost and bewilder'd in the fruitless search;
> Nor sees with how much art the windings run,
> Nor where the regular confusion ends.

11. Soothe.

12. Unidentified.

13. Soothe.

14. Vickery's own poem, "To CONTENT," which appeared in the *Massachusetts Spy* on March 24, 1802. The wording of some of the lines has been altered. See page 183 of this edition. Most of the poems quoted in Emily Hamilton are enclosed in quotation marks, but this poem and a few others are not. Since "To CONTENT" is clearly Vickery's creation, it is possible that the absence of quotation marks indicates those other, heretofore unidentified poems are also hers. I thank Colleen Clark for drawing my attention to the discrepancy in the use of punctuation.

15. Unidentified.

16. In the collection of church songs published by the Reverend Isaac Watts (1674–1748), lines 13–18 of hymn 144 read:

> But sinners scorn the grace,
> That brings salvation nigh:
> They turn away their face,
> And faint, and fall, and die.
> So sad a doom, ye saints, deplore,
> For O! they fall to rise no more.

17. New Hampshire.

18. Unidentified.

19. By "friends" Mary means her grandparents, her guardians. Emily similarly refers to her parents as "friends."

20. The first book mentioned is likely *Celestina*, the third novel written by Charlotte Turner Smith (1749–1806); the second book is possibly *The Wedding Ring, or, the History of Miss Sidney*, an epistolary novel published anonymously by the firm of F. and J. Noble in London in 1779.

21. Unidentified.

22. Despaired.

23. Original reads "I will."

24. Original has a semicolon, not a comma.

25. Showing.

26. That is, her widow's weeds, mourning attire (from the Old English word "waed," meaning garment). Frequently the outfit consisted of black clothing and a veil.

27. New York.

28. Even though Mary Carter has married George Gray, Emily addresses her as "Miss" rather than "Mrs." Emily switches to "Mrs." in letter 39. Whether this oversight originates with the author, the publisher, or the character, I leave for the reader to decide.

29. Unidentified.

30. Despairing.

31. William Cowper (1731–1800), "Ode to Peace," lines 1–3.

32. East Indies.

33. Thomas's 1803 edition employs double quotation marks inside double quotation marks, which for clarity have been altered throughout this publication to conform with the modern practice of single quotation marks within double quotation marks.

34. Thomas Parnell (1679–1718), "The Hermit," lines 206–7. Vickery misquotes these lines: "Yet taught by these, confess th' Almighty just, / And where you can't unriddle, learn to trust."

35. Prey.

36. Timothy Dwight (1752–1817), *The Conquest of Canaan*, book 9, lines 583–84.

37. Unidentified.

38. Rehearse.

39. A Masonic song that can be found, for example, in *Masonic Constitutions, or Illustrations of Masonry; Compiled by the Direction of the Grand Lodge of Kentucky*, which was printed in Lexington, Kentucky, in 1818. Obviously, Vickery must have been drawing on an earlier and (most likely) more local publication of Masonic songs.

40. Unidentified. There is also the possibility that Vickery is simply enclosing a commonplace phrase in quotation marks.

41. John Logan (1748–88), "Written in a Visit to the Country in Autumn." Vickery has quoted about two-thirds of the entire poem, omitting stanzas 3, 4, and 6; she has also altered various words in the poem, changing, for example, "Oh" to "Oft" in the tenth line.

42. William Cowper (1731–1800), "An Epistle to Joseph Hill" (1785), lines 10–11: "True. Changes will befall, and friends may part / But distance only cannot change the heart."

43. Sir Richard Steele, *The Tatler*, number 104: "An inviolable fidelity, good-humour, and complacency of temper outlive all the charms of a fine face and make the decays of it invisible."

44. Dissipate.

45. Play by Arthur Murphy (1727–1805), published 1772.

46. Farce by George Coleman (1732–94), published 1763.

47. Riveted.

48. Unidentified.

49. Unidentified.

50. Willises.

51. John Cunningham (1729–73), "Delia, A Pastoral," quoted in its entirety but with several misquotes throughout.

52. Sometimes known as "Ganges," this popular song is from the collection of church songs published by the Reverend Isaac Watts (1674–1748).

53. That is, a stepmother.

54. No comma in original.

55. Risked.

56. Charlotte Turner Smith (1749–1806), *Celestina* (1791).

57. Derogatory name for the French.

Poems Published in the Massachusetts Spy

1. The title of the poetry column in the *Massachusetts Spy*.

2. Matthew Lyon (1749–1822), U.S. House member from Vermont and sharp critic of President John Adams. He was the first person convicted under the 1798 Sedition Act for criticism of Adams and the government. Once convicted, he was ordered to pay just over $1,000 in fines and was jailed for four months, during which time he was reelected to his House seat. The "Letter" to which Vickery refers is most likely *To the Freemen of the Western District of Vermont* (1798).

3. Another name for the United States.

4. George Washington had just died in December 1799.

5. While the first word in each published poem originally appeared in capital letters, some abstract concepts were also capitalized. Since it is unclear which of these practices was followed in the original, the capitalization has been retained here.

6. Hesperus, the evening star, the planet Venus.

7. Soothes.

8. Helen of Troy, known for her great beauty and as the major catalyst for the Trojan War.

9. Greek and Roman god of the sun and patron of poetry and music, he is often associated with the Muses.

10. Roman goddess of the moon and the hunt; known for her virginity and called Artemis by the Greeks.

11. John Barnard Bennett identifies Miss H. as Relief Hobart, who died July 6, 1801, in Leicester.

12. Peru's profitable mining industry includes copper, silver, and gold.

13. From "To Theodorus," page 164, line 18.

14. Roman goddess of springtime and budding fruits, flowers, and crops; also known as a fertility goddess.

15. From the previous poem, line 32.

16. Original has a period, not a question mark.

17. God.

18. Source of quotation unidentified.

19. Roman god of wine; known to the Greeks as Dionysus.

20. The nine Muses: Greek patron goddesses of the arts, including poetry.

21. Greek and Roman god of the sun and patron of poetry and music, he is often associated with the Muses.

22. Anna Matilda, an admirer of Della Crusca (Robert Merry). Her actual name was Hannah Cowley, and she and Merry corresponded poetically in British periodicals. A more detailed discussion of Della Cruscan poetry can be found in the introduction to this volume.

23. A district in Boeotia (in ancient Greece) that contains Mount Helicon, the location of the springs Aganippe and Hippocrene, both sacred to the Muses.

24. Bedimmed.

25. Compare with "To Fidelia," page 169, line 6. The willow tree is associated with poetic inspiration, and the image of a lyre hanging on a willow tree has long been poetically popular. It can also be found in Psalm 137: 1–2: "By the waters of Babylon, there we sat down and wept, when we remembered Zion. On the willows there we hung up our lyres."

26. Pieria is a district in Macedonia that includes Mount Pierus (home to Orpheus and the Muses) and Mount Olympus (residence of the Greek gods). The Greeks believed that drinking from the Pierian Spring brought knowledge and inspiration.

27. Mount Parnassus, in central Greece near Delphi, is sacred to Apollo and another home of the Muses.

28. The original places a period at the end of the stanza, but a comma clearly makes grammatical sense.

29. God.

30. Quote unidentified.

31. John Barnard Bennett identifies Miss E**** as Eliza Elliot, also known as Betsy Elliot, who died April 2, 1802, in Leicester.

32. Oliver Goldsmith (1728–74), "The Traveller," lines 37–38: "When thus creation's charms around combine / amidst the store, should thankless pride repine?"

33. Apollo, Greek and Roman god of the sun.

34. Although as a metaphorical image "bubbles" makes sense, Vickery might have meant this to be "baubbles."

35. The nine Muses, Greek patron goddesses of the arts, including poetry.

36. The United States.

37. Sarah Wentworth Morton (1759–1846), one of the most respected women poets of her generation.

38. The title of a popular poem by Sarah Wentworth Morton dealing with a love triangle involving a Native American couple (Ouabi and Azakia) and a European (Celario).

39. Greek and Roman god of the sun and patron of poetry and music; he is often associated with the Muses.

40. Fraught.

41. From the previous poem, line 13.

Unpublished Manuscripts

1. Guard.

2. Britain.

3. The United States.

4. Roman goddess of war and variously understood as the sister, wife, or daughter of Mars. She is frequently depicted wearing a helmet and armed with a spear and torch.

5. Gen. Joseph Warren, who died leading colonial troops at the battle of Bunker Hill, June 17, 1775.

6. Every.

7. E'er.

8. Yields.

9. Most likely Vickery meant "O'er whelm'd" (that is, "Overwhelmed").

10. Guard.

11. The manuscript is smudged here. Leaving no blank for the smudge, John Barnard Bennett's transcription obviously interprets the smudge as a cross-out. I have accepted his interpretation of the smudge, since an additional word would upset the poem's meter.

12. Vickery used this letter nearly verbatim in letter 30 of *Emily Hamilton*. At the top of the manuscript appears "By Susan Vickery, author of Emily Hamilton."

13. William Cowper (1731–1800), "An Epistle to Joseph Hill" (1785), lines 10–11: "True. Changes will befall, and friends may part / But distance only cannot change the heart."

14. Alexander Pope (1688–1744), "Eloisa to Abelaird" (1717), line 290: "Rise *Alps* between us! and whole oceans roll!"

15. The manuscript is faded to illegibility—possibly Vickery wrote the next few words and then struck them.

16. Vickery originally wrote "sup" and then struck it out and replaced it with "cup."

17. There is another strikeout after this word, probably a misspelling of "person."

18. Vickery underlined "he was" in the manuscript.

19. Guard.

20. The manuscript is torn at this place, but the writing seems to match the wording found in *Emily Hamilton*.

21. Vickery originally wrote "recieve," then struck it out and replaced it with "receive."

22. Off.

23. Clothes.

24. Reparation.

25. The manuscript is torn here, but *Emily Hamilton* uses the word "gently," which corresponds with the visible handwriting.

26. Vickery double-underlined this word in her manuscript.

27. Soothe.

28. Thomas Campbell (1777–1844), "The Pleasures of Hope" (1799).

29. The manuscript is smudged before "July."

30. A-nights.

31. Sometimes.

32. Every.

33. The manuscript reads "Arouse. indignant, spurn him from thy breast." A comma, however, after "arouse" makes grammatical sense.

34. The nine Muses, Greek patron goddesses of the arts, including poetry.

35. View.

36. A phrase commonly found in the Bible, including in the story of the Creation.

37. Vickery originally wrote "straight," then struck it out and replaced it with "strait."

38. Skeins.

Appendix 1

1. Latin for "musical (or melodious) trifles."

2. Unidentified.

3. Robert Southey (1774–1843), *Joan of Arc* (1796).

4. Della Crusca is the pen name of Robert Merry (1755–98); he and Hannah Cowley corresponded poetically in British periodicals. A more detailed discussion of Della Cruscan poetry can be found in the introduction to this volume.

5. Alexander Pope (1688–1744), "Eloisa to Abelard" (1717), lines 169–70.

6. Lines 57–60, translated as:

> So excellent is your song to me, divine poet,
> As rest on the grass to the weary, as in summer heat
> To quench thirst with sweet water from a bubbling stream.

Appendix 2

1. Susanna Haswell Rowson (1762–1824) was a leading novelist, most famous for her authorship of the bestseller *Charlotte, A Tale of Truth* (1791), commonly known as *Charlotte Temple*.

Suggestions for Further Reading

Altman, Janet Gurkin. *Epistolarity: Approaches to a Form*. Columbus: Ohio State UP, 1982.

Baym, Nina. *Woman's Fiction: A Guide to Novels by and about Women in America, 1820–1870*. 1978. Urbana: U of Illinois P, 1993.

Bennett, John Barnard. "A Young Lady of Worcester County." Master's thesis. Wesleyan U, 1942.

Berkin, Carol. *Revolutionary Mothers: Women in the Struggle for America's Independence*. New York: Knopf, 2005.

Branson, Susan. *These Fiery Frenchified Dames: Women and Political Culture in Early National Philadelphia*. Philadelphia: U of Pennsylvania P, 2001.

Brown, Herbert Ross. *The Sentimental Novel in America*. Durham: Duke UP, 1940.

Charvat, William. *The Profession of Authorship in America, 1800–1870*. Columbus: Ohio State UP, 1968.

Cott, Nancy F. *The Bonds of Womanhood: "Woman's Sphere" in New England, 1780–1835*. New Haven: Yale UP, 1977.

Davidson, Cathy N. "Female Authorship and Authority: The Case of Sukey Vickery." *Early American Literature* 21 (Spring 1986): 4–28.

———. *Revolution and the Word: The Rise of the Novel in America*. New York: Oxford UP, 1986.

Fetterley, Judith. Introduction. *Provisions: A Reader from 19th-Century American Women*. Bloomington: Indiana UP, 1985.

Fliegelman, Jay. *Prodigals and Pilgrims: The American Revolution against Patriarchal Authority, 1750–1800*. New York: Cambridge UP, 1982.

Hargreaves-Mawdsley, W. N. *The English Della Cruscans and Their Time, 1783–1828*. The Hague: Martinus Nijhoff, 1967.

Kelley, Mary. *Learning to Stand and Speak: Women, Education, and Public Life in America's Republic*. Chapel Hill: U of North Carolina P, 2006.

Kerber, Linda K. *Women of the Republic: Intellect and Ideology in Revolutionary America*. Chapel Hill: U of North Carolina P, 1980.

Lewis, Jan. "The Republican Wife: Virtue and Seduction in the Early Republic." *William and Mary Quarterly* 44.4 (October 1987): 689–721.

Norton, Mary Beth. *Liberty's Daughters: The Revolutionary Experience of American Women, 1750–1800*. Ithaca: Cornell UP, 1980.

Petter, Henri. *The Early American Novel*. Columbus: Ohio State UP, 1971.

Rothman, Ellen K. *Hands and Hearts: A History of Courtship in America*. New York: Basic Books, 1984.

Rust, Marion. *Prodigal Daughters: Susanna Rowson's Early American Women*. Chapel Hill: U of North Carolina P, 2008.

Weyler, Karen A. *Sexual and Economic Desire in American Ficiton, 1789–1814*. Iowa City: U of Iowa P, 2004.

Winans, Amy E. "Sukey Vickery." *American Women Prose Writers to 1820*. Ed. Carla Mulford, Angela Vietto, and Amy E. Winans. Vol. 200 of *Dictionary of Literary Biography*. Detroit: Gale, 1998. 380–84.

Zagarri, Rosemarie. *Revolutionary Backlash: Women and Politics in the Early American Republic*. Philadelphia: U of Pennsylvania P, 2007.

To order or obtain more information on these
or other University of Nebraska Press titles,
visit www.nebraskapress.unl.edu.

CPSIA information can be obtained
at www.ICGtesting.com
Printed in the USA
LVHW082039021222
734479LV00002B/243

9 780803 217850